SKELETON KNIGHT IN ANOTHER WORLD

I

written by **Ennki Hakari**   *illustrated by* **KeG**

Characters

Lauren

Lahki

Marca

Rita

A magic circle appears beneath the giant basilisk before a blade of light erupts from the ground, tearing through the beast as it shoots up into the sky.

"SWORD OF Judgment!"

SKELETON KNIGHT IN ANOTHER WORLD

I

written by
Ennki Hakari

illustrated by
KeG

Seven Seas

Seven Seas Entertainment

SKELETON KNIGHT IN ANOTHER WORLD VOL. 1

© 2015 Ennki Hakari
Illustrations by KeG

First published in Japan in 2015 by OVERLAP Inc., Ltd., Tokyo.
English translation rights arranged with OVERLAP Inc., Ltd., Tokyo.

Seven Seas press and purchase enquiries can be sent to
Marketing Manager Lianne Sentar at press@gomanga.com.
Information requiring the distribution and purchase of
digital editions is available from Digital Manager CK Russell
at digital@gomanga.com.

Follow Seven Seas Entertainment online at
sevenseasentertainment.com.

TRANSLATION: Jason Muell
ADAPTATION: Peter Adrian Behravesh
COVER DESIGN: KC Fabellon
INTERIOR LAYOUT & DESIGN: Clay Gardner
PROOFREADER: Kris Swanson, Stephanie Cohen
LIGHT NOVEL EDITOR: Nibedita Sen
MANAGING EDITOR: Julie Davis
EDITOR-IN-CHIEF: Adam Arnold
PUBLISHER: Jason DeAngelis

ISBN: 978-1-64275-064-5
Printed in Canada
First Printing: June 2019
10 9 8 7 6 5 4 3 2 1

SKELETON KNIGHT IN ANOTHER WORLD

I

❖ CONTENTS ❖

Cean River

Furyu Mountains

Grahd

Rata

Rubierute

Xpitol River

Lalatoya

Febient Marsh

Diento

Calcut Mountains

Port Bulgoh

*Great Canada
Forest*

Branbayna

*Riebing
Mountains*

Olav

Selst

Dartu

Anetto Mountains

*Hibbot
Wasteland*

Houvan

Lamburt

Tiocera

Limbult

Telnassos Mountains

Librout River

Port Aldoria

Lydel River

**South
Central
Sea**

World Map

KINGDOM OF
Rohden

Great Revlon
Empire

Holy Revlon
Empire

Rhoden
Kingdom

Great
Canada
Forest

Map

Nohzan
Kingdom

Dukedom of Limbult

Prologue

A LONE, HORSE-DRAWN CARRIAGE sped down an unevenly paved road, flanked by a contingent of horse-mounted guards. The thunder of the horses' galloping hooves echoed through the night, broken only by the occasional crashing sound of a stone bouncing off a wheel and into the body of the carriage.

A servant peeked out of the carriage's rear window, looking down the road behind them. To the right was a sprawling riverbank; farther along, the serene, orange glow of the setting sun reflected off the surface of the Xpitol River. To the left rolled gentle, sloping hills, where herds of animals could be seen grazing in the distance. Trees and other shrubbery lined the road intermittently, casting long shadows on the ground before them.

Nothing seemed out of the ordinary, and the only

sounds that could be heard were the rumbling wheels and the galloping horses. However, those inside the carriage, and the guards riding alongside it, were blanketed in a thick, oppressive silence, undoubtedly due to the series of bizarre circumstances they had just encountered.

The carriage bore the mark of the Luvierte family, royals from the Rhoden Kingdom. Lauren Laraiya du Luvierte, the eldest daughter of the Luvierte family, sat inside, a pensive look on her face as she watched the scenery roll by through the window.

A young woman of just sixteen years, Lauren had long, chestnut-colored hair, though her current unease seemed to have robbed it of its usual sheen and luster. Beneath long eyelashes lay wavering, ephemeral hazel eyes set deep in her delicately shaped face. She was dressed in a beautiful gown made of powder-blue silk, which was accented by the deep reds from the rays of the setting sun cast through the carriage's window.

Lauren had attended an evening ball held by the Diento family, serving as a representative of the Luvierte. On her way home, a gang of bandits—at least twenty by Lauren's count—had been lying in wait for her. Nine of her guards fell back to hold off the bandits' advances, though they could no longer be seen. Now only the carriage, its five-guard contingent, and one knight remained.

The servant who sat inside the carriage with Lauren was Rita Farren, a chambermaid who served the eldest Luvierte daughter. She had short, red hair and distinct green eyes that projected a strong sense of determination. Rita sat quietly next to Lauren, taking the uneasy girl's hand in her own.

"We're safe now, Miss. I don't see any pursuers, and we're nearly back to town." Rita held Lauren's gaze, smiling at the girl and stroking her hand in the hopes of comforting her.

"Thank you, Rita. You're... You're right. We're almost at Father's estate." Lauren smiled and squeezed Rita's hand back, though her anxiety remained.

Suddenly, the carriage slowed down dramatically, and the horses could be heard whinnying lightly from outside. The carriage driver opened the small port behind him and turned to Lauren.

"I'm sorry, Miss, but the horses can't keep running like this. We'll need to go at a walking pace the rest of the way."

The horses had taken off at a full gallop to pull the carriage away from the bandits' ambush. Now, it seemed, they could no longer keep up the pace. Even carriage horses had their limits, though the burden on the horses carrying Lauren's guards must have been even greater.

Rita glanced out the carriage window where she spied a middle-aged man riding alongside them, affectionately patting his horse. His name was Maudlin, one of the Luvierte family's knights, and he oversaw the contingent of guards accompanying the carriage. Though born a peasant, Maudlin's talent for battle had been discovered at a young age, and he was trained to be a knight.

Maudlin reached down and wiped away the sweat from his horse's neck with a towel. Complementing his short-cropped hair and carefully groomed mustache, his well-toned and muscular figure could be seen even through the light armor he wore over it.

"Do you think we lost the bandits, Sir Maudlin?" Rita stuck her head out of the carriage's window, looking back behind them as she addressed the knight.

"Few of the bandits had horses, so if they haven't followed us this far, I dare say we should be fine. Pass the message along to the madam." Maudlin gave Rita a wide, toothy grin in the hopes of putting her at ease.

"In that case, perhaps we can finally breathe easy." Rita's expression relaxed as she let out the breath she had been holding. She glanced up the road.

A dense clump of trees stood along one side of the road ahead. On the other, the sloping hills seemed to encroach even closer. The sight of that alone left Rita with an indescribable feeling of being confined. Her eyebrows narrowed as the muscles in the back of her neck tensed.

Noticing Rita's expression, Maudlin also began scanning the scene in front of them. He seemed to spot something, but before he could get any words out, a volley of arrows cut through the air toward them. The carriage driver screamed as two arrows struck him in the chest.

At the same moment, one of the carriage's wheels struck a stone, sending the driver's body out of his seat. Rita, who had been watching through the window, was thrown back onto the carriage's floorboards. The driver's lifeless body got caught in the carriage's wheels, causing it to grind to a halt.

Another volley of arrows flew from the woods, this time striking two of the guards.

"Damn, another ambush?! This can't be happening!"

The sound of galloping hooves filled the air as six mounted bandits crested the hill and rushed in for the attack. They closed the distance to Lauren's guards, whose backs were exposed as they defended against the onslaught of arrows, swiftly dispatching two who had been injured by the arrow volley, along with a third.

A bandit galloped toward Maudlin, though the knight used his sword to knock the rider off their horse. Maudlin spotted two men running out of the forest and approaching the carriage.

"Miss Rita, take the reins!"

Brought back to reality by the sound of Maudlin's voice, Rita hurriedly hopped out of the carriage. She found the driver's body lying between the front and back wheels, so she shoved him farther under the carriage to prevent him from catching on the back wheels. As she was about to climb into the blood-drenched driver's seat, a hand roughly grabbed her servant uniform from behind and forcefully threw her to the ground.

Rita's back hit the earth with a thud, knocking the air from her lungs and sending her into a coughing fit as she gasped for breath. At the edge of her vision, she witnessed yet another guard being surrounded and killed. She also saw a bandit—likely the one who had thrown her down—standing over her with a crude grin on his face.

"Grwaaaaawh!"

Just then, Rita heard a man scream out in agony. When she looked toward the source of the scream, she was met with a sight that defied belief: One of the guards had stabbed Maudlin in the back, right where the plates of his armor met.

Maudlin seethed, his raw hatred for the man behind him apparent in his contorted expression. "Causdah?!

Why you traitorous…!" He raised his sword as he turned, ready to strike down the disloyal guard who had stabbed him from behind. However, Causdah merely grinned as he ran his own horse into Maudlin's, sending them to the ground from the force of the impact.

A handsome man—or at least, as handsome as bandits got—came rushing in on his horse. Upon dismounting in front of the fallen knight, he ran the rest of the way on foot and stabbed Maudlin in the neck. Blood sprayed everywhere, staining the earth under the knight red.

"Go get the lady out of the carriage, and be nice to her while yer at it."

The handsome bandit's yellow teeth shone through his sneer as he ordered the others about. The man had a square jaw and long, unkempt hair tied off in the back. His chin and neck could hardly be seen through his un-tamed beard. His arms were adorned with several old scars, and, in his hand, he held a large, curved blade. He was clearly the leader of the bandits.

Upon hearing their boss's orders, the other bandits dismounted from their horses in unison and made a dash for the carriage. They tore the door open and ripped a terrified Lauren from her seat.

"Eeeek! Let go of me!"

Lauren resisted with all her might, but two men held

her arms down, even as she twisted her body about in an attempt to wrench free. Two other men grabbed Rita and dragged her over.

The bandit leader yelled out to the men holding Lauren, "Better not rip them clothes when ya take 'em off! They'll fetch us a nice profit when we sell 'em!"

One of the men turned toward the leader as he removed Lauren's dress. "I can play around with 'er, right, Boss? We're just gonna kill 'em anyway."

"What're ya blabberin' on about, idiot! I've got first dibs, and you all get what's left!"

Causdah's expression clouded with indignation upon hearing this. "W-w-wait a minute! I betrayed them, so I should get to go first!"

The leader's eyes lit up with anger at Causdah's retort. Then, he rammed his curved blade coolly through the ex-guard's mouth.

"Gyaugh!" Causdah made a gasping noise as the sword burst out of the back of his head. The other bandits smiled venomously as they watched him fall to the ground like a marionette whose strings had been cut.

"I never planned to give you a share anyway," the leader spat as he kicked the man hunched over on the ground. An awful sound erupted as Causdah's skull cracked, his neck twisting around.

Lauren, who had been watching this all unfold, let out a short scream. A yellow puddle appeared under the young girl, now stripped down to nothing but her corset and drawers.

One of the bandits holding her took notice. "Looks like the li'l lady just gone an' dirtied herself!"

Hearing this, the rest of the men broke out into crude laughter.

"In that case, I'd be happy to take them soiled undergarments off!" The leader stepped forward and pulled the soiled drawers off Lauren with a single tug. The men stared lecherously as Lauren's damp, chestnut hair came into view.

"No! Let me go! Rita! Riitaaa!!!"

Lauren thrashed frantically to avoid the men's gaze, kicking her legs about to get free. The leader ordered one of his men to grab her legs as he pulled down his own pants, exposing himself to her.

"Unhand her this instant! You know what they'll do to you?" Unable to put up with these ruffians any longer, Rita screamed at the men even as they restrained her. Her efforts, however, only made them laugh harder.

"You best not worry about her," one of the men holding her down responded. "You've got your own problems!"

He grabbed her servant's uniform and began tearing

it apart, exposing Rita's underwear and breasts for all to see. After squeezing and pawing at her exposed chest, the bandit threw Rita to the ground.

"We're gonna make sure you and the miss feel reeeeeal good. Gahahaha!"

Rita could smell the stench of the man's breath as he laughed, pulling down his own pants. She could see Lauren out in front of her, arms pinned to the ground by two bandits, with another man holding one of her legs. The leader of the bandits leaned over her, about to push himself between the girl's thighs.

Enveloped by the sounds of ear-splitting laughter, and with no one left to save them, Rita and Lauren could do nothing but scream and cry, praying to the gods to help them.

Then, a massive shadow fell across the bandits. A knight appeared right behind the bandit leader as he laid himself atop Lauren.

The knight was covered from head to toe in gleaming, silvery armor decorated in exquisite detail with white and blue accents. On his back was a billowing cape as black as the night itself, almost as if it had been ripped straight from the sky. His face was completely covered by his helmet, the only opening in his mask a pitch-black visor that obscured any emotion his eyes may have held.

In his right hand, he held a massive longsword which emitted an eerie, azure light. He looked just like the type of Holy Knight one would read about in legends.

Rita couldn't comprehend what had just appeared right before her very eyes.

Without a moment's hesitation, the knight's sword flashed, sending out a blast of light that seemed to slice through the air, right between the bandit leader and the other man holding Lauren's leg. The knight took a large step forward and followed through with a horizontal slash, sending out another blast of light that disappeared between the two men holding Lauren's arms down.

It was all over in an instant.

The top half of the bandit leader split free from the rest of his body. The man next to him, who had been holding Lauren's leg, now ended at the neck, his head rolling to the floor and facing the setting sun. The men who had been holding her arms down were now missing half of their heads. Geysers of blood spurted out like fountains, spattering the grass around them, painting the already sunset-dappled scene an even deeper shade of burgundy.

The top half of the bandit leader tumbled down onto Lauren. She screamed as she frantically kicked it away to the side. The bottom half gushed blood like an overflowing well, forming a crimson lake on the ground.

The two men who had been with Rita—one of whom was still straddling her, his member exposed while the other held her down—finally realized that something was wrong.

"Wauugh! It's a gh-ghost!"

It was every man for himself as the remaining two bandits scrambled to escape. However, the half-dressed man crashed back to the ground next to Rita as his legs tangled in his pants. The next thing Rita knew, the knight swung his sword down and impaled the man, leaving the man stuck to the earth like a skewered frog. The silver knight pulled his blade from the dead man and pointed it at the man's escaping comrade.

"Wyvern Slash!" A deep, muffled voice echoed from within the helmet as the silver knight took a sudden step forward, swinging his massive sword in a horizontal slash.

It appeared to all watching that he had simply swung his sword in the air while the escaping man continued to run away. However, moments later, the man dropped where he stood, his body splitting into two halves, cut cleanly at the waist.

In the course of three blinks of an eye, the entire group of bandits had been reduced to mounds of flesh.

The knight gently shook the blood from his sword and slid it back into the sheath strapped to the back of his armor. He faced the two women, a dispassionate voice calling out from deep within the visor-covered helmet.

"Are you all right?"

The setting sun reflected off the silver knight's armor, making it look like he was entirely enveloped in flames. Lauren and Rita completely forgot about their own state of undress as they stared blankly up at the knight.

CHAPTER 1

Journey to a Mysterious World

WHEN I CAME TO, I didn't know where I was or what I was doing there.

Grassy hills stretched all around me. The sun was still high in the sky, so it must have been a little past noon. Wind blew across the vast sea of green, creating waves of grass that flowed toward where I sat on a rock. The breeze carried with it the scent of fresh vegetation and moist earth. Behind me, I could hear the wind rustle its way through a forest as it moved between the trees.

I stood up from the rock and surveyed the expanse that lay before me. A city dweller most of my life, I'd rarely been exposed to such a tranquil scene. All I could do was stand there and take it all in.

That was when I finally noticed my body.

I was covered from head to toe in silvery-white armor, accented with exquisite blue and white detailing. Such impressive armor was usually reserved for the knights you read about in fairytales. My cape, black as the night, whipped in the wind. Its lining glimmered slightly, making it appear as if the fabric had been ripped straight from the star-filled sky. On my back was a large, round shield decorated with an elaborate design and, below that, a sheath that contained a massive, two-handed sword that gave off a mysterious aura.

Despite this being a rather extreme departure from how I usually looked, I was actually quite familiar with my appearance. The last thing I remembered was playing an online game and falling asleep in front of my computer, which was something I often did.

The next thing I knew, I'd woken up here as Arc, my in-game character.

"What's happened?!" I screamed at the top of my lungs. The voice that echoed from my helmet was far deeper than my own.

Considering how desolate the location was, I didn't exactly expect a reply. However, I couldn't suppress the desire to shout something, anything, any longer.

On a whim, I drew the sword from the sheath on my back. It was a double-edged sword that emitted a pale azure light, reflecting the sun's rays. The blade itself was at least a hundred centimeters long and quite wide, giving it a rather hefty presence. I brought the sword up to eye level and slashed down in a powerful sweep.

"Whoa!" I shouted again.

It was so incredibly light, I could hardly believe the object I was holding was truly a metal sword. The weight of it defied my expectations, and I was able to easily swing it around repeatedly.

Next, I tried swinging the sword around with one hand. Despite being outfitted entirely in armor, my body felt light, allowing me to move around gracefully, unimpeded by the armor.

"Wyvern Slash!" I shouted the name of an in-game attack as I swung the sword.

The blade released a blast of energy straight into the forest. A moment later, a tree with a trunk as wide as a child began falling, making a rustling sound on its way down as its leaves brushed against the trees around it. The birds nesting in the surrounding branches took off flying, and, a moment later, the tree hit the ground with a dull thud.

"I guess this is actually real..."

I finally started to calm down, though I still had no idea what was actually going on. Still somewhat drowsy,

I considered the possibility that this may all be a dream. After all, here I was, a Holy Knight outfitted in the weaponry and armor from the in-game character I had been playing moments ago.

This mythical-class, silvery-white armor I was wearing was from the Belenus Holy Armor series, which could only be worn by Holy Knights. Made up of five pieces—head, torso, arms, waist, and legs—the armor reduced light and fire attacks by half, restored my health at regular intervals, boosted defense, and increased attack power. It was pretty overpowered.

On top of all that, the cape billowing in the wind behind me was the Twilight Cloak, also mythical-class. In addition to reducing the effect of dark attacks, it also restored my magic at regular intervals.

Attached to my back was the mythical-class shield, the Holy Shield of Teutates. Not only did it offer a high defense stat, its resistance to status effects increased with every level I gained.

Many users were highly critical of the incredibly high stats of the Holy Knights' defensive items, leading to the developers of the game making a few changes. However, rather than changing any of the items' stats, they decided (oddly) to make it so Holy Knights were unable to equip accessories. With this restriction on modifying their abilities, the already limited number of Holy Knight players began dwindling. These days, they were incredibly uncommon.

The last of my equipment was my two-handed sword, the Holy Thunder Sword of Caladbolg. It boasted a high attack stat and provided an agility boost. Each mythical-class weapon also came with its own attack skills, but these were really just additional buffs on top of the rest.

Upon sliding the sword into its sheath on my back, I held my right hand up to the sky, summoning Fire. Just like in the game, a flame engulfed my right hand, and fireballs began shooting out of my fist.

Actually, no. This wasn't quite like the game.

I knew for a fact my main class was Holy Knight and my sub-class had been set to Priest before I went to sleep. Fire was a base Mage skill, and Wyvern Slash was a mid-tier Knight skill. If this were just like the game, I shouldn't be able to use them with this class setup.

So why could I use both Mage and Knight skills?

Still uncertain if this was just an incredibly realistic dream, I banged on my helmet. However, I wasn't any closer to waking up. That was when I forced myself to ask the question I'd been dreading: What if this wasn't a dream, or even a game, but reality?

The very thought seemed absurd, even to me, but as I took in what lay before me, all five of my senses providing additional information, I started doubting this was a dream. It all seemed too real.

If this wasn't a game, then that may explain why I could use all of the techniques I had learned, regardless of class changes. After all, it wasn't like a judo practitioner would lose his ability to use all the judo techniques he had learned the moment he started practicing boxing.

In that case, I wondered if this meant I could use the top-tier class skills I had learned.

Before becoming a Holy Knight, a top-tier class, I had previously leveled up nine other classes. In order to become a Holy Knight, I needed to have the top-tier classes of Summoner, Sacred Knight, and Priest. To get those, I needed the mid-tier classes of Magus, Knight, and Bishop. Those required the base-tier classes of Mage, Soldier, and Monk. After those nine classes, that made Holy Knight my tenth.

I didn't learn every skill from every single class, but I had still acquired quite a large number of techniques.

With all these skills at my disposal, I just may be able to survive in this unknown world. The fact that I wasn't limited to my main class would alone be a huge help.

To be honest, the Holy Knight class was basically a love letter from the developers. Holy Knight Swordsmanship was the only ability available, but it allowed you to equip a two-handed sword in one hand, then gave additional attack bonuses if you equipped one in both. With its ample equipment options and high attack and defense stats, the class seemed perfect for tanking. Unfortunately, it was difficult to use as a main class, since it lacked any ability to attract enemies.

The romanticism and the Holy Knight name itself were what drew me in. Having gone through all the effort to attain this top-tier class, I felt a certain affinity for it. Though, even I had to admit it was hard to use. But, on the other hand, the class was certainly more than powerful enough to win in a straight-up fight with its weapons alone, no special techniques needed.

I slowly exhaled while I thought this over. I realized I couldn't just keep idling my time away on top of this hill. I needed to find a person, a town, *something*. I began thinking about what I would do next.

Even though I found myself in this impossible situation, I was a little proud of how calm I was.

I summoned another spell, just as I had done earlier. This time, it was Transport Gate, a Magus support magic skill, which caused a three-meter-wide, pale blue column of light to appear at my feet. This spell allowed players to instantly transport to any town they had previously visited.

In the game, a prompt would typically appear that

allowed you to select the name of the town you wanted to transport to. However, the space in front of me remained blank. I thought for a moment about what I should do. Suddenly, the world around me grew dark. The next moment, I was greeted with the same scene I had seen just moments ago. Looking down at my feet, I guessed I had moved ahead maybe three meters. It seemed the spell wouldn't work without me having a distinct image of where I wanted to go in mind.

I wasn't sure where I was in this world, so perhaps I wouldn't be able to travel very far. It wasn't like I knew any areas other than where I currently stood.

"Well, this sucks," I muttered as I looked up at the sky.

Though, there may be other options. I punched my fist into my open palm as I remembered a different transport skill I could use: Dimensional Step, a supplemental Mage skill. After executing the skill, players could move to any location of their choosing with a click of the mouse. Often used in the early game to get out of range of an enemy's area-of-effect attack or to make a quick escape from hordes of enemies, the skill became mostly useless around mid-game. The area of effect of attacks by large monsters and bosses was simply too large to escape. The skill was basically only useful for adjusting your position, or for consuming MP as you darted across the screen.

I focused on a location in front of me then executed Dimensional Step. An instant later, the world around me began moving. Looking over my shoulder, I could see where I had been standing just moments ago; it was quite a distance away, maybe about 500 meters or so.

In the game, the skill would only allow you to teleport as far as the edge of your screen. Here in the real world, however, the spell made it possible for me to instantly travel to any location I could see. It was pretty convenient to be able to fly about like an esper without needing to put a bead against my head each and every time. Plus, the short recharge time between uses made it a pretty useful transport spell.

I alternated between waiting for the spell to recharge and using Dimensional Step to teleport. My mood started picking up the farther I traveled.

The day wore on, and the sky began taking on a crimson glow as the sun drew ever closer to the horizon. Assuming the sun was west of me, that meant I was traveling southwest.

As I progressed from one grassy hill to the next, a large river came into view. I teleported down to the riverbank and looked across to the other side. The river seemed to be about 200 meters wide. The only sound was the gentle flow of the water, its glass-like surface reflecting the deep orange sheen from the setting sun. The river's water was clear, giving me a view into its depths, where I could see schools of fish swimming past.

I suppose it's about time I take a break and drink something, I thought as I unclasped my helmet from my armor.

Now that I thought about it, it was a bit odd that I didn't feel any weight—or even warmth—from the armor, despite the fact that I was completely encased in metal. With that in the back of my mind, I leaned over the surface of the water.

My face...was completely white.

"What the..." The words escaped my lips before being quickly drowned out by the sounds of the burbling river.

I locked eyes with the face staring back at me from the river. Well, that wasn't entirely accurate. There were no eyes in my reflection. Nor was there a nose, or even skin.

Light blue flames flickered deep within a pair of dark, eyeless sockets, gazing back at me emotionlessly. The skeleton reflected in the water's surface was wearing the same exquisite armor that I was.

It had completely slipped my mind. If my abilities here were just as limited as they had been in the game, I probably would have noticed sooner. However, without this reminder, I had completely forgotten which avatar I was playing.

My usual in-game avatar was based on a humanoid that I had customized down to the last detail. The system allowed players to make all sorts of customizations to their appearance, even inventing your own species. You could give your avatar elongated ears to make an elf, or maybe a pig-like nose to make an orc, just to name a few.

For a fee, you could gain access to even more avatar customizations, one of which was a skeleton avatar.

My friends had criticized me for choosing such a meaningless customization. It may have been a paid avatar, but it wasn't like anyone would be able to see it, since I was covered in armor.

Even I hadn't noticed until I removed my helmet and saw my reflection in the water...

I shook my head and tried clearing my thoughts to refocus myself, though the shock was more emotional than anything. I was surprised at how calm I continued to be, though that provided little comfort considering the situation I found myself in.

This is going to be a pretty big problem, I realized.

There was no way I could remove my helmet in front of people, not looking like this. Someone may think I was some sort of monster and try to kill me.

I also wasn't sure where I stood in terms of strength in this world. Considering that my appearance in the game had transferred over here, it was almost certain there were other monsters out there who'd transferred as well—monsters I wouldn't be able to defeat alone.

I glanced around at my surroundings as the weight of the situation finally began settling in. As far as I could see, nothing but a serene expanse lay in front of me. I didn't see anything that may pose a threat. Knowing that I had a spell like Dimensional Step to escape any dangers at least provided me with some comfort.

But now I needed to think about my next step.

I decided I should lie low and try not to stand out. That was really my only option. Considering my appearance under the armor, it didn't really seem like a good idea to go near any populated areas. On the other hand, it wasn't like I could just wander for the rest of my days, hiding out in a world I knew nothing about. Perhaps I wouldn't need to take my armor off right away, even in populated areas. But even if that were the case, the armor itself was far too extravagant; it would draw plenty of attention on its own. And, again, it wasn't like I could just take it off.

The only things I truly had in this world—a world I didn't even know the name of—were my armor and weapons. I'd lost all my in-game items and money. So, first and foremost, I needed to find a way to start earning money and put together some sort of lifestyle.

I could feel my head heating up the harder I thought, so I stuck it into the river. The chilly water immediately began cooling me as it flowed past my exposed skull.

I hesitantly took a drink. I could feel the water flow down my throat and spread throughout my body. However, when I brought a hand to my throat, all I felt was the vertebrae that made up my neck.

How was a skeleton able to drink water, and where did it even go? And how was I able to taste it?

I figured it was best not to worry about the little things right now. I could feel my head starting to overheat again.

First, I needed to pull myself together and begin looking for a village or town. If I followed the river downstream, I was bound to find some sort of human settlement.

I took my helmet from under my arm and put it back onto my head, resuming my travel with Dimensional Step.

There was a road running alongside the river, so I figured I couldn't be far from some settlement or other. Even at my most charitable, I couldn't call the road nice, or even well taken care of. It consisted mainly of compacted dirt, and I could see where carts had passed through from the ruts etched into the ground. Judging by the road, and the surrounding environment, whatever civilization lived in these parts didn't appear to be very advanced.

As I continued using Dimensional Step to travel downstream, parallel to the road, I spied a horse-drawn carriage and several horses stopped around it. I should have been excited about finally encountering some people from this world, but something about the situation felt very disconcerting.

I transported to a spot above the scene with a good vantage point, where I could watch over the carriage and its surroundings.

I saw a hulking figure clad in leather armor stab another man—one of the carriage's guards, it seemed—straight through the mouth. Around them, five other men who appeared to be guards lay motionless on the ground. There were also a few unkempt men sprawled out among them. The hulking man who'd stabbed the guard and five other men clad in similar clothing—mercenaries, bandits, or something similar—were all that remained. There were also two women, whom the bandits were handling roughly.

Judging by the looks—and the lecherous smiles—the bandits were giving these women, it was apparent where things were going next.

The whole scene further reinforced my impression that I was in a distinctly non-modern world. Horses and carriages were still being used as a means of transportation, and the men's clothes were straight out of a medieval play. What's more, they were just casually killing people with swords in the middle of the day.

But, I thought as I glanced down at my gleaming armor with a sigh, *others would probably say the same about me.*

The gleeful laughter and shouts of the bandits tearing away clothing mixed with the screams and pleas of the pinned-down women.

I couldn't simply stand by and watch. But to save these women, I'd have to take on six bandits, and I'd already seen them kill without hesitation. It wasn't like I could just walk on up and tell them to cut it out.

Assuming I had the same strength and abilities that I did in-game, I was sure I could take them on in a straight fight. But I had no idea if I was stronger—or possibly even weaker—than I was in the game. If I was weaker, well, it could all be over for me the moment I entered the fray. Either way, if I wanted to ensure my victory, I would need to make a plan and get the drop on them.

First off, I needed to take out as many bandits as possible in my initial strike. I hoped the odds were in my favor. After all, attacks made right after Dimensional Step were a nearly instant deathblow; in the game, at least.

The most basic step in any good strategy was to take out the most powerful enemy first. My target was the hulking man currently pulling down his pants. His backside was facing toward me, and he was right in my line of sight.

I pulled my sword out of its sheath. Though I may not have been able to use it with finesse, the mythical-class Holy Thunder Sword of Caladbolg shouldn't have a problem performing here, especially considering the power it had shown earlier when it cleaved through that tree with a single slash.

No, I couldn't worry about things like finesse right now. Those luxuries were reserved for seasoned soldiers.

I took a deep breath and squeezed the sword tightly in my hand. These people were murderers. There was no need to hesitate. Still not totally believing the situation I'd found myself in, I tilted my head to the side, and I focused my gaze on the hulking man.

In the next instant, I used Dimensional Step transportation spell to teleport myself behind the group of bandits and swung my sword at their unprotected backs.

The surprise strike was a massive success. Overpowering, even.

Before they were even aware of my presence, four of the bandits had already been taken out of the fight. As the remaining two attempted to run, I finished them off effortlessly. I hadn't originally intended to kill the escaping bandits, but as I got swept up in the flow of battle and saw the men turn and run, my body moved before my mind had a chance to catch up.

You often hear that showing your back to a bear will entice it to attack you, but this experience made me wonder whether the phenomenon was limited to bears. Until today, I couldn't have imagined actually striking a man down with the Wyvern Slash. Still, I didn't feel any strong emotional or physical reaction to having taken human lives. It was, after all, for the sake of saving the women.

Was this due to my new form?

I felt as if I was on the brink of catching a glimpse of some deep and bottomless emotion lurking within me, only for it to be replaced by an emotion equally lacking in significance. I couldn't tell what the hidden emotion was, but it was hardly the time for introspection. Now that I'd dealt with the bandits, I needed to help the women. Hopefully, they could show me to the nearest town.

I turned my gaze to them. They both looked as if they'd seen better days, so I decided to say something to put them at ease.

"Are you all right?" I spoke just as I would have in the game.

That's right. Just as if this were all a game.

The way I spoke when I played this character came out naturally, like a long-formed habit. Whenever I typed out in-game conversations in front of my PC, I'd mutter the words aloud to myself. Maybe that's why it didn't feel strange when I spoke the words here.

According to my character's backstory, he was an all-around nice guy in his early forties who'd been certified as a Sacred Knight before a curse was placed on him, turning him into a skeleton. He was now on a journey to wander the land in search of a cure.

The two women—actually, the one with the chest-nut-colored hair was still a young girl—gazed ahead blankly, drenched in the bright red blood of the bandits.

They must have been through a lot.

The girl in chambermaid clothing looked to be in her twenties and wore her curly, red hair short, cut off at the nape of her neck. Her strong, determined, green eyes stared back at me. She held an arm across her chest, where her clothing had been. She'd somehow avoided much of the blood spatter.

"You should go get washed up at the river. I'll stay behind and take care of any remaining bandits."

"Th-thank you... Come with me, madam."

The chambermaid responded to my suggestion with a slight bow before running over to the carriage and pulling out a large cloth from their bags. She walked over to the girl—the one she referred to as "madam"—and wrapped the girl in the cloth, then escorted the little madam toward the river.

After seeing them off, I surveyed my surroundings.

In all, there were nine dead bandits and six more bodies that appeared to have been guards. It was a gruesome scene.

In addition to the four horses hitched to the carriage, there were another twelve in the vicinity. Judging by the gear the horses carried, six of them had belonged to the bandits. Horses were probably a luxury in this place, akin to a passenger car in my own world.

Since I was trapped in a world I knew nothing about, I figured money was the first thing I needed to take care of. No matter what time period—or world—we were talking about, money was a universal necessity to life. Whether I planned on heading into town with the women or just wandering the lands as a vagabond, I'd need to get some other resources together as well.

First, I decided to take the bandits' horses and sell them in town. That would hopefully give me a fair amount of coin. I could probably take the weapons from the dead bandits and sell those too. I'd guess that blades in particular were pretty expensive in this time period, seeing as they were big chunks of metal.

The leather armor didn't seem like it'd net me much on the open market, so I decided to leave it all behind. It was all pretty roughed-up and drenched in blood, so I wasn't even sure I could sell it.

As I knelt to search the nearest bandit, I noted how difficult it was to tell the bad guys from the good. A wry laugh echoed from deep within my helmet.

I found a leather pouch tied to the bandit's waist. Inside, there were four silver, hundred-yen-sized coins and fifteen more that looked similar in size and color to the old ten-yen coins. They all bore the same mark on them and appeared to be the local currency. Silver and copper? They were poorly minted compared to the coins used in Japan, but they certainly fit with the rest of the world. I went about collecting money from the rest of the bandits.

The man with his backside sticking out—the leader, I supposed—had six gold-colored coins approximately the size of one-yen coins. The gold, or at least what I believed was gold, was surprisingly heavy for its size.

All told, the nine bandits had six gold, thirty-one silver, and sixty-seven copper coins. Whether this was a significant amount or not, I couldn't say yet. I didn't know anything about the cost of goods here.

After that, I collected a total of six swords, one

mace-like club, and three short swords. I tied them all together and put them into a burlap sack tied to the back of one of the bandits' horses. Then I piled all the bandits' bodies up in the grasslands next to the road. I was surprisingly calm about the whole thing. Maybe all those foreign medical shows I'd been watching had desensitized me to seeing bodies like this.

Figuring that the bodies would just start rotting if I left them like this, I cast Fire. Flames burst from my right hand, bathing the mound of corpses in a continuous stream and incinerating the bandits' remains.

I moved upwind of the flames and smoke to watch the scene unfold. As they burned, I thought about how even miserable excuses for humans like these could eventually become fertilizer and provide some sort of benefit to the grass and flowers once they were reduced to ash.

The two women returned from the river, and their complexions were notably better now. The chestnut-haired girl was wrapped in a large cloth and supported by her chambermaid. She was still somewhat pale as she made her way toward me, bowing her head slightly when she arrived.

"Th-thank you for saving me from such...dire circumstances."

Tears formed at the edges of her eyes. She must've been absolutely terrified. Despite all that, the very fact that she could approach a mysterious, armor-clad man and express her gratitude made it clear to me that she wasn't some simple, young girl.

"You have certainly met with a great deal of misfortune here. Though my words may ring hollow, I am relieved that you are safe."

After hearing my response, the chambermaid next to the girl bowed her head and spoke up. "Please allow me to also express my gratitude. Now, madam, let's get you into the carriage. I will bring you a change of clothes."

With that gentle prompt, the young girl walked to the carriage and climbed inside.

The chambermaid stepped behind the carriage, removed one of the leather bags tied to the luggage rack, and began searching for spare clothes.

"I've burnt the bandits' bodies. What would you like me to do with the guards?"

She stopped her search and thought for a moment.

"Put them to the side of the road." She bowed her head daintily as she replied. "We will send soldiers to collect their bodies. The weapons and horses will be coming back with us. I would greatly appreciate your assistance in gathering them together."

"Understood." I tilted my helmet curtly in reply and began moving the guards' bodies.

The chambermaid took the change of clothes inside the carriage and pulled the window curtain shut.

I gathered together the guards' weapons in a separate burlap sack, which I then put into the carriage's luggage compartment. The harnesses on the guards' horses seemed sturdy enough, so I used some rope the bandits had been carrying to tie them to the back of the carriage, hoping it would be able to pull them along. Then I tied together five of the bandits' horses and mounted the sixth, the sturdiest-looking one.

It'd been awhile since I'd ridden a horse—probably not since I'd taken a few lessons at my friend's riding school—but I felt comfortable at least getting the horse to walk. Running would be an entirely different story, as I'd never tried that before. Nor was I sure I could lead the other horses all the way into town.

All the horses were massive, nothing like the thin, streamlined thoroughbreds I was used to seeing. The muscles in their legs and throughout their body were thick and round, and the one I sat astride had little difficulty supporting my nearly two-meter-tall, hulking frame. It just looked back at me and my heavy armor as if I was some sort of annoyance.

A short time later, the chambermaid stepped out of the carriage in a new set of clothes and approached me.

"I would once again like to express my gratitude to you for rescuing us from that awful situation." She clasped her hands together at her waist and bowed her head deeply as she spoke.

"No thanks needed, I simply happened across you. However, I will gladly accompany you to the next town." I spoke with a slight air of arrogance as I redirected the discussion to my actual goal—getting to the next town.

"Thank you!" The chambermaid didn't seem to notice anything amiss and was rather cheerful as she thanked me before moving up into the driver's seat. She gave the reins a light snap, causing the horses to once again resume their march down the road.

Once the carriage had begun its silent procession forward, I brought my own horse alongside it. The horses tied together behind me dutifully clopped along in stride.

Looking up at the sky, I could see that the sun was now low and night was rapidly approaching. The horizon to the west was bathed in a deep burgundy, meaning we probably had another hour or so until it was completely dark.

"It seems I've forgotten my manners." The chambermaid, now driving the carriage, looked over to me from where she sat and bowed slightly in introduction. "My name is Rita Farren, chambermaid to Madam Lauren Laraiya du Luvierte, of the Luvierte family." Rita's green eyes were locked on my helmet. She seemed to be waiting for me to introduce myself.

"Hm." I cleared my throat once to give myself an air of importance. "They call me Arc. I'm but a simple wanderer." Of course, I opted to use my in-game name. Clad completely in armor like this, I found it much easier to put on an act and play someone other than myself.

The girl in the carriage was apparently the daughter of some type of nobility. It seemed my plan to lie low had failed right out of the gate. If I didn't get back on track soon, things could slide even farther downhill.

"What brings you to Rhoden, Master Arc?"

Rita's question broke me out of the introspective train of thought I'd drifted into, lulled by the gentle sway of the horse. It also brought many more questions with it, which floated about inside my head.

Was Rhoden a region? Or maybe a kingdom? It certainly wasn't a name I'd ever heard when playing online. My mind continued racing.

"I am simply wandering wherever my feet take me. I have no specific destination."

It was an answer I came up with in the spur of the moment. However, considering my character's backstory about traveling the land in search of a cure to his curse, it made sense for me to gloss over the specifics.

Looking ahead to the horizon, I could see that night had already settled into the hills, bringing with it a solemn atmosphere. Doubts were also rising from the darkest corners of my mind. What was going to happen to me? It wasn't like I had a particularly strong attachment to my life in the real world, but it'd also be rather difficult to live as a skeleton in some world I knew nothing about.

I'd gotten caught up in all the magic manipulation and sword wielding, forgetting about the harsh reality of my situation. But with things beginning to calm down a bit, the fear of uncertainty edged its way in.

Thankfully, Rita didn't seem to pick up on any of this. She simply nodded.

"Is that so? We're currently on our way to the town of Luvierte, which is controlled by Miss Lauren's father, Master Buckle. I'm confident he will be overjoyed to hear that you have done away with the bandits. I'd be honored if you would accompany us to his residence."

She must have picked up on some of my uncertainty, because she punctuated her invitation with a warm smile.

Alas, this wasn't an invitation I could accept. Meeting with someone of high status, like a land-owning noble, was simply out of the question.

First and foremost, I would have to take off my helmet; you can't just meet nobility with your helmet still firmly on your head. In modern terms, that'd be like meeting with the prefectural governor while wearing a motorcycle helmet. Nowadays, you can't even go into a convenience store with your face completely covered like that.

In any case, I needed to avoid that situation at all costs.

"I appreciate the offer. However, I do not need a reward. Your gratitude is enough."

I tried ending the conversation there, but her face only clouded over as she continued insisting.

"After having saved Miss Lauren and myself like that, I couldn't imagine not providing you with a reward. Perhaps you should speak with Master Buckle."

Well, this was making things difficult. It didn't look like refusing a reward was an option she was willing to accept. Maybe if I just told her something that I wanted, we could end it there. I wracked my skull as I tried thinking of something to request.

"Very well then. I'd appreciate it if you could provide me with something that would ease my passage as I continue my journey."

Assuming I'd need some sort of papers to travel about freely, I tried suggesting that. I highly doubted they had anything as advanced as a passport in this world, but I figured they might have something similar.

In response to my request, Rita furrowed her brow and looked ahead at nothing in particular.

"Provide you with... Ah! I think I know just the thing. Please, take this. It is my copper travel pass. Only the noble family themselves possess silver passes. So long as you show this, you should be able to travel anywhere you like throughout the domain."

She pulled a copper medallion, just slightly smaller than a business card, from her breast pocket and reached out from the driver's seat to hand it to me.

I took the medallion and looked it over. In the center was a crest—the noble family's crest?—as well as a number of symbols I'd never seen before etched onto its surface. It seemed well made, and could probably even be used as a decoration.

"Much appreciated."

After thanking her, I put the travel pass into the burlap sack on the back of my horse, with all the goods I'd liberated from the bandits.

Rita called out to me again, this time with a more cheerful tone in her voice. "Up ahead is the town of Luvierte, Master Arc."

I glanced ahead of the carriage, and, sure enough, I could see a town down the hill from us. The outskirts were marked by a moat approximately three meters across, filled with water from the river passing along its perimeter. An expanse of farmland surrounded the moat, grains rippling about as the wind blew across them. Beyond the farms was another moat, to provide an additional layer of protection.

The stone wall around the town was probably five meters in height and appeared to be well constructed. It would have been woefully short for a castle, but it seemed good enough for a town.

Luvierte appeared to be somewhat on the large side, considering the time period. Ahead of us on the road lay the town's gate. Approximately five meters across, it was flanked on either side by guard towers built directly into the wall. I had no doubt the towers housed numerous guards keeping a lookout. Immediately in front of the gate, a stone bridge crossed the outer moat, quite a departure from the drawbridges usually found at in-game towns.

The toll of a bell rose from somewhere inside this town that had appeared out of the darkness, the winds carrying each peal all the way to us.

"Master Arc, that bell marks the closing of the gates. We should hurry."

It seemed like the gate wasn't going to be shut immediately after the bell finished tolling, but Rita still wanted the carriage to reach the town before it did. Considering that the carriage held a noble's daughter, I was almost certain they would have opened the gates up for her regardless, but she was probably worried about making extra work for the gate guards.

We seemed to be approaching the east gate, in front of which stood several guards with spears. We'd been noticed.

One of the guards' demeanor changed instantly when he recognized Rita.

"Miss Rita, what happened?!" He ran over. "Where is Sir Maudlin and the other guards?"

Upon hearing his cries, the other gate guards also made their way over. The first man to approach was the only one wearing a helmet, perhaps their captain.

"We were ambushed by bandits about an hour up the road. Master Arc here defeated them, but, unfortunately, Sir Maudlin and his fifteen-guard contingent were all murdered."

"That can't be!"

The captain of the gate guards exchanged looks with Rita, utter bewilderment etched upon his face. The other guards began murmuring among themselves as they heard the news.

"We put the bodies of Sir Maudlin and five of his guards in a safe place. I'd like you to go collect them.

Now, I must take the madam back to her estate and notify Master Buckle of what has happened."

"Understood! I will form a group to recover the bodies at once. Please secure permission for us to depart from Master Buckle."

The captain offered Rita a swift salute before taking off in a run to give orders to his men.

Rita dropped down from the driver's seat and approached me, bowing her head again. "Master Arc, I'd like to once again express my gratitude to you. If there is anything I can ever do, please call on me, Rita Farren, chambermaid of the Luvierte estate. I promise I will do my utmost to assist you."

"Well, there is one thing... Could you tell me where I could sell these?" I gestured to the horses I'd taken from the bandits. Traveling around with six horses would be an incredible hassle, so I wanted to sell them as soon as possible. The only problem was that I didn't know where to do that.

"Enter the east gate then immediately turn right. There you will find Dando's stable. He will buy your horses. I'm sure he'll work out a deal quickly if you mention my name."

"Much obliged."

I thanked Rita and walked the horses through the east gate. We parted ways at the first junction, her turning left while I headed right, waving goodbye to them before continuing on.

The stable Rita had mentioned was made of wood, and beside it stood a sign with the image of a horse on it.

I tied the horses to a nearby pole and entered, where I found a stable hand. Though only 160 centimeters tall, he seemed a strong man with a stocky build, judging by the arms that bulged out of his rolled-up sleeves. He was bald, with a bushy beard that extended down to his chest. Assuming this was the shop owner, I cut to the chase and told the man what I wanted.

"Miss Rita of the Luvierte estate told me to come here. I'd like to sell some horses."

He looked surprised for a moment, but after giving me a quick once-over, his expression changed to a gentle grin as he approached me.

"Well, well. I be Dando, the owner of this fine establishment. Do ye have a letter of introduction, kind sir?"

"I have no letters, but Miss Rita told me this was the best place to sell horses. She wasn't exactly in a position to put pen to paper."

The stable owner raised an eyebrow, as if trying to unravel the meaning behind what I'd said. I didn't know if I could discuss what had happened with the bandits, but, in any case, I had an introduction from a person working for the estate. Since Dando almost certainly had some form of relationship with Rita, he should be able to trust me.

"The Luvierte daughter came under attack earlier this evening from a group of bandits. I happened to be nearby, so I lent them a hand. You could say the six horses are my loot from the bandits. Will you take a look?"

"Attacked? Miss Lauren?! This is certainly all news ta me. And six 'orses ye say... Well, I suppose we should go check on them."

Dando raked his fingers through his beard as he exited through the front of the stable to inspect the horses. He grabbed a lamp hanging next to the shop to get a better look, inspecting them one by one, stroking their coats as he went. He appeared to be running the numbers in his head.

"I can offer ye forty-five sok for the big one 'ere and thirty sok each for the rest. For the saddles...'ow does one sok for the lot sound?"

I still had no idea how much anything cost, or even the units of currency, but I assumed this would at least cover my initial travel expenses. Figuring he probably wouldn't make an unfair offer to a man fully clad in armor—though this was probably an overly optimistic outlook—I accepted.

"Glad ta 'ear it! Wait right 'ere, I'll be back with yer money. 'Ey, boys! Come get these 'orses an' bring 'em inside!"

With a quick nod of his head, Dando turned toward the shop and yelled inside. Two young boys came running out and went immediately to the horses, moving them to the stables.

I passed the time watching the boys move the horses until Dando returned, this time with a cloth sack. He began arranging the contents on a nearby table, stacking up the one-yen-sized gold coins in groups of ten. Apparently, gold coins were known as sok. In total, there were nineteen gold towers and six coins.

"That'll be 196 sok in all. Feel free ta check."

At Dando's prompting, I gave the coins a quick count before taking a few into my hand as if inspecting them. I couldn't really say either way, but there didn't seem to be any issues.

I put the coins into my small leather coin pouch, which quickly took on some heft. Despite how tiny the coins looked, each weighed about as much as a five-hundred-yen coin. They didn't look to be pure gold, but whatever metals they were made of were pretty heavy.

"Thank you. You don't by chance know of a place where I could spend the night?"

"An inn? Well, there's Marla's in the center of town, off the main thoroughfare. But I'm not sure if there's any place in these parts where a person like yerself could stay." Dando once again glanced over my armor, then gave me an apologetic look.

"I am but a wanderer. All I need is a place where I can lie down, out of the wind and rain."

After thanking the stable owner, I made my way toward the town's center.

The sun had now completely set, blanketing the town in darkness. I encountered several people walking quickly along the roads, but it seemed that few townsfolk went out after dark. Each time I passed someone, they looked taken aback when they saw me. I imagined it must have bene pretty terrifying to see an armor-clad man roaming the streets at night.

In the center of town, I found a thoroughfare about ten meters across. It seemed the town of Luvierte only had gates to its east and west, though this road connected the town's center to its southern part, meaning there was no direct route from the gates to the road.

Two-story, wooden houses and shops lined the thoroughfare, spilling light from their windows onto the road. In front of one shop hung a sign with the image of a barrel on it, which I assumed to be a bar. Loud, male voices could be heard echoing from within. I approached and called out to a man stumbling around near the bar's entrance.

"I am searching for Marla's inn. Could you tell me where to find it?"

"O-over there, S-s-sir Knight, sir!"

The drunk man stared wide-eyed at me as he slurred his words, pointing to a building across the road. I thanked him and made my way toward it. A bell rang as I stepped through the door, prompting a surprised-looking middle-aged man to hurry over from behind the counter to greet me.

"Ah, Sir Knight! What brings you to our humble establishment?"

"I'd like to stay the night."

"Here?! You want to stay here, in a place like this?" The innkeeper's voice squeaked, betraying his surprise.

I imagined I looked like a mighty knight from some far-flung region. But I confirmed my intention, and the innkeeper handed over a room key, his hand shaking ever so slightly.

A night's stay cost one sek—a silver coin. Firewood for cooking cost an additional sek. It must have been some sort of discount inn if people had to bring their own food, buy firewood, and cook their own meals in the kitchen.

To be fair, the concept of a meal coming with your stay had only started around the Edo period in Japan. In the west, food was still typically a separate charge, so I supposed it made sense here.

Next to the counter, a flight of stairs led up to the second floor. The stairs creaked under the weight of my armor as I ascended. Once at my room, I turned the knob only to find that the door wouldn't budge. Maybe it was just poorly made, but I heard a light thud as I pushed. It felt as if the door was caught on something. Putting a little more force into it, I heard a snapping noise as it came right off its hinges. The door was now suspended in the air, held up only by the doorknob in my hand.

"Wha?!" I gasped in surprise.

After checking to see if anyone was around, I began picking up the nails that had held the hinge to the door. I pushed them back into their holes, hoping to make the door as good as new. I opened and closed it a few times, and it seemed fine.

While I was glad to learn I was strong enough to push nails in with just a finger, it would have been nice not to have knocked the door off its hinges in the first place. Ultimately, though, I decided it was better to have more strength than less.

The room consisted of a small, wood-framed window

next to a simple, wooden bed covered by a large, thin blanket. I set the oil lamp I'd been given on the window sill and sat down on the bed to relax.

What today lacked in physical exertion, it made up for in emotional exhaustion, I thought to myself.

Despite not having eaten anything all day, I still wasn't hungry, nor did I feel particularly tired. It seemed there was so much left for me to learn about my skeleton body. I wondered if I might be able to function without rest.

I decided to sleep anyway. Not only did it seem pointless to wander the town while everyone slept, it wouldn't do much to help my reputation as a wandering skeleton, either. What's more, I'd seen few lanterns in the street when I was out earlier. Only faint moonlight illuminated the town. Even though the sun had just set, it may as well have been midnight as far as the town was concerned.

It was time to get some healthy, restful sleep. Whether or not a skeleton body needed a healthy, restful lifestyle was a question for another time.

My biggest issue for now, however, was whether I'd be attacked in my sleep. The inn didn't appear to have any form of security, so I'd decided not to take off my armor. I extinguished the lamp's flame and sat on the bed, resting my back against the wall. The wooden frame creaked in protest at my weight, but I ignored it and crossed my arms, letting my eyes fall closed.

How did I close eyes that I didn't even have anyway?

This question continued repeating itself in my mind as I lost myself to the darkness.

After parting ways with the armored knight, Arc, at the east gate, Rita directed the carriage down the road toward the estate at the center of town. The sun had already set, and there were few people milling about.

She could see the estate's large gate in front of her. The estate was surrounded by a four-meter-tall stone wall, at the center of which was an iron-reinforced wooden gate. Three guards stood watch out front.

Upon seeing the family crest on the carriage, one of the guards waved the gate open. Rita guided the carriage through and brought it to a stop in the garden next to a large, stone-built manor.

She could tell the guards were shaken. And why wouldn't they be? After all, the carriage returned without a driver or its accompanying guards. If that wasn't enough, the six horses tied together and trailing behind it would make anyone wonder what happened.

But it seemed the news had made it back ahead of them. No sooner had Rita stopped the carriage in front of the manor than the Luviertes' head butler came rushing outside.

"Rita Farren, just what happened here?!"

The head butler had thin white hair, complimented by a white mustache. Though usually a calm man, he was frantic as he pressed Rita for information.

Before she could answer, the carriage door opened and Lauren stumbled out. The daughter of the great Luvierte family looked as if she had seen better days. All the servants who had followed the head butler outside stood speechless, shocked at what they saw.

Not only was Lauren's face pale, but all the makeup that had been finely applied when she'd left earlier that day was now a mess, her hair in disarray.

Rita dropped down from the driver's seat and came to Lauren's side, supporting the young girl as she walked.

"We were ambushed by bandits. Miss Lauren and I were barely able to escape with our lives. Sir Maudlin and his contingent of guards fought valiantly, but they were struck down. I'd like to report the events to the master at once. Please hurry and make the necessary arrangements."

Upon hearing her report, the head butler went white and the other servants fell silent. But the head butler soon came to his senses and began issuing orders.

"Rita, go inform the master. He is in the study, as usual. The rest of you, look after the madam! I will notify Master Boscos of what has happened."

Despite his age, the head butler took off at a run toward a house separate from the main manor, but still within the estate.

Once the head butler was out of earshot, Lauren turned her gaze to her chambermaid. "Rita, I... I would also like to go see Father."

Rita hesitated for a moment before nodding her assent. She took Lauren's hand and led the girl into the manor's entrance hall.

Rita and Lauren climbed the stairwell up to the second floor, passed through the central reception room, and took a left down the corridor. From there, they proceeded along the west hallway before stopping in front of an elegantly-carved wooden door. Rita knocked lightly and waited for the person on the other side to give permission to enter.

The two slid silently into a room illuminated by several magical lanterns. Tall bookcases lined each wall, leading up to a large desk at the end where the master of the study sat, writing on a piece of paper.

The man had thinning brown hair styled with oil and a well-manicured mustache that complimented the soft, round features of his face. His eyes, however, carried within them that sharpness that often marks nobility. Those eyes drilled into the very souls of those he spoke with.

The man was Viscount Buckle du Luvierte, Lauren's father and the owner of this domain. He set down his quill pen. After inspecting Rita's face with apprehension, his eyes widened in utter bewilderment as they fell on his daughter, stepping out from behind the chambermaid.

His surprise was understandable. It was typically not Rita's responsibility to notify the viscount of his daughter's return. This would usually be done by a guard or Sir Maudlin, either reporting to the viscount himself or to the consul, Boscos, who would then relay the news. What was more, Lauren's expression was devoid of its usual graceful smile.

"Rita, Lauren, did you just get back from Diento? What happened to the two of you?" Buckle attempted to contain his shock as his eyes moved between the two women, though a hint of it could still be heard in his voice.

Rita took a step forward and told him what she'd told the head butler.

"What?! Lauren, are you all right? Are you hurt?"

No sooner had Rita finished making her report than Buckle sprang up from his chair and rushed over to his daughter, pulling her in close. Hardly any man could remain calm upon learning that his daughter had just been attacked by bandits.

"I'm sorry for causing you to worry, Father. Someone came to our rescue right when the situation was most dire." Lauren struggled to end her response with a smile, trying to not upset her father.

"Whatever do you...?"

Before he was able to inquire further into what his daughter had just said, they were interrupted by a knock at the door. After Buckle gave permission, a middle-aged man quickly entered the room.

The man stood around 180 centimeters tall with a slim build. His salt-and-pepper hair was cut close to his scalp, his face accented by long sideburns. Deep wrinkles lined his forehead, making him appear ten years older than his forty-or-so years of life. This was Boscos Futran, consul to the Luvierte family.

"I just heard the news from the head butler. Attacked by bandits... What sort of insolent fool would attack the viscount's carriage...?! But I am pleased to hear that Miss Lauren has returned safely."

Boscos furrowed his brow, causing the wrinkles to deepen even further as he stroked them with his right hand. He bowed deeply to Lauren, who responded in kind. The consul's words softened the expression on

Buckle's face. He turned back to Rita and spoke. "Tell us more about what happened, and the events leading up to it."

"We were first ambushed shortly after we left Corna by a group of around twenty bandits. Nine guards stayed behind to hold them back while we escaped with Sir Maudlin and the remaining guards. However, we were ambushed once again by a group of nine bandits the moment we stopped our horses."

"You were ambushed twice?!"

"That's correct. I suppose the first ambush may have been meant to draw our guards away."

Upon hearing this, Boscos crossed his arms, and his face contorted into a scowl. He cleared his throat before speaking. "Sir Maudlin and the five remaining guards were killed in the second ambush by just nine bandits? These men must have been highly skilled."

Rita responded, to the best of her ability and memory, as Boscos asked for more details on the attack.

"I can't believe it. A traitor in our midst?! Boscos, I want you to find out everything you can about this Causdah. If he has any family, I want them brought before me!" Buckle's veins bulged as he gave the order.

"Y-yes. Understood." Boscos gave a quick bow and left the study.

Returning to his desk, Buckle dropped back into his chair and let out an exhausted sigh. "A gang of bandits with six horses... I've never heard of any groups like that in this region."

The viscount groaned slightly as he looked out the study's window and into the darkness. The idea of mounted bandits was unbelievable to him. In addition to food and water, the bandits would also have needed shoes, saddles, and even training to prepare each horse for combat, all of which would have cost great amounts of money. A small-scale gang would have had a difficult time supporting six horses, but if a large group had moved into his domain, he would have at least heard rumors.

"It seems the bandits' objective was to kill Miss Lauren. It's possible they had been hired by someone."

Rita spoke her theory to the viscount's back. He continued groaning lightly as he glared out the window in front of him.

It was dangerous for bandits to attack a carriage belonging to a noble family. Though rare, abductions and ransoms did occur, but bandits generally wouldn't go out of their way to commit murder and make an enemy of the nobility. The noble society within the kingdom was a surprisingly close-knit group, and if bandits were to draw attention to themselves like that, they would be pursued across the entirety of the Rhoden Kingdom. They wouldn't do such a thing unless they had some sort of ace up their sleeve.

"Perhaps...this is a shake-up by the supporters of the second prince?" Buckle's round features contorted into a mixture of shock and anger as he hit on this possibility.

Behind the scenes, a vicious battle raged in Rhoden over who would succeed the elderly king. Dissent was spreading among the supporters of the three major factions: the first prince born to the king's second-class wife; the second prince born to his first-class wife; and the second daughter born to the actual queen.

Considering how far away Luvierte was from the capital, up near the northern border, the viscount had believed this battle had nothing to do with them. Rita tilted her head at Buckle's theory, but, being a simple chambermaid with little knowledge of political affairs, this was beyond her area of expertise. Lauren looked over at Rita and cocked her head to the side as well, also ignorant of the political world.

Sensing the confusion from the looks on the girls' faces, Buckle turned the conversation back to the man he heard about earlier, the one who saved them from the direst of circumstances. "And this armored knight who saved you from the second attack, did he make any specific demands?"

"We offered him our sincerest thanks, but...all he would accept was my copper travel pass. What shall we do?"

"If he says that's all he wants, then we shall leave it at that. I am eternally grateful to the man who saved my daughter, but I can't shake the feeling that anyone who would come at such an opportune time is somehow in consort with the supporters of the second prince."

The viscount couldn't overlook the possibility that this knight, who had appeared by the road at exactly the right time, had done so in order to build favor with the noble family. It all just seemed too suspicious.

Of course, Rita, who had interacted directly with the knight, insisted passionately that this was not the case. However, she was unable to change Buckle's mind.

"Rumors will spread once we collect the bodies of Maudlin and his men and begin sweeping for the remaining bandits. Please, take your leave and get some rest."

Rita and Lauren both bowed.

Once out of the study, Rita let out a sigh as she recalled the knight, his image etched into her memory. The knight—a self-proclaimed wanderer who spoke with a low, despondent voice—didn't strike her as being aligned with any particular faction. However, his magnificent armor reminded her of that worn by the guardians of the nearby Revlon Empire. Its overbearing presence made him feel like some sort of warrior deity.

Though she'd never actually seen his face, she hoped the fates would smile upon them and grant her a chance to meet him again. When she mentioned this to Lauren, the young girl's expression softened a bit, and she nodded firmly in agreement.

"You look happy, Rita."

"S-sorry, madam. I just feel like I've met a knight straight out of a fairy tale."

Seeing Rita's excitement wither under the belief that she had been chastised, Lauren apologized and bowed her head repeatedly. However, as she continued watching Rita, the edges of Lauren's lips turned up in a peculiar grin.

"Well, as punishment, I suppose you will be sleeping with me tonight."

Rita stood there, blinking at Lauren's response. The girl had never made a request like this before. However, considering the events that had unfolded earlier, it was no wonder that she was scared.

Locking eyes with Lauren, Rita took on a serious demeanor and nodded. She took the girl's cold fingers into her own, in an effort to warm them, and led the way back to Lauren's bedroom.

The next day, I awoke to find the morning sun straining its way through the gaps in the wooden shutters, faintly illuminating the room.

I stood and stretched my body in an attempt to loosen it up after spending a night with my back against the wall. Since I didn't have any muscles to loosen, it was more a habit than anything else.

After twisting the vertebrae in my neck left and right, I stood up from the bed and opened the window, filling the room with bright sunlight. The window faced the thoroughfare, and, outside, I could see the town below me already bustling, despite the early hour.

At the center of the thoroughfare sprawled a morning market, where many people had gathered. Customers milled about among a variety of merchants, including farmers offering up fresh vegetables, vendors hawking roasted meat, and craftspeople selling beautifully dyed cloths and other goods.

I checked the money in my waist pouch and the contents of my burlap sack, then made my way out of the room.

Down on the first floor, the check-out counter was empty, the other guests nowhere to be found. I guessed that would make sense, considering we'd all paid up front. Strange way to run a business, though.

Out on the thoroughfare, I threw the burlap sack over

my shoulder. All eyes were instantly on me, making me feel more than a little uncomfortable. Maybe walking around fully clad in armor wasn't the norm in this world. No, that couldn't be it; I could see a few others similarly outfitted. Maybe it was my rather ostentatious armor that was drawing attention.

Time to get myself together. First things first, I needed to find an armory to sell my loot.

I walked a ways to the west before spotting a shop with a sign bearing a crossed sword and axe. Inside, the shop was dimly lit, its cramped interior covered wall to wall with metal weapons and armor.

As I was browsing, a middle-aged man, who I assumed to be the shop's owner, stepped out from the back. At first, he was startled by my appearance, but he then flashed a cheerful smile.

"And what can I do for you, dear sir?" the shop owner asked, rubbing his hands together as he spoke.

"I'd like to sell these. What are they worth?"

I lowered the burlap sack from my shoulder and undid the cord holding the flap shut, placing all the items I'd plundered from the bandits—six swords, one mace, and two of the three short swords—onto the counter. The third short sword seemed like it might come in handy, so I left it in the bag.

The shop owner inspected each of the items, removing the swords from their sheaths so he could examine their blades. Finally, he placed his hand to his chin, as if signaling that he'd settled on a purchase price, and turned back to face me.

"I'll give you fifteen sok for the curved blade and five each for the straight swords. The mace'll get you seven sok and five sek, and I can pay one sok and five sek for each of the short swords. I can sell the curved blade straight away with a little sharpening, but I'll need to hammer out the rest of the swords to work out the imperfections. No one around here really uses maces, so that's the best I can do."

I was satisfied with the shopkeeper's explanation and agreed to his offer. "That will be fine."

"Fifty sok and five sek it is then."

He pulled fifty gold coins and five silver ones out of a cabinet and set them down on the counter. I put the money into my leather waist pouch.

Between the money from the horses and the money from the weapons, my pouch was feeling pretty full. Last night's stay had cost me a silver coin—one sek—and each of the gold coins seemed to be worth ten of the silver ones, meaning each one would provide me ten nights with a roof over my head.

However, I didn't know when or where I might need

money in this strange world. It would probably be best for me to find a way to earn more while I still had some financial stability.

The shopkeeper was facing away from me as he busied himself putting away the weapons he'd just purchased.

"Apologies, but do you perchance know of a way to earn some good wages to fund my travels?"

The shopkeeper stopped what he was doing and turned to look at me, tilting his head to the side slightly.

"Wages? Well, if I were to make a suggestion based on your magnificent armor there, I suppose I'd go with the mercenaries. Then you could enter and leave town without paying taxes, too."

So, there was a mercenary guild in town. If I registered with them, I'd receive a mercenary license I could show to the guards. I had no idea taxes were levied just for coming and going through the gates, since I'd entered the town with the Luvierte family's carriage.

By the nature of their job, mercenaries enter and exit towns often, so it'd be impossible to make a living if they had to pay taxes every time. Shopkeepers who registered with the merchant guild also fell under the same system, but they still had to pay taxes on the goods they sold.

I thanked the shopkeeper and left.

The mercenary guild office was right across the

thoroughfare from the weapon's shop, next to the merchant guild. It was a plain, two-story, timber building, its only distinguishing feature a sign depicting a sword crossed over a shield. Upon entering through the double doors on the first floor, I found myself at a counter completely fenced in by iron bars that went straight up to the ceiling, like a cage.

Inside the cage sat a lone bear. Not actually a bear, but a man who could pass for one. Sporting short black hair and a face that hadn't seen a razor in some time, the man wore a black eyepatch and had a large scar that ran across his forehead. Muscular arms protruded from his shirt, and tufts of black hair pushed out around his open collar.

So far, the only people I'd seen at reception desks or in shops had been burly men. I guessed women's rights hadn't yet advanced all that much in this world.

The eyepatch-wearing bear glared at me as I approached the counter, but this was understandable, considering I was completely decked out in weapons and armor.

"I'd like you to issue me a mercenary license."

The corners of the bear's mouth twisted into a grin when he heard my request, though he continued to glare at me through his cage. I supposed this was his best effort at a smile, something he wasn't quite used to doing, but it was still off-putting.

"Judgin' by yer equipment, ya don' seem to be in any

need of money. Besides, if ya want a mercenary license, ya need to pass a test. A test of strength, basically. All ya need to do is bring back proof that ya killed three beasts, monsters, or bandits. Which ones and the order is up t'you. Real simple, yeah?" The bear guarding the reception desk shot me a bold smile.

Beasts sounded normal enough, but apparently there were also monsters in this world. I'd noticed herds of animals out in the grasslands and on the hills as I made my way here, but I hadn't seen anything like a beast or monster. It had all struck me as a rather tranquil scene.

What's more, bandits were also included on the list. Would severed heads serve as proof, then? I'd already cremated the corpses of the bandits I'd killed yesterday, so those wouldn't do.

"Understood. I'll be back with my three bounties."

I made a mental note of the test criteria before thanking the bear and leaving the mercenary guild office.

Despite how crowded the thoroughfare's sprawling morning market was, the path immediately in front of me was surprisingly clear. I walked easily through the crowds and headed toward the west gate.

On my way, I stopped at a stall selling a variety of leather goods, ranging from small coin pouches made from hardened leather to leather carrying cases. I picked up a large leather waterskin in the shape of a gourd, with a cork pressed into the top to serve as a stopper. This was an absolute necessity for any traveler. I handed the stall owner three silver coins and received five copper coins in change. Considering how full my coin pouch was already, I knew fishing out copper coins would quickly become a hassle. Pretty soon, I'd have to start sorting my coins into different pouches based on their denominations.

At another stall, I purchased a large leather sack for one sek, so I'd have something to put my upcoming bounties in. This time, I opted to pay in copper coins to lighten the weight of my coin pouch.

As I continued, I passed a stall whose delightful aroma filled the thoroughfare. A simple fire pit in front of the stall displayed roasted meats covered in finely-diced herbs. The smell made me quite hungry.

My interest piqued, I turned to a man smoking a pipe in front of the stall. "Shopkeep, what type of meat is that?"

The man seemed to have swallowed some smoke as I spoke to him. His eyes swelled red and he coughed as he offered up his response. "Hyack! Th-this is herb-roasted rabbit meat, Sir Knight."

What I'd assumed was chicken was apparently rabbit. I'd heard it was a staple of French cuisine, but I'd never tried it before.

"I'll have one then."

The man skipped past the selection of cooked, leaf-wrapped meats lining the front of his stall and instead grabbed some fresh meat. He began cooking it in front of me, but the flame in the fire pit was already dying down. The man obviously wanted to offer me something freshly cooked, but I couldn't help getting annoyed at how long it was taking. I'd stopped by the stall because I was hungry *now*. One of the cooked meats would have been fine.

I decided to be appreciative and wait. As I let my eyes wander, I watched the old man stretch out his hand toward the wood in the fire pit and begin chanting quietly. "Fire, heed my call and burn. Fire!"

A fireball erupted from the man's hands and set the firewood ablaze.

"Wha?! Are you a magic user?" I could hardly contain my surprise. The sight was even more impressive than when I'd used magic myself.

The man rubbed the back of his neck, his pride barely concealed by his attempt at modesty. "Well, it's just a little fire magic, nothing special."

"That's right, Sir Knight. A magical fire rod would be just as useful as him and his magic," a woman selling dried beans one stall over poked fun at the man.

"You don't need to be so blunt, Ma. Besides, this is

much more convenient. Unlike magic rods, I don't need any rune stones."

"Why, even a goblin's rune stones would last a while in a fire rod. I hardly see a difference."

It seemed like the woman one stall over may be his wife. He objected weakly, but she just cackled as she continued without mercy.

Magic was evidently a relatively normal occurrence in this world. It sounded like even people who couldn't use magic were able to use magic-imbued items. From those used in day-to-day objects to ones made for use on the battlefield, I could only imagine the wide array of rune-stone-powered items that must be out there. Hearing popular monsters like goblins brought up in normal day-to-day conversation also made the fact that I was in an alternate world feel all the more real.

The man, now hunched over after being so thoroughly browbeaten by his wife, handed me the freshly roasted rabbit. I thanked him for the meat and paid. It looked to be a whole rabbit's worth of meat, but it only cost me two copper coins. The smell of it was overpowering, but there was no way I could take my helmet off and eat here. I'd need to take my lunch outside the town limits while I searched for my bounties.

As I made my way west down the thoroughfare, I took

a detour to look at some of the houses and soon stumbled upon a small, open area in front of the west gate. There, I found a stone waterway that poured water out into another aqueduct below. The water appeared to be drinkable, as I watched peddlers entering the gate fill their flasks. Women from the surrounding houses came and went as well, filling various bottles and jars with water.

Downstream, in the lower aqueduct, people washed vegetables and the like, and even farther down, women washed clothes. The east gate probably had a similar setup, but it had been night when I arrived, which was why I hadn't seen anyone.

As I approached the aqueduct, the people fell quiet and spread out to make way for me. I gave my water skin a quick rinse before filling it up, then popped the cork in it and returned it to my burlap sack. I then made my way toward the west gate.

Merchants stood with their horse-drawn carts at the west gate as their goods were inspected by the guards. I also spotted the occasional man in leather or metal armor milling about, likely serving as hired protection for the peddlers. There were surprisingly few people lined up at the gate, possibly due to the taxes imposed by the town.

As I approached, a guard—obviously terrified out of his mind by my appearance—slowly approached me.

"S-sorry, sir, but if you're leaving town, you'll need to pay the exit tax of three sek or show me your travel pass."

The guard was young. Behind him, I could see several older guards talking to each other as they watched. It seemed like they'd volunteered him to come over. The guard's voice squeaked as he spoke.

I reached into my bag and pulled out the travel pass I'd received the night before and handed it over. As soon as he saw it, the young guard quickly saluted, then handed the travel pass back. Apparently, this was my permission to leave, so I made my way through the west gate.

Crossing the stone bridge over the moat, I saw a vast field, much like the one at the east gate, sprawled out before me. I continued following the road west, spying the occasional farmer tending crops as I went.

I would've preferred to speed things up using Dimensional Step, but I wanted to avoid doing anything too flashy while people could see me. I stood out enough as it was. Magic may be regarded as a relatively normal part of life in this world, but it was unlikely that spells involving zipping through the air were a common occurrence. If they were, then people wouldn't need horses. No, I decided to walk on my own two feet.

The road sloped gently uphill. When I made it to the top, I was able to get a good look at my surroundings.

To my left, a massive river meandered across the country-side to the southwest. A little farther down the hill in front of me, the road branched off into two directions. One continued following the river, and the other stretched off to the northwest. The fields I'd walked through ended at the hill, and there were no signs of human habitation in the distance.

I figured I could use my teleportation magic to travel along the northwest road. However, since I didn't have a map, and there weren't any buildings to use as landmarks, it was best not to stray from the roads, lest I get lost.

Dimensional Step was quite convenient. When I had a good view of the countryside, I could easily travel up to a kilometer or so. On the other hand, the better my view, the more easily I could be seen.

After moving along the northwest road a ways, I came across a small forest just off the path. Figuring I may be able to find some sort of beast there, I teleported to the tree line and entered the forest. But my search may prove more difficult than I'd anticipated. In addition to the sounds of my footsteps as I walked through the under-brush, the birds were chirping noisily.

Plus, if I ran across any dangerous monsters, my only real option was to retreat.

I continued my search through the forest, teleporting

as I went. My vision was far more obscured here than it was on the plains, so the distances I teleported were naturally shorter.

I proceeded through the forest with care, ever vigilant of my surroundings, so as not to get lost in the forest. But, being a novice hunter, I knew finding any sort of beast wouldn't be easy. The fact that I was wearing gleaming, silvery-white armor also didn't help matters. While I lacked a hunter's stealth, I made up for it by providing a huge target to other hunters.

At the very least, my armor meant that I still had a chance even if a wild animal caught me in its jaws.

I finally found two small, boar-like creatures near a stream a little ways off. They were around a meter long and covered in short, grayish-brown hair. Two long tusks arced out their mouths. The animals weren't moving much; they were probably resting. I watched them from a distance through the gaps between the trees as I drew the Holy Thunder Sword of Caladbolg from its sheath on my back.

The sword made a slight scraping noise, unleashing an azure glow as I drew it. The boars didn't seem to notice, though their ears perked up slightly. Sword firmly in hand, I used Dimensional Step to move right up next to them in an instant.

As soon as I reappeared, I hacked at the boar closest to me. The sword easily severed two of the boar's legs—one front and one back—the bones offering no resistance. I then teleported to the second boar and again chopped off the front and back legs on one side.

The boar-like creatures collapsed next to the river, squealing as they fell. As soon as they hit their sides, I pierced their stomachs. The squealing grew even louder as blood poured from their bellies and severed limbs. The water in the creek took on darker and darker shades of red as the boars' cries began to weaken.

These boars were undoubtedly edible, so I figured I could turn a decent profit by taking them back and selling them somewhere after I passed the trial for my mercenary license.

I remembered hearing someplace that leaving blood in a body would make the meat smell bad, so you needed to cut the animal's stomach open while it was still alive and drain the blood. As such, I lined the boars along the incline of the creek to allow the blood to flow away.

I knew it'd be pretty cold-hearted to enjoy a hunk of meat now, surrounded by the boars' ever-weakening death cries. Yet, for some reason, looking down at them reminded me of the herb-roasted rabbit I'd bought that morning. I sat on the rocky bank of the creek and, after a quick check to make sure I was alone, took off my helmet. The only sounds around me were those of the rustling trees and the quiet burbling of the stream. After taking a deep breath of the fresh air and stretching for a bit, I pulled the package of herb-roasted rabbit from my bag.

"Bless this meal." I put my hands together in thanks for the rabbit I was about to eat.

I unwrapped the leaves and grabbed the meat with my hand, taking a big bite out of it. I had no complaints about the smell of the herbs or the slightly salty meat, and, actually, it tasted pretty good—much like chicken, though the texture was a little rubbery, which I could definitely get used to.

In no time at all, I'd eaten an entire rabbit's worth of meat. I then pulled out the leather waterskin I'd purchased that morning to bring some moisture back to my throat after all that salty meat. It was still a mystery to me where all the food and water actually went, but I was happy enough that I could eat and drink.

"Thank you for this gift." After putting my hands together again in thanks, I washed them in the stream and sat down on the rocky bank to rest.

I propped my head up in my hands as I let the sounds of the wind rustling through the leaves and the water flowing over the rocks wash over me. I looked around at the forest around me. I'd assumed this was a parallel world, but it lacked most of the hallmarks of a fantasy setting. But it didn't feel like I'd traveled back to the Middle Ages either.

There were no floating continents, no dragons, and I hadn't yet encountered any fantasy staples like ogres or elves during my travels. I'd heard there were goblins and other such monsters, but the beasts lying in front of me next to the creek looked like nothing more than boars with larger-than-average tusks.

Up till now, the most fantasy-like thing I'd encountered was myself. A skeleton that could eat, drink, and even use overpowered magic. It made the magic the man at the food stall used look like nothing more than a cheap card trick. I grumbled to myself that until I truly saw a monster, I still wouldn't be totally convinced about where I was.

Right at that moment, I sensed something approaching from deep within the thicket on the other side of the creek. As it drew nearer, I could hear heavy footfalls and a sound akin to that of a screeching pig.

Out from the thicket came three large pigs, each around 160 centimeters tall, walking upright on two feet.

They had hunched backs and massive arms, each holding thick, crudely constructed clubs. Their skin was a ruddy color, and they wore no clothes. The pig-like creatures stumped toward the stream on tiny legs, their protruding bellies wobbling as they moved.

That right there was all the convincing I needed. This was *definitely* a fantasy world.

Though similar to the orcs I was accustomed to in video games, these were slightly different. They were completely naked—possibly due to limited intellect—and lacked any type of armor or metal weaponry. In the game, these would be your typical, run-of-the-mill monster, probably somewhere between Level 20-40.

I was sure I could easily dispatch them. After all, I'd leveled up my current character to Level 255, the maximum achievable level. Level 250 was the maximum with normal experience points alone, but the game offered a system that would increase the limit by one every time you completed certain massive player events. Each unlocked level beyond 250 granted the same amount of benefits as ten normal levels, meaning I was actually equivalent to Level 300.

I also had the mythical-class weaponry that I'd just used in my encounter with the boars, which made me quite formidable in combat.

The three orcs made snorting noises, apparently communicating with each other. It looked like they were pointing at the boars lying next to the creek and saying, *Looks like we found a great catch.*

Just then, one of the orcs noticed me sitting on the rocky embankment and let out a high-pitched squeal.

"Squeeeeee!!!"

"Hroink?! Hraffa oink froogrho!"

The other two orcs responded in kind with their own menacing cries. They lifted their clubs and ran toward me, footfalls thundering as they approached. Rather, to call what they were doing "running" was probably an overstatement. Regardless, waves rippled across their protruding bellies as they moved.

I put my helmet back on and teleported behind the orcs. Pulling my sword from its sheath, I jammed it into the back of one of their necks, right through the cervical vertebrae.

"Hruaugh?!"

The orc I'd stabbed died instantly. Just like in the game, it seemed they weren't all that much of a challenge.

The remaining two looked around desperately for a moment, still surprised that their foe had disappeared right before their eyes. Slowly, they became aware of my presence behind themselves.

I twisted the wide blade from side to side, effortlessly slicing through the dead monster's meaty neck and sending its head tumbling down. Blood burst out of its huge body as it fell, hitting the ground with a massive thud.

"Froink?! Hroooink!"

Upon witnessing the death of their comrade, the two remaining orcs let out terrified squeals and stumbled over themselves to escape into the forest.

I didn't bother pursuing them, since the two boars and the one orc I'd already killed satisfied my three-bounty requirement.

I took the orc's severed head to the creek and washed away the blood. Even though I knew it was an orc, it looked just like a normal pig without its body. I put the head into the bag I'd bought for my bounties. Hopefully it'd serve as enough proof. I then tied the hind legs of the boar creatures together and threw them over my shoulder. They must've weighed at least a hundred kilograms together, but I had no problem carrying them, thanks to my leveled-up strength.

Alternating between walking and teleporting, I made my way out of the forest. I got lost, albeit briefly, but eventually made my way back to the main road.

I wasn't very good with directions, so I needed to be careful here. Otherwise I'd never make it back to town. It wasn't like there was anyone around for me to ask for directions, or even a police box.

Back on the road, I let out a sigh and looked up at the sun. It looked like it was around three in the afternoon.

Keeping an eye out for any people nearby, I made my way back toward the town of Luvierte using short teleportation jumps. When I reached the place where the road forked, I began seeing other people heading into town. It looked like I'd need to walk the rest of the way in.

About an hour later, I arrived at Luvierte's west gate.

The people I passed looked surprised when they saw me with two animals hanging over my shoulder. I imagined it was uncommon to carry that much weight so effortlessly, and over one arm at that.

I stepped through the open double doors of the mercenary guild office. The place was empty except for the eyepatch-wearing bear manning his cage at the counter and another man deeper inside doing administrative work. As I approached the counter, the corner of the bear-like man's mouth twisted up into a sneer as he glared at me through his cage. I was sure the bars around the counter were meant to protect the employees from ruffians, but from where I stood, it looked like this man was a dangerous caged animal that couldn't be let loose.

"Back so soon, huh. Didja get anything?" The bear called out to me with that awkward smile still on his face.

In response, I took the bound animals off my shoulder

and set them on the ground. I removed the orc's head from my bounty sack.

"That makes three. Will you be issuing me my mercenary license now?"

The bear's eyes widened slightly, and a low noise emanated from the back of his throat, possibly out of admiration.

"Well, I'll be. I never expected ya to get all three in jus' a half days' time. Two bull boars and an orc, huh? What'd ya do with the orc meat and his rune stone?"

Apparently, the boar-like creatures were called bull boars. As for the orc, I was surprised to learn the meat was edible.

The man went on to explain that orc meat was worth five sek—the silver coins—and since orcs were monsters, there was a black stone in their hearts called a rune stone. When I told him I'd never taken a rune stone before, the man laughed.

"Well, ya certainly aren't hurtin' for money, are ya?"

The rune stones found inside orcs were the size of a pinky finger and were only worth around one silver sek. Even so, it seemed like such a waste when that same amount could buy me one night at a cheap inn. I decided from then on to do my best to get those stones.

After his inspection was finished, the man placed

a gold medallion around the size of a dog tag on the counter between the bars.

"Here's your mercenary license. That'll run ya three sek. Also, I need yer name."

"My name is Arc."

I pulled three silver coins out of my wallet and paid the man before taking my gold mercenary license in hand. On the license was a five-digit number followed by a string of unfamiliar characters. It also had three stars etched into it. I stared at the characters for some time until suddenly, despite not having seen these characters before, the translation popped into my head. "Luvierte Mercenary Guild, Rhoden Kingdom." It was a peculiar feeling.

Thinking about it, I realized I'd been able to converse with those around me this whole time. I couldn't believe I hadn't thought about this before. But there was no downside to being able to understand the language at least.

"What are these?" I pointed to the three stars etched into the right side of the mercenary license.

"That's yer skill level, assigned to you by our staff. Being able to single-handedly take down an orc puts ya at three stars. The highest level is seven stars, but there ain't too many around like that." The eyepatch-wearing bear flashed a toothy grin, giving the impression he might be one of those rare few.

Three out of seven wasn't bad at all. I hadn't been aiming for a rank, but "average" was fine with me.

"Roaming mercenaries usually look for jobs on the hiring board over on that wall."

He pointed over toward a board hanging next to the entrance. Several wooden tags with letters written on them hung from it. At first glance, they looked like the picture tablets hung up for offerings at shrines. I took one of the tags into my hand and stared at the letters. The words slowly began translating in my mind, and one by one, I was able to understand what they meant.

It seemed like each of these tags was a work order. Judging by the difference in color between the sides and surfaces, once a request was completed, the surface was shaved clean and a new order was written on it. It seemed paper was probably still a luxury in this world. I took a look through all of the hanging tags and read the requests.

"These are pretty much just chores."

Most of the requests were boring tasks, like ridding fields of vermin, helping cultivate farmland, transporting rubble, or cleaning the aqueducts. Not only that, but the pay was bad too. Was this a mercenary guild or a help-wanted one?

"A town's mercenary troupe gets first dibs on the really good jobs and those that'll need a lot of men. If yer looking for somethin' on the higher end, you'll wanna join a troupe. The folks who take requests from the guild office are members of the troupe with some downtime trying to earn extra pocket money or wandering mercenaries like you."

Joining a mercenary troupe and taking on job orders with other members was out of the question. I wouldn't be able to hide my identity forever in that case. On the other hand, it would be difficult to spend the rest of my life never interacting with people.

I decided to take on a random job, just to get a feel for how the system worked.

I looked through the job board again and grabbed a request. It was from a person in the village of Rata who wanted someone to stand guard while they picked medicinal herbs. The pay was low—just one sek—but I wanted to see what herb-gathering was like.

In the game, picking medicinal herbs was a common fetch quest. Here, however, I'd be protecting those doing the picking. It made sense when I thought about it, since it'd be tough for someone without any knowledge of herbs to go out looking for them. Mercenaries wouldn't know how to tell the difference between herbs and similar-looking grasses, or even where they typically grew.

When I took the job request to the counter, I was met with a confused look from the bear-like man.

"Are ya serious 'bout takin' this one? The pay is low for what they're askin'."

"That's fine. I'm interested in the process."

This was entirely a flight of fancy on my part. In addition to the low likelihood that I'd encounter any notable danger while watching over someone searching for herbs, this also felt like the most quest-like job of the lot.

"Yer a strange one. Be sure to treat the requester nice, yeah? Not that that'd be a problem for the likes of ya." The smile pulling at the corners of the bear's mouth looked much more natural this time around.

The man was a pretty rare breed. How many other people in this world would have treated me normally if I stood in front of them fully outfitted in armor?

The bear finished registering the job to me and handed back the tag. He said the requester was a thirteen-year-old girl living in the village.

"After ya finish the request, be sure to have her give ya a completion tag. Ya get paid by submittin' the request tag together with the completion tag."

I asked the bear how to get to Rata, thanked him, and left the guild.

My next stop was the merchant guild office next door. The bear told me they'd buy the boars and the orc's head off of me.

The merchant guild office was much larger than the mercenary guild, and even included spaces to park carriages out front, as well as a vault to store merchandise in the back. It also had far more staff members than visitors.

Much like in the mercenary guild, the counter was surrounded by iron bars. However, unlike the mercenary guild, there were many people bustling about behind the counter. I called out to one of the receptionists, a middle-aged man, as I approached and asked to sell my loot. He told me that purchases were made by the vault in back and pointed out where to go.

The inspection went quickly, and I was able to sell the bull boars for seven silver and five copper coins each and the orc's head for a single copper coin. I put the coins in the leather pouch, thanked the staff member, and was on my way yet again.

When I stepped outside, it was already dusk. I decided I'd stay here for another night and make my way to Rata tomorrow.

The town of Diento was built to serve as a strategic point on the road leading to the capital, which was located at the center of the Rhoden Kingdom.

Travelers from the northern border had two routes available to them when making their way to the capital: the western route which wound its way through the Calcut mountain range that spread to the south of the capital; or the eastern route.

Though the western route offered a shorter journey to the capital, it was bordered on the western side by the vast Hibbot wasteland. Due to the difficulties in securing water, and the limited number of towns along the road, traveling with large groups was no easy task.

By comparison, the eastern road was longer, but it ran parallel to the Lydel River. The river flowed all the way down the eastern side of the Calcut mountain range and straight into the capital, providing a vast water supply along the way.

The relatively flat land also provided for larger towns along the eastern route. Though travelers from the Furyu mountain range would need to cross the Lydel River twice, both up- and downstream, it was still the easier of the two.

The town of Diento was on the eastern route and stood in front of the expansive, three-hundred-meter stone bridge that crossed the Lydel River upstream, leading straight to the town's east gate. Due to Diento's strategic importance, it also served as a fortress, and was surrounded by two stone walls.

Marquis Tryton du Diento was the ruler of this town. His well-constructed castle stood at the center of Diento and doubled as its military fortress. In addition to the two walls, it was also surrounded by dual moats.

In one of the rooms of the castle stood a desk, behind which sat Marquis du Diento, who was busy shuffling through assorted papers. This was his study, where he spent many of his days. Sporting a mane of white hair that flowed down his back and a bushy white mustache, Marquis du Diento was a plump, older gentleman, dressed in the finest of clothes.

A hollow knock echoed at the study door. Without looking up from his work, Marquis du Diento gave permission for the person on the other side to enter.

"Pardon me, sir."

Celsika Dourman, consul to the Diento domain, entered the room. Celsika was a thin man with a nervous, pale complexion. He wore his hair long, combed over on top to hide the fact that his hair was thinning. After a slight bow, he made his way over to the desk, brushing his drooping hair back into place as he did.

"The Luvierte...matter...ended in failure..."

Tryton raised an eyebrow in response to Celsika's report and looked up from his papers, breathing a heavy sigh. He slumped back into his chair. "I seem to recall you saying you had entrusted this to someone most skilled."

"Apologies, sir. My man *was* skilled. He slayed all the guards. However, fates turned, and a wandering mercenary killed him and his bandits."

"So, they were just bandits after all. Your plan was lacking in the most important of details. And what of the monsters we received from the east to set loose in Luvierte?"

"I've yet to receive any reports. However, since the first plan has already failed, it's unlikely the second will shake Viscount Luvierte. The odds are even better now that he will handle the monsters."

"Damn!" Tryton's face contorted. "Well, even so, I imagine two giant basilisks will at least rack up a hefty number of casualties."

Celsika nodded in agreement. "But why would His Highness Dakares want to cause turmoil in Luvierte?"

"Who can say? Perhaps it's a demand from the east. They're protecting His Highness's back after all. If Luvierte were to fall in line with Dakares' faction, it would reinforce the east's position and allow him to focus his attention on Revlon to the west. We have so much trade with the east, so it would benefit us as well."

"True. Luvierte currently supports the west, putting him in His Highness Sekt's camp. We haven't yet publicly committed to any position, so it's doubtful they know about our involvement in this incident."

"If no one knows, then we shall leave it that way. It's more important that you secure the products. We need to send them out soon. For now, focus only on nobility within the kingdom that we're certain are paying attention to us. No matter what, we need to ensure that Her Highness Yuriarna does not learn of this."

Tryton shifted his heavy frame, pulled a cigar from a desk drawer, and lit it. Smoke billowed out of his mouth with each exhale. Between puffs, he asked Celsika about the status of the products.

"We currently have four of the elven...products...in the basement of the shop. We have a group out looking for more now."

"It's growing harder and harder to get our hands on them it seems. Perhaps they're finally becoming suspicious. I want you to speed up your efforts. And where is that idiot son of mine? I haven't seen him around lately."

"Master Udolan? When I checked on him this morning, he was wearing his sword. He may have accompanied the group to acquire more elves."

A vein bulged in Tryton's forehead when he heard this response, and he pounded his fist down on the desk. "That idiot! This isn't a game! He can hardly use a sword as it is, he'll be nothing but a hindrance in the elf forest! I've heard enough. Leave at once."

Celsika responded by bowing courteously and quietly slipping out of the room.

Tryton took a deep pull on his cigar before aggressively extinguishing it in his ashtray. He glared down at the papers splayed across his desk.

SKELETON KNIGHT IN ANOTHER WORLD

CHAPTER 2
The Wandering Mercenary

I WOKE UP THE NEXT MORNING to the sounds of people bustling about as they walked along the thoroughfare.

I'd come back to the inn again, spending another night on the creaky wooden bed with my back against the wall. After loosening up my stiff joints, I picked up my bags and went downstairs.

The counter was unmanned, just like yesterday. After exiting the inn, I merged into the crowd of people on the thoroughfare and made my way toward the east gate.

Today, I was heading to the village of Rata—about a half day's journey by horse—to carry out the job I'd taken from the mercenary guild office.

I passed through the morning market and refilled my water skin at the aqueduct in front of the east gate.

Nearby, a group of armored men stood gathered together, watching me out of the corners of their eyes. The town's mercenary troupe, perhaps?

At the gate, I showed my travel pass and was waved on through, just like the day before. After crossing the stone bridge, I walked along a raised dirt path that ran between the wheat fields and the moat, following along the town wall as I made my way north.

Every time I ran across a farmer, they would bow their head and step out of my way. They probably assumed I was a royal knight from some far-flung region, so I made sure to nod my head and acknowledge them as I passed.

Once I reached Luvierte's northern boundary, the dirt path grew into a much larger road that stretched off into the distance. I continued following it, and, once I was out of the fields and could no longer be seen, I began using Dimensional Step to quickly traverse the picturesque landscape.

After traveling north for a bit, I hit my first juncture in the road—the landmark I was looking for. The bear had told me yesterday to take a left and follow the road into the village. Looking ahead, I could see one of the paths had massive stakes running along both sides. In the other direction, a dirt path covered in undergrowth stretched off into the northwest. It was more of an animal trail than a road, though in my world, neither of these options would have passed for roads.

I continued teleporting along the animal-trail-like path until I saw a field surrounded by a wooden fence and an empty ditch. Beyond the field lay a village surrounded by a moat, and inside that, a large mound of dirt with logs bound together and stacked on top formed a wall. The gate consisted of several massive logs strapped together and suspended over the entrance by a sturdy-looking rope. The villagers would probably cut the rope to drop the gate whenever they were under attack.

Outside the gate, two old men with poorly made spears talked animatedly. One of the men noticed my approach and notified the other. They both began babbling and gesticulating wildly as they watched me.

Eventually, one of them made his way over to me, tottering along with his bent back and using the spear as a cane. To be honest, these men didn't seem like the best choices for gate guards.

"Sir Knight! May I ask what business you have with our simple village?" the old guard spoke in a stilted, high-pitched voice. He must have been nervous.

"Please don't misunderstand. I am a simple mercenary. I came here to perform a job at the request of a Miss Marca."

"Marca? Seona's eldest daughter, right?" The old man

blinked several times, the look of surprise at my unexpected response apparent on his face.

"Could you please show me the way to Miss Marca's home?"

"R-right away! Follow me." The old man replied excitedly and led me toward the gate, gesturing to the other guard as we passed to let him know everything was fine. I finally entered Rata.

All eyes were on me in an instant. Not only was it likely rare to have an outsider come visit, but they were probably put even further on edge by my armor. The reaction was consistent everywhere I went.

In contrast with the wooden houses I'd seen back in town, the dwellings in the village looked more like mountain cabins. The old man walked up to one of these dwellings and knocked on the large wooden door before announcing our presence.

"Seona, you in there? You've got a visitor!"

I heard a woman reply and, a moment later, saw the door open a crack. However, there was no one there.

I lowered my eyes a bit and noticed a girl of around ten staring up at us. She wore her blonde hair in a bob and regarded the old man and me with large, brown eyes.

"Hello, Herina. Where's your mother? This knight here has some business with her."

"Umm..."

The young girl—Herina, according to the old man—shook her head slightly and frowned. She stepped back, as if to hide in the darkness behind the door.

"Oh, right. She's probably working in the fields." The old man scratched his head and made a face, as if deep in thought.

I could hear the sound of someone approaching. Then the door flew wide open.

"Mother is in the fields right now. Whaddya want?"

The new girl who'd appeared was older, around thirteen or fourteen. She was probably 150 centimeters tall and had light brown hair tied into shoulder-length pigtails. With her tanned skin and well-worn clothes, she certainly looked the part of a farm girl. She stared up at the guard with large, clear blue eyes.

As her gaze shifted from the old man to me, her eyes grew even larger. "Whoa! Are you the one who took my job, Mister Knight?"

Her eyes lit up when she realized what I was there for, though as she looked me over, she began tilting her head to the side, growing more uncertain. I imagined my armor didn't really fit the image of a mercenary; she'd even referred to me as a knight.

"My name is Arc. I am no knight, just a simple

mercenary. Are you Miss Marca?" I tried to put her at ease by asking her name.

She hurriedly bowed her head and took a step back inside before replying. "Yes, that's me! P-please, come in!"

The gate guard bowed once and turned back toward the gate.

"Thank you."

Once inside, I could see that the house was quite small. Immediately next to the entrance was a cooking area, consisting of a stone-lined hole surrounded by compacted earth with a pot suspended above it. Several wooden utensils were organized neatly in a simple cupboard. Farther inside, the floor was flat and lined with stones, on top of which rested a sparse few pieces of wooden furniture, including a table, four chairs, and two beds in the back.

"Herina, Mister Knight and I have some business to discuss. Go play for a bit, okay?"

The young girl—likely Marca's younger sister—hid behind Marca as her large, brown eyes looked me over with great interest.

"Please sit down, Mister Knight." Marca motioned toward one of the chairs in front of the table. I thanked her and did so.

Marca sat in the chair across from me, looking up at me as she spoke. "Didja really agree to take my job? The guild told me they weren't sure anyone would want to. I could only put up what little money I had in my allowance."

The girl still seemed uncertain about what she was seeing. If our roles had been reversed, I would also have a hard time believing a person like myself would work for such an amount.

"Please, call me Arc. I'm simply interested in the art of picking medicinal herbs."

Upon hearing my reason for taking her request, the girl looked surprised. Then a smile spread across her face, her cheeks flushing a light pink. She bowed her head again, her pigtails moving with the gesture.

"Thank you! So, um, Mister Arc... Are you ready to go? I just need to grab a few things."

I nodded, which sent the girl off running. She grabbed a large cloth hanging from the wall and wrapped it around her neck like a scarf, then picked up a basket near the door. Finally, she took Herina's hands, looking her straight in the eyes as she spoke.

"Herina, Sissy's heading to the forest. Can you keep an eye on the house for me?"

"No problem!"

Herina puffed out her chest and gave a sharp nod in response. Marca smiled and patted Herina's head, running her fingers through the little girl's hair.

"Mama will be back soon. Tell her I hired a bodyguard to take me out into the forest, so there's no need to worry."

"Okay!" Herina replied again with a firm nod.

I followed Marca out of the house while Herina watched us from the door, waving the whole time. Marca waved back to her sister then led the way toward the village gate.

"Did you not tell your mother about this?" I looked down at the young girl, her basket firmly on her back.

She responded by turning around to look at me, a slight frown on her face. "I mean, there's no way she'd let me go if I told her."

Marca ducked out of the village gate, her face set in a slight scowl. The two old men guarding the gate from before bowed and watched as we left.

"People have been seeing large monsters in the fields near the village lately. But that was only after I made this request and paid the guild."

"And your father?"

Marca's pace slowed slightly as she walked north along the village wall.

"Papa was real sick. He died last year. Mama, my sister, and I work in the fields, but things are pretty tough." Marca's face clouded over, and she averted her eyes, though her ever-present smile remained.

"I apologize for my thoughtless question."

She responded by breaking into a slow run. When she finally turned around, her sad expression had been replaced with the same cheerful look from before.

"It's okay! 'Sides, I wanna surprise Mama and help her out!"

I could tell she was just a normal, happy young girl, no different from anyone else her age. She also had a beautiful smile.

"The herbs are used for making medicine. I can sell them for a pretty good price in town, which will really help Mama. I used to go out with Papa to pick herbs, then we'd go into town to sell them."

The look of nostalgia on her face made me want to do whatever I could to help her out. At the same time, she also reminded me of what I was like at her age, much to my chagrin. I laughed quietly under my helmet.

I've gotta help this girl and her family, I thought as I adjusted my outlook. This was no longer a simple pleasure jaunt.

"Well then, we'll just have to collect a ton of herbs to make things easier for your mother."

"Definitely!" The girl exuded excitement, her mind focused entirely on her family.

"Are we heading somewhere dangerous?"

"The forest up ahead stretches way out to the south-west, along the base of the Furyu Mountains. Deeper in the forest, I heard there are wyverns, dragons, and other dangerous monsters. But Papa said it's safe as long as you don't go too deep into the forest."

Still, it seemed like there were more monsters than usual in this forest, so it'd be best not to overstay our welcome.

I continued walking behind Marca as she explained where we were. Apparently, the steep, snowcapped peaks I could see to the northeast were part of the Furyu mountain range.

The empty plain soon gave way to the occasional tree, the vegetation growing denser and denser as we walked on toward the forest. I decided that if we encountered any monsters I couldn't handle, I'd escape with Marca using Dimensional Step. I continued following in her footsteps with my head on a constant pivot, scanning for any dangerous monsters in the area.

On the western side of Rata, a woman stooped in one corner of the vast fields outside the village, tending to vegetables.

Her long, curly blonde hair was tied into a ponytail that draped past her shoulders, and her bright blue eyes and freckles gave her face a gentle look. She stood around 170 centimeters tall and wore a patch-covered dress. The woman stopped her work to wipe the sweat from her brow before looking up at the sun; she was certain she'd heard someone call her name. She scanned the tree line to the north.

"Did you hear something?"

She looked over at the muscular woman working next to her. The second woman stopped her work as well.

"I didn't hear a thing. What was it, Seona?"

The first woman, Seona, listened closely as she once again scanned the surrounding fields. Just then, she saw two men—hunters, judging by their garb—rushing, panic-stricken, from the forest to the north. She could see several villagers emerge from the fields to surround the hunters, but she was too far away to hear what they were saying.

"I wonder what happened." Seona's voice betrayed her concern as she looked back to the woman next to her.

"Maybe it was one of the fang boars that came by before. Why don't we go see?"

The brawny woman also looked worried jogging toward the hunters and villagers. Seona took off after the woman, feeling a sense of unease deep in her own chest.

"I'll go tell the village chief!" One of the villagers who had been talking to the hunters sprinted back toward the village.

The rest of the villagers drew closer to the hunters, who were now sitting on the ground catching their breath.

"What happened?"

One of the hunters looked up at Seona's question, his voice a mixture of fear and excitement.

"A monster! It was a huge monster!"

Hearing this, the woman who had come with her looked back skeptically, cocking her head to the side. "You mean the fang boars?"

The other hunter responded this time. His face was pale and white, though he was just as worked up as his comrade. "Not even close! This one was real huge, nearly eight meters long! I never seen nothin' that size before!"

The nearby villagers' expressions changed to looks of shock and concern.

"You mean you saw that massive thing this close to the village?"

"Maybe that's what's been chasing the fang boars out this way?"

"If we report this incident to the viscount, I wonder if he'll send his troops out."

The other villagers looked concerned as they chattered among themselves. The burly woman glanced at Seona, a worried expression on her face.

"It's just your girls at home, right, Seona? You should go make sure they're safe."

"You're right. I'm going to head home right now!"

The other woman's words had no sooner left her mouth than Seona was running back to her spot in the field. She threw her tools into her basket and hoisted it up onto her back. Then she took off along the dirt path toward the village.

The guards at the gate looked confused as Seona approached, but she ignored them and ran straight to her home. Out of the corner of her eye, she could see a young man on a horse galloping out of the village. The chief had probably sent a messenger to notify the viscount of their impending emergency.

Seona threw the door to her house open and rushed inside. Seona found Herina sitting on a chair at the table, kicking her legs about. Herina looked surprised at first, but her face lit up as soon as she recognized her mother. She dashed to the door and threw her arms around Seona.

"Mama!"

Seona pulled the girl in close and picked Herina up, her eyes scanning the house for her other daughter.

"Herina, do you know where Marca went?" She brushed Herina's cheek with one hand as she held her daughter.

Herina tilted her head to the side. "Sissy went to the forest. But she said it's okay, 'cause she has a bodyguard!"

Herina looked proud of herself at having been able to pass along her sister's message.

Seona, however, felt dizzy, and her legs grew weak. She put Herina down and began interrogating her daughter. "Did she say why she was going to the forest? And who is this bodyguard?!"

Herina looked confused by all of this and began pouting. Seona tried hard to control her emotions and asked her daughter once again in a gentler manner this time.

"Did Marca say why she went to the forest?"

"Nope..." Herina shook her head.

"All right then. Do you know who the bodyguard was?"

"He was a knight, wearing huuuge armor, who came to our house. He left with Sissy." The girl stretched out her arms as she spoke, trying to convey how massive the armor was.

Seona had a pretty good guess as to why Marca had gone off into the forest. Around this time every year, Marca used to go out with her father to collect medicinal herbs. Marca had once told Seona about a certain species of fragrant flowers that only grew deep within the forest.

"Oh no. She went to the mountains to pick herbs! Listen, Herina, Mama needs to leave the house again, and I need you to stay here. Don't leave the house for any reason, okay?"

Seeing the anger in her mother's eyes, Herina's face stiffened as she nodded.

Seona rushed back out of the house, making her way toward the village gate. The old men who stood guard before were now accompanied by a group of young men with spears. As soon as they saw Seona rushing toward them, the men moved quickly to stand in her path.

"Where are you going?"

"My daughter, Marca, she went out to the forest! I need to go find her!" Annoyed at the men blocking her path, Seona tried explaining the situation as best she could.

However, the men just exchanged glances, uncertain expressions on their faces.

"The village chief said not to let anyone leave."

As he spoke, the old man put his hand on Seona's shoulder to stop her. She shrugged him off in a desperate attempt to leave the village, but the other men stepped forward to hold her back.

"No, there's a dangerous monster out there! We can't let you go into the forest!"

"Let me go, please! Just let me go!"

"And what about your little Herina at home?! What will she do if something happens to you?"

Already on the edge of hysterics, Seona dropped to her knees.

"Marca has a magnificently armored knight with her. She'll be fine." Seeing what the desperate mother was going through, one of the old guards attempted to comfort her. Unfortunately, the words had little effect.

"This way, Mister Arc!"

Marca had been leading the way through the forest when she found something and took off in a half-run toward a slight depression in the earth scattered with rocks. Between the rocks, small, rooted plants spread across the ground like a green carpet. Marca entered the depression and began gathering the plants, throwing them into her basket. Each of them had numerous lotus-like petals branching off.

"These are called cocora. They help cure wounds and skin conditions." The girl's pigtails bobbed about as she explained the herb's medicinal effects, all the while continuing to pick the cocora plants from the ground.

I looked around, but there didn't seem to be any danger

nearby, so I dropped down into the depression to help her. Marca gave me a peculiar look and laughed. It must have been a pretty funny sight: a hulking suit of armor nearly two meters tall sitting on the ground pulling weeds.

About an hour later, Marca's basket was half full of cocora. There were still plenty of plants in the pit, but Marca said we should look for another location. The villagers used these herbs for ointments, so she wanted to leave some for anyone hurt by the recent increase in monsters. The next place we'd be heading was apparently our main objective.

As we moved deeper into the woods, the undergrowth began taking over the path, and the leaves on the trees grew ever denser, almost claustrophobic. Most animals that made it this far in would certainly have picked up on the oppressive feeling and turned around by now. However, we still hadn't run into any of the monsters I'd been so worried about.

Marca led us into a clearing filled with gentle, sloping hills that were dotted with trees. The branches were blanketed with white flowers, almost as if they were covered with fluff. The wind carried with it a delightful scent as it passed through the trees and across the flowers.

"Great! They're in full bloom! Can you believe how white the kobumi trees are?" I could hear the happiness in the young girl's voice as she ran gleefully toward the trees. But something felt off. I narrowed my gaze and began looking around. There was a rock-like lump on the other side of the flowering kobumi trees, but it didn't look like any normal mountain rock. It seemed to be moving, almost imperceptibly, as if it were alive.

I called out to Marca to get her to stop. "Wait, Miss Marca! There's something hiding over there!"

"Huh?"

Possibly responding to Marca's appearance, or maybe even my yelling, the thing that had been hiding behind the kobumi trees slowly stood, trembling, as if it were loosening up its muscles.

It was a massive, lizard-like creature, a little over eight meters in length from its head to the tip of its tail. It stood on six thick, muscular legs, and was covered in green and gray scales. The monster looked like a chameleon, its huge eyes casting about in every direction before finally locking onto us. It had a green, crown-shaped crest on top of its head and thorny scales running down its back, all the way to the tip of its tail.

The monster opened its mouth wide, showing off rows and rows of sharp teeth as it let loose an unnerving growl from deep in its throat.

"Groooooooaaaaaal!"

The massive lizard continued its low growl as its forked tongue darted out of its mouth, moving about as if it were a snake. Its massive eyes then settled on me.

"Eep!" Marca let out a short scream.

I remembered seeing this chameleon-like creature back in the game. This was the giant basilisk, a Level 150-170 monster. With its low defense and attack stats, it wasn't so bad to deal with once you were used to it, though it could be quite a challenge for newly minted, mid-tier players. Between its petrifying stare, poison fog, and paralyzing claws, it could unleash a status-effect combo and easily wear a player down until it killed them.

I could see how this monster would be a real challenge for normal villagers to deal with. But I had to wonder, was this one of the magical monsters I kept hearing about?

After seeing the basilisk appear in front of her, Marca stopped her dash toward the kobumi trees and turned to run back. The giant basilisk took off after her, shuffling along the ground on its six massive legs. However, before it reached her, it suddenly stopped moving, as if it had given up the chase. It began moving its head up and down, its crest turning red.

This was just like in the game!

It was going to do its petrifying stare, an area-of-effect status attack; though, the name was a misnomer as it was hardly a stare. The attack unleashed damage on anyone standing in a wide, wedge-shaped area in front of the monster, followed by multiple shockwaves. I didn't know whether the attack would also turn its victims to stone, like in the game, but I wasn't eager to find out.

Marca got her foot tangled in something and tumbled to the ground with a loud crash. This was bad; she was just in range of the monster's petrifying attack.

I tossed my bags to the side, pulled the Holy Shield of Teutates off my back, and ran toward her. She was holding her right ankle and looked about ready to cry. I grabbed the girl and pulled her behind my shield, then turned to face the giant basilisk.

The higher your level, the greater the resistance mythical-class items like my shield offered against status effects. If my level was higher than my enemy's, then the shield would block most of their attacks outright.

I lifted the shield and took a defensive stance. The next moment, the air vibrated with a low droning noise as the shield began shaking. I glanced down to see Marca curled up behind the shield with her eyes shut tight and her hands over her ears. She seemed to be fine. It looked like we'd made it through the petrifying stare safe and sound.

In the game, it took a while before the giant basilisk could use this attack again, but I wasn't sure if that was the case here. I also wasn't too excited about the idea of pushing the monster's limits just to figure out its attack patterns.

"Graoooooooaaal!" The giant basilisk seemed annoyed at having its petrifying attack blocked. It rushed toward us, closing the short distance in a matter of moments.

I stepped forward, keeping Marca protected behind my back, and slammed my shield into the massive lizard.

"Graoooaaaaaaoool!" The monster howled as it was hit, the shield resonating with a dull thud. The giant lizard, all eight meters of it, tumbled end over end as it flew through the air.

The basilisk's eyes wandered about as it raised its head and tried to refocus. It started turning crimson as it glared my way. The hit seemed to have really annoyed it.

I pulled my sword out from its sheath at my back with one hand and raised it above my head. With Marca behind me, I figured my best bet would be to use a long-range strike. If I hit its weak point with a concentrated attack, I should be able to defeat it. I wasn't going to go down easy.

"Sword of Judgment!"

This was a Sacred Knight skill that let you attack a single enemy from a distance. Since it was technically classified as a magical attack, it was fairly effective against enemies with high resistance to physical attacks.

Giant basilisks in the game weren't resistant to physical attacks, but since this one's body was covered in scales, I decided to go with this skill, just in case.

My sword took on a phosphorescent glow as I swung it around. Once this glow was nearly blinding, I swung the sword down.

A magic circle appeared beneath the giant basilisk before a blade of light erupted from the ground, tearing through the beast as it shot up into the sky.

"Graaoaooooooooooooal!"

The blade pierced the giant beast's stomach effortlessly. It continued growing six meters up into the air, then made a noise similar to a tuning fork being struck against metal before shattering like glass into thousands of fragments.

The clearing fell quiet, the only sound that of the giant basilisk's body trembling as it slumped to the ground. I watched for a few moments with my sword still drawn, but the monster didn't make a move. I looked back down at the sword in my hand, eyes wide with surprise.

That skill shouldn't have been strong enough to fell a giant basilisk on its own...

Now that I thought about it, the light sword created by the Sword of Judgment was much larger than it should have been as well.

I knew that my skills relied on the strength I put into them, so maybe that was what had powered it up? I mean, in real life, the more strength you put into a skill, the greater its effect. If that were the case, then even mid-tier Sacred Knight skills could become high-powered techniques.

Marca peeked out from behind me to see the fallen basilisk. She shouted with excitement as she looked up at me, like I was some sort of shining hero.

She was beginning to make me feel embarrassed, so I decided to change the subject.

"How's your leg, Miss Marca?"

Marca's expression quickly changed, as if she'd just remembered something. She stooped down and started holding her right ankle again. I gently pried her hand back. Her skin was red and beginning to swell up.

"I'll be fine, it's no big deal." Her brow furrowed, but she somehow managed to force a smile. But it was obvious her ankle wasn't okay. I thought through all the class skills I'd learned as I examined it. The question was, could recovery magic actually heal injuries?

My sub-class, Priest, was largely a support class and the highest tier of the Monk line. It covered a wide variety of spells, from recovery to lifting curses. But before I tried using the high-powered recovery magic from the Priest class, I should see what sort of effect the low-level Monk recovery spells may have.

I hadn't been injured since coming here, nor had I needed to use my healing spells. All I'd used was the Mage attack spell, Fire.

"Hold still. I'm going to use some magic."

I held my hand over Marca's hurt ankle and chanted quietly to call upon the Mending Heal spell. A gentle glow began emanating from my hand, the light surrounding her ankle before dissipating.

"How's that, Miss Marca? Does it still hurt?"

The red swelling was already beginning to die down as I watched. Marca's eyes went wide, and she began rubbing her ankle and moving it around to make sure it was all healed. She looked up at me with a smile.

"This is amazing! You can even heal people, just like a real cleric!"

The girl was so overjoyed that she began hopping up and down right there, a big grin on her face.

"It's been some time since I used the spell. I wasn't certain it would work. However, I'm glad you're healed."

It's been some time was an understatement—this was the first time I'd ever used a healing spell in this world. But I figured I'd play it off like it was nothing.

Judging by the girl's reaction, there were at least some

people who were able to use healing magic. But there must not have been all that many, given that she referred to them as "clerics."

I put my musings on the particulars of healing magic to the side for the time being and turned my attention back to the massive corpse sprawled next to me. "Say, Miss Marca. Was this thing the monster you said had recently appeared near the village?"

"Naw, I'd never seen anything this big before." Marca's braids swung around behind her as she shook her head. "The ones that've been coming to the village were fang boars. They've got big, nasty tusks." She pointed both her index and middle fingers straight up and put them at the edges of her mouth, imitating a fang boar.

"I see. Then perhaps we'd best not mention this encounter to anyone else."

Marca watched me as I stood up, a quizzical expression on her face. "Why not?"

"Your mother would only worry if she heard about the attack."

Even if we hadn't been attacked, no parent would be comfortable with the idea that their child had snuck out of the village while fang boars were running rampant nearby, regardless of whether they'd hired a mercenary.

I shook my head. It had been careless of me to take

a child out of the village without getting her mother's permission. Hopefully it'd be all right if I at least got her home before sundown.

I'd have to worry about that later. For now, I decided to check the surroundings to ensure nothing else was lying in wait. After I was sure that the coast was clear, we went back to picking herbs—the whole reason we were there in the first place.

"Miss Marca, are you here to collect the kobumi?"

My question seemed to bring her back to her senses, as Marca ran straight to the base of the kobumi tree and began plucking the white flowers off the lower branches, putting them into her basket.

I glanced back at the corpse of the giant basilisk. The eight-meter-long monster was sprawled out on the earth, blood from the hole in its stomach staining the dirt red. I wondered if it had a rune stone inside it.

The problem was that I didn't know where to find its heart. Considering how massive it was, it may be like searching for a needle in a haystack. In the end, I decided to just go for it.

I shoved the giant corpse with all my might, rolling it onto its back. I was impressed at my physical strength, as it was relatively easy to move the hulking mass. If the basilisk was anything like an alligator, its heart would be in its underbelly, near the front legs. I didn't think the short sword in my bag was up to the task, so I used the Holy Thunder Sword of Caladbolg to stab into the hole in its belly and cut up to where I figured the heart should be.

It felt greatly similar like dissecting a giant frog—not exactly a pleasant sensation.

Upon pulling open the basilisk's belly, I discovered that I'd found its heart on my first try. At the base of this massive, muscular organ was a stone about the size of a baby's fist. I pulled it out and held it up to the sunlight, letting out an excited gasp as it took on a semitransparent, violet hue. My first rune stone.

I looked over the basilisk's corpse once more but figured there was no way it could possibly be edible like the orcs. Orcs were at least tangentially related to pigs, whereas this was just an oversized, grotesque chameleon. I couldn't imagine it would taste any good. It'd also be a hassle to drag it back to town, so I decided to leave it where it lay, to decompose and give something back to the forest.

"Hey, Mister Arc, can you get those flowers up on top?" Marca interrupted my thoughts to ask for help.

I put the rune stone into my bag and made my way over to where she was standing, near a kobumi tree.

The kobumi were small, five-petal flowers that grew all across the tree's branches. An enticing scent emanated from them, filling the air with their aroma. Marca was busy picking all the flowers off the lower branches.

"What are these used for?"

"Hmm, Papa never told me. He just said they were only used by adults, and that they could be sold for a lot of money if you dried them out and crushed them into powder. They're medicinal herbs, so I figure they must be for some sort of sickness. Do you know of any adult sicknesses, Mister Arc?" Marca didn't miss a beat picking flowers as she asked me the question, her head tilted to the side.

Adult sicknesses...like some sort of stress disorder?

But that didn't make sense. Those were usually brought on by day-to-day life; and besides, kids could suffer from those too. Nothing else really came to mind.

"I'm afraid I don't know."

"Huh, I guess I'll just have to ask someone who does. People may try to take advantage of me if I don't know about the product I'm selling!" She ended her sentence with a giggle.

Working together, we were able to finish filling her basket in no time at all. We put the rest of the kobumi flowers into my large bounty sack. Marca's face beamed as she hefted the sack up.

"We got a whole bunch of 'em!"

I nodded in agreement and hefted the bag over my shoulder as I prepared to leave.

Marca led the way home. There was no way I could have made it out on my own. Since I'd never been in this forest before, everything looked the same to me. But Marca seemed to know her way from various landmarks and the general lay of the land.

A short time later, the trees grew thin, and I could tell that we were nearly to the fields on the outskirts of the village.

That's when I saw it—a large, black boar, its massive body moving from side to side as it used its front legs to dig into the soft earth around it.

"A fang boar! That's the one that attacked the fields! But that's strange... He wasn't here when we left."

I couldn't tell if he'd heard Marca's voice or maybe just sensed our presence, but the fang boar stopped digging, slowly raised its head, and let out a cry.

This thing was on a completely different level from the bull boars I'd encountered before. Over two meters long and nearly as tall as Marca, it reminded me of a small mountain. Four tusks shot straight up out of its lower jaw.

The beast poised itself on its hind legs and let out

another cry before rushing toward us in a mad dash. By the time I dropped my bag and turned to face it, the fang boar was nearly upon us.

Fortunately, even at full speed, the fang boar wasn't exactly fast. I braced myself, grabbed its tusks in both hands, and used my sheer strength to shove its jaw into the ground. I yanked out my sword and stabbed it in the stomach, further enraging the beast. It put all its strength into its legs as it tried forcing its way back up, but I was able to easily keep its head down.

"A-are you okay?"

Marca watched with concern as I wrestled with the fang boar. I punched it twice in the head, which seemed to slow its movements.

"Mm, this is hardly a challenge for me. By the way, are these edible, Miss Marca?"

I continued holding the massive boar's head down as the blood flowed out of the wound in its stomach. Marca slowly made her way over toward me.

"Y-yeah, they are. I've never eaten one, but the adults in the village say they taste real good."

"Hmm, in that case, why don't we bring this one back with us?"

I lifted the boar up by its tusks and threw it over my shoulders. The weight itself wasn't an issue, but I figured it'd be hard to carry something this massive over one arm. Marca's eyes went wide as she watched.

"I'm sorry to ask this of you, but could you carry my bag, Miss Marca?"

"Of course!"

The girl ran over to my bounty sack and hefted it up, hurriedly returning to me.

"Much appreciated."

We continued toward the village, the fang boar hanging over my shoulders. Marca stole the occasional glance at me as she walked alongside.

When we finally made it back to Rata's gate, we were greeted by a large gathering of the village's young men, all armed with spears. The atmosphere was thick with tension. One of the young men yelled out, pointing in our direction, "Marca's back!" prompting the other men to respond in unison, turning to look our way.

"Someone hurry and tell Seona!"

I watched as one of the young men rushed into the village. Judging by the men's reactions, it was clear they'd been worried about Marca. I turned my attention back to her, the grimace on her face suggesting that Seona was her mother's name.

It looked like Marca and I both had some apologies to make.

While I thought this over, an older man with a bow under his arm came running up to us. He looked dumbfounded.

"S-Sir Knight, is that a fang boar you're holding there?"

All the men who'd been watching Marca turned their attention to the object on my back. The fang boar was no longer bleeding, the blood having drained out during our walk back, so I hefted it off my shoulders and dropped it in front of the gate. The villagers let out a collective gasp of astonishment.

"We ran into it just outside the village. I figured I'd bring it back."

While I explained the situation to the villagers, a woman came rushing out through the crowd.

"Marca!"

She ran over to us and scooped the girl up into her arms.

The woman had long, curly blonde hair tied back in a ponytail. Her eyes were the same shade of blue as Marca's, but the surrounding skin was red and puffy. I assumed this was Seona, Marca's mother.

"Where did you go?!"

Marca tensed up as looking into Seona's tear-filled eyes. Seona stretched out her hand and brushed Marca's cheek, as if to make sure her daughter really was safe and sound. Held tight in her embrace, Marca let out a sob.

"I'm so sorry, Mama..."

"Don't ever go out to the forest again without telling me, okay?"

After Marca acknowledged her with a nod, Seona finally relaxed, the hint of a gentle smile beginning to form. She turned to me and bowed her head, her face betraying the turmoil she was feeling.

It wasn't exactly what I'd call a look of gratitude.

My appearance probably gave me the air of someone important, making her hesitant to criticize me outright. No matter how unfair a class society might be, those on the bottom had no choice but to accept it.

Even through her daughter had gone behind her back and hired someone who'd taken the girl out of the village without her knowledge, Seona chose to accept this in silence. Or, at least, so I assumed.

"I apologize for my lack of consideration. It was incredibly reckless of me to take Miss Marca out into the woods without informing you first. I deeply regret my actions."

I bowed my head. It was true; it was incredibly thoughtless on my part, and I would've been reported to the police immediately if this had happened in my own world. I considered taking off my helmet to bow, but I figured that would only make the situation more complicated.

Seona looked taken aback by this. She averted her gaze for a moment.

"Mister Arc didn't do anything wrong! I was the one who sent out the job request." Marca stepped between us and tugged on her mother's sleeve, trying to mediate. Seona smiled down at her and stroked her cheek before looking back at me.

"I'm sorry that my daughter dragged you into this. But thank you for accompanying her."

Seona lowered her head in a slight bow. Marca and the rest of the villagers let out a collective sigh of relief.

A burly woman stepped out of the crowd and slapped Seona on the back, a wide smile on her face. "Don't worry 'bout it! When I first heard there was a big monster on the outskirts of the village, I knew it'd all work out one way or another!"

The rest of the villagers nodded in agreement and told Seona how glad they were to have Marca back safe and sound.

It was then I remembered the fang boar at my feet. "Is this the giant monster you were talking about?"

A man—a hunter—stepped out of the crowd. "That's not 'im. The one I be seein' was 'uge! Even its eyes were 'uge, and it 'ad six legs. Never seen nothin' like it before!"

Hearing his description, Marca and I exchanged looks.

She seemed to want to speak up, but I shook my head. She quietly nodded before turning to look up at her mother.

This wasn't the right time to talk about the giant basilisk. It would only make Seona worry more, and further fan the flames of her anger toward me and Marca. The young girl and I reached an unspoken agreement to avoid all that.

"We sent a villager to notify the viscount. With any luck, he's dispatching a force to hunt for the beast as we speak."

While Marca and I continued our unspoken conversation, the villagers discussed how they'd deal with the monster.

Though I'd already taken care of the giant basilisk, so it'd be a waste of time if the viscount put together an army.

On the other hand, there was no way to know for sure that the monster I'd killed was the same one the hunters saw. If a force went into the forest and rid it of any other monsters, that would be great news for the village.

The hunter interrupted my thoughts, inspecting the beast by my feet while he spoke. "What do ya plan on doing with that 'un there, Sir Knight? Its 'ide can be used for all sorts o' things, and the tusks are worth quite a bit of coin. The meat's pretty good, too. If yer gonna take it all the way to town, could I ask ya to hire some villagers to help you?"

"Hm, this is a monster, yes? I'd like you to tan the hide and give it to Miss Seona as a gift. You may take the tusks and magic rune as payment."

"Wha?! Ya sure 'bout that?" The hunter stared at me in surprise.

I simply nodded in response, then turned to look at Seona. She wore a confused expression on her face.

"I apologize for all the trouble I've caused you, Miss Seona. Please accept this hide as a token of my apology."

"Wow, you're giving us its hide, Mister Arc?" Marca responded before her mother even had a chance. She looked excitedly between the fang boar on the ground and her mother.

Seeing the enthusiasm on her daughter's face, Seona looked torn for a moment before bowing her head and accepting the gift. "Thank you, sir. I appreciate it."

I had no idea if a fang boar hide was suitable for this type of apology, but I could think of no other use for it at the moment, and it was all I had to give.

"And divide the meat up among the villagers."

The townsfolk responded with a resounding cheer, each one thanking me in turn.

Apparently, the village had been in trouble recently,

what with the increase in monster appearances in the fields. They'd been discussing whether to send out hunting parties or pool their money to hire the mercenary guild.

I wondered if the giant basilisk had been the one pushing the fang boars out of the forest and closer to the village.

The fang boar I'd killed was taken to the meat shop, next to the hunter's house. As the villagers rolled the giant beast over on a cart, others who'd heard the news took turns stealing peeks at the catch. Even the village chief came to express his gratitude.

When all was said and done, the sun had begun to set.

With my tasks finished, I left the tanning and division of meat up to the hunters and villagers and followed Marca and her mother back to their house. I needed to drop off the kobumi flowers, which were still in my bag.

"We're back, Herina."

The moment Seona opened the door, Herina came running through the house and dove into her mother's arms. Seona picked the girl up and apologized for leaving her alone.

As this all unfolded, I turned back to Marca.

"Miss Marca, if my duties are now fulfilled, could you provide me with the completion tag?"

The mercenary guild office had told me the job

wouldn't be considered complete, and I wouldn't receive payment, if I didn't obtain a tag from the requester.

"Oh, right!"

Marca reached down into her pocket and retrieved a wooden tag, about the size of a business card, and handed it to me. It had the request number and other information written on it.

"Thank you for everything, Mister Arc."

Marca dipped her head in an adorable bow. Her mother followed suit.

"I am sincerely sorry for the trouble I caused. Alas, it's time for me to take my leave." I offered a deep nod in appreciation.

I put Marca's wooden tag into my bag, threw the bag over my shoulder, and left the house. Marca ran to the doorway to wave goodbye, to which I waved back, then turned around and began walking.

I could hear jovial chatter coming from the hunter's house. They were probably still butchering the fang boar. Looking up at the orange-painted sky, I could see birds flocking together as they flew off toward the forest.

If I didn't get back to Luvierte soon, the gates would be closed. Of course, I could use Dimensional Step to teleport past the wall and into town, but I was saving that as a last resort.

I passed villagers returning home from a day in the fields as I made my way back to the road. Once past the fields, I was alone again, the only sounds those of the rustling grass and trees.

I decided to give the Transport Gate skill another try. The last time I'd used it, I could only teleport a few meters, perhaps because the spell only allowed me to travel to a location I had clearly in my mind.

This time around, I focused my thoughts on the hill overlooking Luvierte's east gate. Not only did I have a clear image of it, I figured few people ventured out there. If I was successful, the ability to instantly transport to locations I'd already visited would prove incredibly useful. However, it'd also probably be useless for places where everything looked pretty much the same, like forests and open fields.

Just in case, I decided to memorize the sight of Rata and its surroundings.

I turned back to look at the village. In the distance, I could see smoke billowing from chimneys as families prepared their evening meals.

Then, putting my back to Rata once again, I focused my mind on my destination outside Luvierte.

"Transport Gate!"

As soon as I summoned the spell, a three-meter-wide, pale blue column of light began rising up from underneath my feet. The world around me went dark, and I felt as if I was floating. The next thing I knew, I was standing atop the hill where I'd caught my first glimpse of Luvierte. Behind me, Rata was nowhere to be seen.

It seemed like Transport Gate was a success. So long as I kept memorizing locations, traveling would be much easier. It was a pretty amazing transportation spell.

While grinning like a fool, I saw four horses take off in a gallop from Luvierte's west gate. The horses ran in perfect formation, making their way north toward Rata, the place I'd just left behind.

I wondered if that was the advance squad, or maybe a scouting party, dispatched by the viscount after receiving the report of the giant basilisk. Hopefully, their presence would help the villagers sleep easy tonight.

I made my way down the hill, through Luvierte's east gate, and toward the mercenary guild office. Behind me tolled the bell signaling that the gates would be closed. I'd made it back just in time.

When I entered the guild office, I was met by the now-familiar bear-like man, wearing a sinister-looking grin in his cage. I was surprised that Marca had been able to come here and submit her request to him.

"Mission complete. Here's the proof."

I pulled my request and completion tags out of my bag

and put them down on the counter. After checking them, the bear handed over my silver coin. With that, my job was finished.

I made my way back to my usual inn and thought about what I would do the next day.

Off in a corner of the Luvierte mansion was a room that looked as if a tornado had gone through it. Inside this room stood a man, busily rummaging through the items that had survived the initial onslaught. The older gentleman sported an impressive mustache and a muscular body that his expensive clothing strained to contain. It looked as if he was deep in thought. This disorganized man was Horcos Farren, the commander of the estate's knight regiment.

He was puzzling over a problem as he rummaged through the mountain of books and papers strewn about the room.

Just then, a servant girl arrived. She put her hand to her temple as she faced the man. Though her mouth turned up in a smile, her eyes betrayed her anger.

"Father, why are you tearing apart this room? I just cleaned it!"

The twenty-year-old woman wore her curly red hair

short, cut off at the nape of her neck. Her shoulders tensed as she fixed her determined green eyes on the knight commander.

"Oh, Rita! Have you seen my copy of Carcy Held's *Monster Bestiary*? I put it somewhere around here..." The man ignored his daughter's angry objections as he glanced around the room.

Rita, for her part, let out a sigh and looked at her father as one would at a man in need of help. This was a common occurrence.

"Hmph! I put it back on the bookshelf, which is exactly where important books are supposed to be. It's right here, see?"

Rita pulled a thick, leather-bound book from a nearby shelf and shoved it in front of Horcos's face.

"Ah, so that's where it was!"

Horcos took the book from Rita and began paging through it. Seeing the serious look on her father's face, Rita began cleaning up the mess, her shoulders slumping.

"Why were you looking for that?" she asked as she busied herself picking up the discarded books. His eyes remained fixed on the page in front of him as he replied.

"A gigantic monster has apparently appeared in a nearby village. If I'm remembering right, it's a pretty troublesome monster to deal with."

As the commander of the estate's knights, Horcos was a formidable fighter. For him to think of something as *troublesome*, it must have been rather serious.

Taking notice of the unease in his daughter's eyes, Horcos looked up from the book and gave her a wide smile.

"It's fine. Just a bit of a hassle, nothing more. No need to worry."

"I wasn't worried!"

Rita's cheeks flushed at her father's smile. She looked away, setting her face in a determined scowl.

"I see. Well, I must go visit with Master Buckle. Today and tomorrow will be quite busy."

Horcos put the book under his arm and patted his daughter's head on his way out the door.

Early the next morning, a contingent of the Luvierte army brought together to exterminate the giant basilisk began their march toward Rata. The contingent stood at 140 men, though only around one hundred of them would take part in the actual fighting. The rear of the procession included men in charge of other logistics, such as transporting equipment and food provisions.

Since the battle would take place in a forest, the only horses with them were those used by the carriages and the knights, leaving most of the men to march on foot.

With Rata about a half day's journey by horse, the estate's army was expected to arrive by the afternoon if they continued at their current pace.

Ten soldiers had been sent ahead the previous day to work out the stationing of the troops and other matters with the village chief. This would allow the army to begin their garrison preparations in the village square and dispatch patrols to the forest to look for the monster as soon as they arrived.

At the center of the procession, atop a magnificent horse, rode a man who stood out among them all. That man was Horcos, commander of the knights. In stark contrast to the previous night, he now looked regal, outfitted in a beautifully made suit of armor.

Horcos held his horse's reins in one hand and rummaged around in the bag behind him with the other to retrieve a piece of bread. After a few bites, he took a swig from his leather water skin.

A young knight brought his horse in close and called out to Horcos. "Commander Horcos, eating atop your horse is not exactly becoming of a knight."

The commander smiled back cheerfully in response. "Rural knights like us need not concern themselves with manners! We were so busy this morning, I didn't have time to eat. I could hardly keep my stomach quiet with the tempting smell of my daughter's freshly baked bread wafting from my bag."

"Miss Rita made that?" The young knight looked longingly at the bread in his commander's hand.

"Get your own, Giovanni. If you want my daughter to make you bread, you'd best marry her first!"

"No, I mean... I should establish myself as a knight first, before I..." The young knight mumbled a response to Horcos's rebuke before hanging his head.

Giovanni had soft, blond hair and a good-looking face, marked by a strong nose. His features were thin and delicate, more like that of a noble or a thespian than a knight, making him look rather unreliable. But this good-looking young man was one of the best swordsmen in all of Luvierte.

"She turned twenty this year. If you keep procrastinating, I'll have to introduce her to some other man!"

Giovanni's face went pale at the commander's threat, his voice squeaking as he replied. "No, wait! We'll be wed as soon as this mission is finished. This time for sure!"

He could feel the other men's eyes on him and hear their barely concealed chuckles as they watched the exchange.

The procession of soldiers arrived in Rata early that afternoon.

After Commander Horcos exchanged greetings with the village chief, the army busied itself setting up their tents in the middle of the village square as the villagers had already prepared the large, open space for the army to station themselves. Amidst the large influx of people, scouting patrols began assembling to track down the monster.

There were three patrols, broken into groups of three soldiers each, with an additional person from the village—hunters and other people who had seen the monster—assigned to them as guides. They decided to head toward the forest immediately, while the sun was still high in the sky.

After seeing the scouting patrols off as they entered the woods, Giovanni turned to Horcos, who was watching the trees sway gently in the breeze. "Is there really a giant basilisk in these woods?"

"Who can say? But it's hard to imagine the hunters would confuse such a distinct monster with something else. Even if we hadn't heard similar reports before, it's not like we know about every single creature lurking in the forest."

Horcos stroked his beard, as if pondering the meaning of his own words.

Later that evening, the scouting patrols returned with a surprising report.

"First Squad encountered the monster, the giant basilisk, in the woods. It was large, around nine meters in length."

"Second Squad did not encounter any monsters and has nothing to report."

"Third Squad uncovered the body of an eight-meter, giant basilisk, its stomach cut open. It appeared to have died recently."

After listening to the reports from each of the squad leaders, Horcos crossed his arms and furrowed his brow, a thoughtful expression on his face. The knights charged with exterminating the monsters had assembled in a large tent in Rata's village square, with all of them wearing the same look of concern as their commander.

Giovanni stood at Horcos's side, his eyes narrowed, a serious expression on his face as he spoke. "Two giant basilisks? Now that's hard to believe."

Horcos looked up, directing his gaze at the leaders of the three squad leaders.

"There were two, but the squad members reported that one was already dead. So, what killed it? Could this be the work of another monster? One capable of killing a giant basilisk?"

The leader of Third Squad stood firm under Horcos's gaze and offered up his observations without a moment's hesitation. "It looked to be the work of a human.

The killing blow was a clean strike that pierced straight through its stomach and out its back, and the cut down its belly appeared to be from someone taking the creature's rune stone, which was missing from its body."

The other knights exchanged disbelieving glances with each other. Horcos shared their sentiment, but he couldn't let his own feelings show. Instead, he turned his gaze to Giovanni.

Giovanni assumed the commander was seeking his opinion, but he couldn't believe that a human alone could so easily fell a giant basilisk. There was only one possibility.

"Could this be the work of elves? Their soldiers are incredibly skilled in combat. I've heard they use earth magic to pierce their enemies, and the wind itself to cut them apart."

Several knights nodded along with Giovanni's assessment, seemingly convinced.

There were several clans of elves on the continent. They were renowned for devoting their long lives to improving their martial skills, as well as for their ability to wield powerful magic. The Rhoden Kingdom had a long history of getting into, and subsequently losing at great costs, brutal conflicts with the elves when they encroached on the forests where the elves resided.

One of the knights offered a counterpoint to Giovanni's suggestion. "I heard the elves live much farther to the east. Would they really come all the way out here?"

Several other knights nodded in agreement.

Horcos frowned as he looked at each one of the men standing in the tent. "For now, we should be happy that one of the monsters has already been exterminated and focus on how to take care of the remaining one."

The leader of the third squad spoke up. "Is there some open space where we can approach the giant basilisk and launch our attack?"

"We found it in a wide-open area. It should be fairly easy to assemble and dispatch a regiment."

"Then, tomorrow, we'll head out into the woods and exterminate it?"

Horcos gave a wry smile as he shook his head in response to Giovanni's suggestion.

"Dealing with a giant basilisk isn't so easy. If we aren't careful, we will surely incur massive losses. Tomorrow, we will enter the forest to inspect the area and begin preparations while our patrols continue to follow its movements."

No objections were voiced to the commander's decision. All the knights nodded in agreement and returned to their respective stations.

The normally quiet village square was filled with the

roar of bonfires and the nervous bustling of soldiers waiting for the morning to come.

The next day, over half of the Luvierte army contingent in Rata made its way into the forest, to the top of a gentle, sloping hill. The hillside was lined with unevenly spaced trees, their branches covered entirely in white, fluff-like blossoms. The wind carried with it the delightful scent of the flowers.

Since the army's sheer force of numbers would be near useless when battling in the forest, they had decided to confront the giant basilisk in the open plain they had heard about in the previous day's report.

Giovanni looked out across the hill. "This looks like a good spot."

Horcos crossed his arms and nodded firmly. "We best get started with our preparations."

After their commander gave the orders, the various military elements went off to their respective stations to begin preparations.

To ensure that they could swiftly change their battle formations, the soldiers cut down the grass and rid the area of stones and other objects that would interfere with their movement. Their preparations were manifold, and even included erecting short fences to slow the monster's movements.

Most of the work wasn't finished until well past noon.

"Have the survey patrol cease their activities by nightfall. The rest of you, go back to the village and build up your strength. I don't want you tired tomorrow. And send ten men to collect the fallen basilisk. I want it brought back to the village."

Horcos gazed down at the eight-meter-long body lying at the base of the hill. He had inspected it himself, but it was just as the squad leader had said: there were two cuts, both of which appeared to have been made by a human. The basilisk was otherwise in good condition, with no obvious additional injuries, suggesting the huge monster had been killed with a single strike.

"The question is, what sort of god or devil did this? I'm afraid to even consider which it might be." Horcos spoke in a low voice as he stroked his beard, making sure no one could hear him.

On the second morning after being dispatched to Rata, nearly one hundred soldiers positioned themselves in the forest clearing and waited for the basilisk.

Giovanni looked slightly nervous as he stared up at the sun, high in the sky.

"The squad should be here any minute now, no?"

"Judging by the smoke signal we saw beyond the hill a

short while ago, they're almost here. Don't let your guard down, men!"

The men let out an excited roar in response to their commander's speech. The atmosphere grew tense, and the idle chatter faded into silence. The flower-scented wind rustled the grass as it blew across the hill, giving the whole scene a rather idyllic appearance. However, the wind carried another sound with it as well, which added a sense of foreboding to the otherwise beautiful scene.

A faint, eerie cry could be heard from beyond the hill, causing the men to mutter among themselves. Several soldiers in light armor crested the hill and immediately began running at full speed down the other side.

"It's here! Whatever you do, don't lower your shields!"

"Raaah!" The soldiers in the front line of the formation yelled in unison in response to Horcos' command, their meter-tall, silver, rectangular shields gleaming in the sunlight.

The incoming squad had only made it halfway down the hill when the giant basilisk appeared near the top.

Its massive body was covered in green scales, with a gray pattern running along its entire length. A crown-shaped crest sprouted from its head, and its six lizard-like legs propelled it down the hill. Several arrows were sticking out its back, its huge eyes burning with rage.

The voice of one of the soldiers carried across the clearing like a bell. "It's gotta be at least ten meters!"

It was previously reported to be around nine meters; however, face to face, it looked even bigger.

"Grooooaaaaaaaooooooll!"

The eerie, lizard-like monster let out a roar, its split tongue flicking about. The soldiers hesitated as its cry echoed across the hillside.

"Toughen up, boys! Let down your guard and you'll be leaving here in a casket!" The commander's words brought the soldiers out of their temporary shock, refocusing them on the task at hand.

The squad leader reassembled his men after their run down the hill, saluted Horcos, and rejoined the formation. Horcos nodded back before launching into orders to his various captains.

"Archers, ready yourselves!"

As soon as the words left his mouth, the soldiers at the back of the formation drew arrows from the quivers at their waists and awaited their next order.

The giant basilisk's large eyes fixed on the army at the bottom of the hill. After giving a low, throaty groan, it began running down the hill toward the men. The first wooden fence stalled it momentarily as it searched for a way around.

"Archers, draw your bows!"

"Release!"

Once the order was given, the archers moved in unison and let loose a tremendous volley of arrows, raining them down on the giant basilisk as it continued struggling with the fence. Several arrows managed to pierce its scales, causing the monster to screech in anger, throwing its massive body against the fence. After only a few blows, the simply constructed barrier was nothing but a pile of wood.

"Don't let up!"

As Horcos implored his archers to continue firing, arrows blanketed the hillside like a heavy spring rain, continuing to stick into the giant basilisk. One arrow pierced the monster's eye, causing it to thrash about wildly. A swing of its great tail catapulted the pile of wood toward the army, though the men on the front lines caught it all on their shields, sending up a thunderous racket.

Now thoroughly enraged, the giant basilisk ran straight toward the front line, tearing through fence after fence with its enormous body as it went.

"Shield element, prepare yourselves! Archers, stand down!"

In sync with Horcos's orders, the archers ceased their barrage while the men in front set their feet into position and put their shoulders against the backs of their giant shields. A moment later, the basilisk slammed into the front line with a hideous roar, slowly pushing back the entire formation. Horcos immediately issued his next command.

"Spear element, thrust!"

As the giant basilisk was held fast by the wall of shields in its path, countless spears came stabbing out of the gaps between the shields, leaving several gaping wounds in its scale-covered hide.

The monster responded with a howl of pain, swinging its tail like a club. Plumes of blood shot into the sky as several men were launched back. But the openings in the line were quickly filled by nearby shield-bearing men.

Spears continued thrusting out through the gaps to pierce the lizard. The increasingly enraged monster tried to slice through the shields with its razor-sharp claws, but the mithril-plated surfaces held strong, resulting in nothing but high-pitched screeching noises.

Stepping back from the shield wall, the giant basilisk began waving its head back and forth. Its crown-shaped crest slowly turned red as it filled with blood.

"Shield element, brace yourselves! Everyone else, duck behind the shields!" Recognizing what the giant basilisk was about to do, Horcos yelled out this command before stepping behind his own massive shield. The next moment, a dull thrum seemed to vibrate the very air itself, shoving the entire army formation back. Horcos yelled at his men to push through the shockwave and get back into position. This time, he split the formation into two groups, intending to pincer the giant basilisk from both sides.

Between having its attack blocked and not being able to move due to all the injuries it had sustained, the giant basilisk simply glared at the splitting formation. Surrounded by soldiers, the monster waved its limbs about in an attempt to knock down the shield wall, even as men continued stabbing it. The formation, however, anticipated this and moved constantly, causing the lizard to miss its strikes and become even further infuriated.

The basilisk finally managed to clamp down on the edge of a shield and, with a shake of its mighty head, sent the soldier holding it flying into the air. Before the now-shieldless man could hit the ground, the monster caught him with its mouth and chomped down, spraying blood in every direction. The men froze. Taking advantage of its opening, the giant basilisk found its next target and stretched its neck out.

Giovanni had been waiting for just this moment. He stabbed down into the outstretched neck with all his might.

But the basilisk effortlessly caught Giovanni's mighty blow with its teeth and swung the man around by his spear like a ragdoll. Giovanni let go of his weapon and was spared from being thrown up into the air, though he still landed outside the protection of the shields. As he rolled along the ground, Giovanni reached for his sword.

Unfortunately, his opponent had the drop on him. The giant basilisk stretched its neck toward its prey, its tooth-lined mouth filling his vision.

Giovanni could smell the scent of freshly baked bread, could see the smiling face of the woman he loved.

"Giovanni! Say something, will ya?"

A familiar voice beckoned Giovanni back to reality. The giant basilisk was right in front of him, the hilt of a sword sticking out of its eye. The monster's head lolled on the ground. He could hear the soldiers calling to him, but the commander's voice rang out above the rest. The formation parted for Horcos as he approached.

"My apologies, commander. I let my guard down..." Giovanni pushed himself into a sitting position, head hanging in shame.

"You know, if you play hotshot like that when you're young, you'll never grow old enough to be anything, kid. And look! Because of you, this sword is ruined."

Horcos yanked the sword out of the giant basilisk's

eyeball and showed it to the younger man. Due to the force of the blow, the tip of the blade had bent where it hit the skull.

"I am truly sorry, commander. My rash actions forced you to the front line to save me."

"If that's really how you feel, then I guess it means you'll finally marry my little girl, huh?"

Giovanni had been preparing to launch into a heartfelt apology, but Horcos simply shot him a wide smile and slapped him on the shoulder.

"Three men died in the conflict, and eleven more suffered injuries."

Horcos nodded in response to this report, then closed his eyes and let his shoulders drop. "Considering what we were fighting against, I suppose that's a respectable count."

"If you hadn't read about this rare beast, we wouldn't have stood a chance."

Horcos muttered a response to Giovanni's praise as he surveyed the fallen basilisk. In front of him, men had already begun chopping its body up and loading it onto carts.

"Looks like we've got our offering to the central government."

"The central government?"

"The nobles on the country's borders are required to

give offerings. The basilisk should fetch a high price on the open market. I may even be able to ask Master Buckle for a weapon stipend."

Giovanni turned his gaze back to the giant basilisk.

While it was true the monster's poison was highly prized, especially for its value in hunting other monsters, he wasn't entirely convinced that the central government would be excited to receive it as an offering.

I spent yet another night at the inn, waking up the morning in my usual pose after my day in Rata.

After staring off into space for a moment, I got my bags together, walked past the still-vacant counter, and left the inn.

I felt like there was something different about the town, though nothing seemed out of the ordinary.

I made my way to the mercenary guild office. There were several mercenaries inside, looking through postings on the job board. It was the first time I'd actually seen other mercenaries at the guild.

They glanced toward me as I approached, their faces turning to surprise before they moved silently out of my way. Taking advantage of the unobstructed view, I read through the postings on the board, but they were all small, one-man jobs that wouldn't earn me any more than five silver coins at the most.

Unable to find anything of interest, I decided to head off on my own to spend the day hunting and scouting around the outskirts of the town. I could probably sell whatever I caught at the merchant guild office.

I made my way south, toward the forest on the far side of the Xpitol River.

Dimensional Step brought me to the opposite shore in a flash. With no bridges in the vicinity, I was soon surrounded by silent trees, completely devoid of any signs of human life.

Entering this no man's land all on my own elicited the same excitement I'd felt when exploring a new map in the game.

I spent the day searching around the forest. Or, more accurately, I spent the latter half of the day desperately searching for the way back out.

I ran into a small group of orcs, but after I killed the first one with a single swipe, the rest went running. They were cowardly monsters, it seemed. That one orc was my only real catch for the day.

The rest of my time was spent wandering about the forest with the fallen orc over my shoulders.

There were quite a few animals and monsters in the forest. I was familiar with some, but not others. And unlike in the game, I was hesitant to mercilessly kill everything I saw. After all, it wasn't like I would receive any experience or item drops from slaughtering monsters here.

When I finally stepped out of the woods, the sun was already setting. I slipped through Luvierte's west gate, cut across the carriage parking in front of the merchant guild office, and made my way to the desk at the vault in back.

The man at the counter was the same one who'd helped me last time. I asked him if he was interested in purchasing the orc still draped over my shoulders, and the sale netted me six silver and five copper coins—the same as a meter-long bull boar. The rune stone inside the orc was apparently worth one silver coin, meaning that, pound for pound, the bull boar was worth much more. I wondered if this was because orcs were slower and easier to kill.

Regardless, this didn't bother me, since I wasn't looking for the most efficient method for earning a living. After I accepted the man's offer, he stepped away to get my money.

While I waited for his return, I could hear two merchants talking near the purchase counter. When you know nothing about the world you're in, eavesdropping can be incredibly useful.

"I been hearin' a lotta stories lately about powerful monsters appearin' on the border. Caravans travelin' around eastern Revlon are takin' a lotta casualties."

"That's pretty normal, isn't it, since we're so close to the Furyu Forest? We've always had tons of monsters."

"You stupid or somethin'? It's not like the roads or villages around here often get attacked."

"Well, maybe the dragons are stirring up some trouble up in the Furyu Mountains?"

Hearing these two men so casually talking about fantasy tropes amazed me.

The man behind the purchase counter finally showed up with my money, bringing me back from the images of dragons now flying through my mind. After counting the money, I put it into my pouch and left the building.

I walked through the town for a bit, figuring I'd spend another night at the usual inn. My thoughts wandered as I contemplated what to do with myself. I wanted to set up a place of my own someday, a place to come back to after adventures. So long as I was near civilization, I was stuck wearing my armor for fear of people seeing me without it.

Thanks to my Transport Gate, I could still easily come back to town from wherever I set myself up, be it in the middle of a forest or...anywhere, really. If I found someplace nice, maybe I'd build myself a house.

For now, though, I figured I should continue earning money and learning what I could about where I was. Thus I made a plan for the upcoming week.

The next few days passed rather uneventfully, as I left Luvierte to hunt, check out the surrounding area, and gather information.

Then a day came when I woke up much later than usual. Despite the hour, the inn's counter was still empty, so I walked out without a word and went straight to the mercenary guild office to check the job board. After that, I turned toward the west gate to spend the day earning some pocket money and getting further acquainted with the area.

However, something felt different about the town. There were far more people than usual walking toward the west gate, and they seemed to be excited about something. I found myself walking behind two men and decided to listen in on their conversation.

"Word is the army killed two giant basilisks in the forest outside a nearby town. Apparently, they're on display in the square!"

"No way! I never thought we'd have anything like a basilisk in these parts. I haven't even heard of someone *seeing* one before!"

"These stories are more and more common lately, ya know. Signs of something to come, maybe?"

Apparently, the viscount had sent out his army to ex-terminate the giant basilisks. But if they'd managed to kill two, did that mean there had been three in the forest? Or were they counting the one I'd stopped as their own kill? With how rare these monsters were, I figured the latter was more likely.

My interest piqued, I headed for the square near the west gate.

The paths running along both sides of the square were already jammed full of people. From my vantage point at the edge of the road, I could see a procession of knights and soldiers walking slowly past. Behind them were a line of horse-drawn carts that held the giant basilisks, chopped up into large chunks. It made sense seeing it as such, since there would've been no way to transport such massive creatures in one piece.

I looked over at the large man next to me, who was also fixated on the procession, and asked him a question.

"Is it always such a big ordeal when these basilisks come around?"

The man gasped when he saw me, though he quickly regained his composure.

"When a giant basilisk comes near a settlement, you either have to hire a renowned mercenary troupe or dis-patch the viscount's army to deal with it."

"Huh. Sounds like they're a pretty big deal then."

"I'd say so! A single basilisk could wipe out an entire village. But if you were able to kill one, I hear it'd fetch a pretty hefty sum. By drying out and pulverizing the poison in its body, you can make monster-killing arrows and all sorts of other things."

It sounded like I could've gotten myself a lot of money if I'd brought the one I'd killed back with me. I nodded along to the man's explanation, feeling a little sorry for myself. But, on the other hand, there was no way I could have brought the basilisk's body back on my own, and certainly not without drawing attention to myself.

I kept an eye on the troops as they marched past. I couldn't tell if the giant basilisk I'd killed was one of the two in the procession, but if it was, the soldiers would surely be looking for whoever had killed it.

I wanted to avoid interacting with any influential people if I could, so I decided it was best to move along before anything came of it. I turned around and made my way for the east gate.

During my research over the past few days, I'd learned of a town named Corna, located down the road to the east. Beyond that was a place called Diento, the largest town in the region. It was a three- to four-day trip by horse.

Since I already had all my worldly possessions with me, I decided to make my way toward Diento.

The town of Diento was located to the west of a sprawling forest.

Off in the distance, the morning sun began cresting the horizon and shining its light on the town's walls, slowly waking its slumbering inhabitants. The town had been built around the impressive fortress of Marquis du Diento, and inside one of its rooms sat a plump man with long white hair and a bushy white mustache, holding his head in his hands.

The man's name was Marquis Tryton du Diento.

"How did they do it? We released two giant basilisks into the Luvierte domain, did we not? They should have been reduced to panic in the face of such a threat!"

The cause of Tryton's misery was a report received earlier that morning from an informant in the Luvierte domain.

According to the informant, the giant basilisks he'd unleashed upon Luvierte had hardly caused any casualties, inflicting only minimal losses unto the viscount's army.

"Well, the east's envoy said we shouldn't expect much from the monsters. They were mere experiments, difficult to control over great distances. But even so, with two of them loose in the region, there should have been twice as many casualties in the battle against them." The thin, nervous-looking man sitting across from Tryton ended his speech with a heavy sigh before reaching up to brush his thinning hair back into place. Celsika Dourman, consul to the Diento domain, ran his eyes over the report in his hand.

Tryton's eyes narrowed. "If you had succeeded in the attack on his daughter, the viscount would have certainly been more shaken up by this..."

"Their thirty mithril shields were probably also a factor. I suspect they lowered the number of casualties from what we'd been expecting."

The marquis's eyes shot daggers at his consul. Though Celsika didn't seem to notice and continued speaking.

"According to the report here, we're about to run out of stock of the phantasms we've been using as bait for the elves. Shall I place an order with the usual place for more?"

The expression on Tryton's face contorted even further at Celsika's report. He turned his gaze away from the fidgeting man in front of him and let out a sigh of annoyance.

"Dammit! Not only did you fail in your road-side ambush, you follow it up by demanding money? You're no different from the rest of those useless scum!"

"It's no easy feat to capture a phantasm unless you have the proper skills, so we don't have many other choices. Besides, the procurement costs for trap bait are a mere pittance in the accounting books."

It looked as though steam was about to begin rising from Tryton's head. "You think I don't know that?! The problem is how this whole situation feels!"

Tryton adjusted his plump belly and reclined far back in his chair, crossing his arms and filling the air with a palpable tension. Celsika sighed quietly before slipping out of the room.

SKELET◉N
KNIGHT IN
ANOTHER WORLD

CHAPTER 3
Ariane, the Elf

A YOUNG WOMAN ran on uneasy feet through the moonlit forest.

The surrounding trees were dark, as if the entire world had been painted with an ink-soaked brush. Despite this, the woman's pursuers were slowly but surely closing in on her.

She was around twenty years old, with wispy, shoulder-length, golden hair tinted with green, matching the green of her eyes. As she ran, her hair grew tangled with small twigs and leaves, her cheeks marked by tears. Her breath was ragged, her hands and feet covered in scratches from bushes and trees, as if the very woods were trying to hold her back.

Her elongated, pointed ears—a trait unique to the people of the forest—picked up the sounds of multiple pursuers off in the distance. When she looked around, however, she saw no signs of life.

Had she been a dark elf, one of the other groups inhabiting the forest, she would have been able to see in the dark. For normal elves like herself, however, even seeing things in the forest during daylight was difficult enough. Night was another challenge entirely.

Elves were generally good at sensing the presence of others. Unfortunately, this young woman was still early in her training as a soldier and did not yet have the skills to keep herself calm enough to properly sense her surroundings.

She had tried desperately to escape her pursuers, but she could tell they were circling in closer and closer with each passing moment.

A split second after she registered the sound of something slicing through the air, an arrow pierced her right ankle and she tumbled to the ground.

"Aaaaaaghh!"

Pain erupted throughout her body the moment she saw the wound, her screams echoing among the trees. Her eyes welled with tears as she held her immobile leg, wailing and rolling about on the ground in agony.

Moments later, the bushes around her began moving, and several men stepped out of the darkness.

The men all wore thick, leather armor that covered

much of their bodies. They were armed with swords, daggers, and daggers, and bows, and they quickly closed in on the young woman, menacing smiles on their faces. They were clearly quite skilled at this.

One eagle-eyed man, his hand still holding the sword at his waist, issued commands to the rest.

"'urry up and put a collar on 'er!"

Another man stepped from the underbrush and approached the woman from behind, clasping a collar made of dark metal around her neck. He shoved a gag into her mouth, stifling her cries of pain as he climbed on top of her. As the men finished their well-practiced routine, a thin, well-dressed young man holding a lamp stepped from the bushes.

"Gah, just another brat! We come all the way out here, and all we get is some filthy-smelling forest urchin. This is no fun."

After inspecting the fallen girl under the lamplight and letting his disdain be known, the man pulled an extravagant sword from the sheath at his waist and stabbed her in the upper arm with its tip.

Despite the gag, her scream of pain could still be heard as she writhed about.

"Hey, cut it out! I can't have you scratching up our valuable merchandise!"

The leader of the group drew his sword from its sheath and glared at the young man. The young man glared back, a vein in his forehead bulging.

"You work for my father! You can't tell me what to do!"

The leader of the group looked unimpressed as he exchanged looks with the other men, rubbing his chin all the while. He decided to try to resolve the situation peacefully.

"We can patch her up later. We need to get out of here before the other elves find us." He issued his orders in a low voice before turning his intense eyes to the man next to him. "Did you retrieve the traps?"

The man responded with a slight nod and lifted the cages in his hand, each of which held a small animal. It was too dark to see their contents, but weak cries could be heard emanating from within the cages.

"Good. We'll wait till morning and bring our four prizes back to Diento."

After receiving the signal from their leader, the men, accompanied by the insulting young man with his lamp, carried their bounty back into the dark forest.

After leaving Luvierte, I began using Dimensional Step to travel upriver along the road that followed the Xpitol.

I passed several settlements surrounded by long walls along the way, though they all seemed to be pretty small.

After some time, I finally reached Corna, which looked like a smaller version of Luvierte. I decided not to stop and continued toward my next destination.

A while later, I eventually arrived at the Lydel River, the source of the Xpitol River. To the southwest, I could see the Calcut Mountains extending into the distance. The Lydel River gently traced the eastern edge of the Calcut foothills, apparently leading all the way to the country's capital. If I continued heading upriver, I would reach the town of Diento.

By carriage, this trip would take at least three days. However, I was able to cover the distance in less than half a day thanks to my teleportation abilities.

The town of Diento was just a short ways upriver from where the Xpitol split from the Lydel. At about three times the size of Luvierte, the town also possessed a rather sizeable amount of land for cultivating crops. Dual walls surrounded the town, which sat atop of a hill. Rows and rows of houses lined both the inside and outside of the wall, with dual moats surrounding the whole area. It looked exactly like a castle town.

I lost track of time as I took in the amazing sight of the town walls dyed orange from the setting sun, and the unobstructed view of the fields beyond them. If a town this size still existed in the modern era, it would certainly be a world heritage site.

I shook myself from my daze and began walking toward Diento. The fields surrounding the town were surprisingly busy, filled with farmers working and others hurrying home. I'd have to walk the rest of the way, since I was trying to avoid being seen using teleportation spells.

I was still quite a ways off from the town, though.

Maybe I could at least speed up my pace… I took off in a dash, my cape fluttering wildly behind me. The people ahead of me on the road heard my heavy footfalls, letting out yelps as they jumped out of my way. I wanted to tell them that there wasn't anything to worry about.

To be fair, it was entirely understandable to be afraid of a two-meter-tall, armor-clad man running toward you at high speed.

I slowed my pace as the gate loomed close. I'd definitely draw attention to myself if I ran right up to it.

Seven meters above me, guards walked atop the walls that surrounded the town. After I passed the first gate, the second wall came into view.

The second gate stood slightly uphill from the first. After showing my mercenary license to the guard, I was allowed passage into the town of Diento.

It seemed like everything in the town was made of stone, including the rows upon rows of two- and three-story buildings. Thrust into the massive crowd of people, I was surprised at just how noisy everyone here was, from sellers hawking their wares to the drunks milling about.

It was almost nostalgic...

Roads wove in and out of the buildings from every direction. I could tell that it'd take me some time to get the layout down. Upon entering a nearby bar, I found myself among several people who looked like they'd just gotten off work and were already well into their cups.

I called to the barkeep behind the counter. "Sorry to disturb you, but I'm looking for an inn. Do you have any recommendations?"

The barkeep responded instead with an offer of his own. "Well if it's an inn you're lookin' for, we run one here on the second and third floors! A night'll run ya two sek."

I wondered if I could buy food here and bring it upstairs.

"Can I eat in my room?"

"I don't see why not, so long as ya bring yer plate back down when yer done. It's three suk for a meal. Whaddya think?"

I paid the barkeep two silver and three copper coins

for my room and board and moments later received a tray with my meal on it. I took the tray up the stairwell beside the bar to my room on the third floor.

Upon opening the door, I found a room far better than where I'd stayed in Luvierte. There was a sturdy bed with a blanket, as well as a small table and chair. I placed my food on the table, sat on the bed, and removed my helmet.

It had been a while since I had a proper meal.

The meal on the tray was relatively simple: flat, black bread, a bowl of bean soup, and a salad. It didn't look like there was any meat.

The black bread was tough to chew through, so I soaked it in the soup to soften it up. The soup itself was actually pretty good. It tasted like it was made with chicken broth. The salad was a simple affair consisting of various vegetables on a bed of lettuce and endive, topped with vinegar and salt. I was a bit confused by their choice to serve it on such similar, leafy vegetables.

After I finished eating, I put my helmet back on and took my tray downstairs. The barkeep looked at me a bit funny when I returned the tray, but I couldn't blame him. It must have been odd to see an armored guest take their food upstairs then return the utensils with their armor still on. But at least he didn't say anything about it.

Back in my room, I sat down on the bed with my back against the wall and assumed my usual pose to get some sleep. I pulled the blanket over myself as well, but it hardly made a difference with my armor on.

Early the next morning, I woke to the sound of bells ringing in the distance. Once back on the first floor, I could see the barkeep back in the kitchen carrying out his duties. It looked like this inn was manned in the mornings, unlike the last place I stayed. I set my room key down on the counter, called out to the barkeep, and left the inn.

After asking a person on the street for directions, I made my way to the local mercenary guild office.

It was a three-story, stone building, but the interior wasn't much different from the one in the previous town, other than the fact that there were so many more staff members behind the counter, and there was no caged bear of a man working there.

A group of men who appeared to be mercenaries crowded around the job board. They were incredibly tough-looking, just like the staff. It made we wonder if there were any female mercenaries; at the very least, they could hire a woman to work in the office.

As I looked over the job board, I could hear various discussions between the mercenaries.

"Five members of our troupe went hunting four days ago, but we haven't seen 'em since."

"Think maybe some bandits or monsters got to them? We're close to elf territory. The monsters around that area are pretty strong, so I wouldn't be surprised."

"Nah, they were heading to the base of the Calcut Mountains, toward the capital."

This world was full of dangers, both inside and outside the towns. It sounded like it wasn't uncommon to simply lose track of people the moment they set foot outside.

On the other hand, this was the first I'd heard of an elf species. Up till now, all I'd seen were normal humans. I got the impression that elves lived in the forests and didn't venture out to where the humans lived.

I'd hate to come all the way to this other world and not see one at least.

I continued looking through the job board as I mulled this over, but despite the volume of requests—thanks to the larger population—they were still the same old boring chores. It seemed like I'd need to join a troupe if I hoped to get any of the good jobs.

I left the mercenary guild office, figuring I could head out to the forest again and hunt around for something to sell.

I stopped at a stall selling dried fruits to buy some

provisions. The vendor said he was selling strawberries, but they looked like some type of wild variety to me. Maybe this was what they looked like in Europe.

The man charged me eight copper coins for a small wooden cup full of the dried fruits, claiming it would last me half a year; I didn't think it'd even last me half a day. I put the provisions in a small bag and threw them in my sack.

I asked a nearby pedestrian for directions then made my way to the south gate.

At the inner wall, I showed the gate guard my mercenary license, and he waved me through. I walked downhill and exited the city through the outer wall's gate.

Ahead of me, a stone bridge resting atop six arches spanned the three-hundred-meter-wide river. The bridge could accommodate three carriages traveling side by side, and it was full of people and carriage traffic. Apparently, this was a transportation hub.

After crossing the bridge, I could see the Calcut mountain range, and the forest running along it, off to my right. To my left was a fenced-in area filled with cows, sheep, and horses, probably a pasture of some kind. Beyond that was a field of crops.

Farther up the Lydel River, the forest loomed close, but here on the other side, the land was mostly open.

I decided to make my way toward the base of the

Calcut Mountains to hunt around for a bit. I took a path off the main road and made my way southwest.

The Lydel River rushed off into the forest, though I couldn't see where it went after that. As I walked, the vegetation rapidly grew thicker, closing in around me and blocking out the sunlight. Roots sprouted from the ground everywhere, looking almost like tentacles trying to grab my legs and block my path.

The trees here weren't nearly as thick as those in the forest near the Furyu Mountains, but they made up for that by growing close together. There was no room for me to maneuver my two-handed sword in here. Well, I probably could have, but I'd take half a dozen trees down with each swing. Dimensional Step was also practically useless here in the dense forest.

I saw a few small animals here and there, but, just as quickly as they appeared, they'd disappear back into the underbrush. I'd probably need to set traps to catch anything here.

I wandered through the forest for about an hour before I encountered five men—bandits, I guessed. They stepped out of the underbrush, wearing sinister smiles on their unshaven faces. Their greasy hair suggested they hadn't washed in some time. All five of them were holding short swords.

"Well, well. Where ya going, Sir Knight? Hehehe."

"Just leave yer stuff right there, and we won't need to torture ya to death. We're pretty nice guys, ain't we fellas?"

"Can't believe our luck! Having a fancy knight like this, just wandering around in our woods all alone. Hahaha!"

"And when we kill someone out here, we don't even need to hide the body. Gahaha!"

The men kept jeering, overly confident in the strength of their position. They eyed me up and down, as if calculating the value of all the goods I carried. They were practically salivating.

"So, whaddya think, Sir Knight?"

Two of the men moved in unison, stabbing their short swords into the gaps in my armor at my neck and sides, as if they were used to taking on armored opponents. This wasn't like the game at all. No one would simply strike at someone's armor head on.

"Hng?" I looked down at the swords sticking out of me and grunted.

"Hya hya! Just like fighting a practice dummy."

"The only thing impressive about him is his armor!"

The men continued their mocking banter.

They weren't wrong; this exquisite armor housed nothing but bones. But that meant there were no vital organs inside for their swords to pierce. Now that they'd attacked me, I no longer had any reason to go easy on them.

"Was that supposed to tickle?"

"Wha?"

"Huh?!"

I glanced down at the two men. They looked back at me with blank stares, momentarily stunned into silence.

Pwaah! I punched one of the men's heads, and it went flying with a sound akin to a balloon exploding. His body shook for a second before falling to its knees.

The other bandits' faces contorted in shock. I'd put a little too much strength into that punch... I hadn't meant to knock his head off.

The rest of the fight unfolded as if I were watching it in slow motion. I turned and uppercut the other bandit next to me, my fist punching straight through his jaw and out the top of his skull. Blood exploded from his eyes, ears, and mouth, drenching the earth.

"A gh-ghooost!"

"Save meeeeeeeee!"

A little farther off, two of the other bandits turned tail. I summoned my Rock Shot ability and unleashed a volley at their backs, tearing rock-sized holes through them. Rock Shot was a fairly powerful base magic skill belonging to the Magus class. The leather armor the bandits wore stood no chance against it.

That made four. I spotted the last man weaving

through the trees in a frantic attempt at escape, almost like a monkey swinging through its natural habitat. Given the density of the undergrowth, Dimensional Step would do me no good, so I decided to simply run after the bandit instead.

He was much more familiar with the lay of the land than I was, and he drew even farther away as I shoved through the bushes and trees. I tried closing the distance by avoiding the more densely packed areas and running through the clearings.

Suddenly, my foot snagged on something. In front of me, a large boulder suspended by a rope dropped to the earth, and my leg flew out from under me.

"Heh! Can't believe ya fell for such a beginner's trap!" The bandit had stopped and was looking right at me, as if he'd just caught a major bounty.

I yanked my foot free from the rope, shooting the boulder high into the sky, pieces of rope flying in every direction. A boulder that size was no match for my superhuman strength.

I took off...and ran into another trap. This time, a wall of spears erupted out of the ground, meant to stab any animal that came this way. I let my armor take the brunt of it and rushed through, sending splintering wood everywhere.

Next up was a giant wooden stake that came flying at me through the air. My fist connected with the side of it, pulling the rope taut before the wood exploded in a shower of splinters.

Apparently, the bandits had set up traps all along the open areas. My only choice was to continue through the dense woods and simply smash my way through. I figured if beasts could do it, then so could I.

"Whoooa! I-It really is a ghost!" the bandit screamed in horror before taking off again. Despite being shaken by what he'd just witnessed, the man was still able to deftly navigate the woods.

I continued my pursuit at full speed. I was like a tank as I trampled trees with my body and barreled over rocks. Nothing could make me change my path in my frantic pursuit.

Excitement welled up within me as the pursuit continued, prompting me to yell after the fleeing man. "Hahaha! You think you can get away from me?!"

"Aaaaaaugh!"

Hearing this, I could see the crotch of the man's pants darken, and I caught a whiff of ammonia. I was quite impressed that, despite having peed himself in fear, he could still keep up his escape.

Once we made it out of the woods, I found myself

staring at a cliff face around seven to eight meters high. In front of me, a cave-like opening burrowed into the rock, with a simple fence around it to keep animals away. The bandits' hideout, maybe?

Two men sat on the ground out front, staring into space, seemingly bored out of their minds. They stared in surprise when the man I'd been pursuing appeared.

Wide open areas made things infinitely easier for me.

I used my Dimensional Step to teleport behind the men, drew my sword, and sliced through all three with a single diagonal slash, staining the entrance to the cave with blood and filling the area with the faint odor of rusted steel.

A gentle breeze rustled the forest leaves.

Despite having murdered yet another group of bandits, I didn't feel anything. It was all like an FPS game to me; I was simply exterminating another enemy.

I stared down at my gore-drenched sword through the slit in my helmet, yet still felt nothing. The blood slowly dripped away, and the blade's soothing azure glow returned.

It was like I simultaneously was and wasn't in my own body. And yet, at the same time, I felt oddly certain of who I was. Though, for some reason, I wasn't the least bit shaken by things that should bother me.

I used to role play a character that had been cursed to become a skeleton. It was beginning to feel like that was actually true.

I slid the glowing blade back into its sheath then opened and closed my hand a few times, as if to test the reality of the situation.

That was when I noticed the faint cries of some sort of animal coming from deep within the cave.

Careful not to make any noise, I crept forward and peered inside. There didn't seem to be anything particularly out of the ordinary, so I made my way in.

The cave wasn't very deep. It curved to the left shortly past the entrance then extended for another hundred meters or so. At the end of the tunnel was a large open area, lit by several lamps. It seemed to be where the bandits slept.

There were various knick-knacks strewn about the place, along with a wooden box for storing valuables. It looked much like a treasure chest. Inside, I found a large number of gold coins. Adding them to my purse, I guessed I had over five hundred gold coins now. Despite their small size—around that of a one-yen coin—they weighed as much as a five-hundred-yen coin, adding quite a bit of heft to my sack.

There were also several weapons and other items lying around, so I picked up anything that looked valuable.

I threw everything into my sack, laughing lightly as I considered that there really was little difference between the bandits' actions and my own.

Just then, I sensed something move and raised my head to look around. I noticed a steel cage sitting in the corner of the cave.

It stood in the shadows outside the lamplight, which was why I'd missed it. As I approached the cage for a closer look, I could see an injured animal glaring out at me from inside. I brought the cage closer to the lamp for a better look, revealing a fox inside.

Well, a fox-like animal, at least. It was about sixty centimeters long. Its tail made up nearly half that length and was covered with fur that reminded me of the fluff on a dandelion. Its face looked uncannily like a fox's, with large, triangular ears that perked up attentively. It had fleshy membranes between its legs and body, similar to a Japanese flying squirrel. I couldn't quite tell its color in the dim light, but much of its body seemed to be covered in a light green fur, with white fur on its stomach.

The animal held its tail up as high as the cage would allow, never taking its eyes off me and groaning lightly all the while. I could see a light wound on one of its front legs and a much deeper one on a hind leg, staining its soft fur a deep red.

I figured I'd use my healing magic on its wounds, so I undid the latch on the cage and opened the door. However, it didn't appear like the green fox had any desire to come out. Making sure not to leave any space for it to escape, I reached my arm into the cage to pull it out.

"Kyiii!" The fox let out a short yelp and bit down on my finger. It didn't hurt at all, thanks to my armored gloves, but the fox continued glaring at me, growling deep in its throat. It showed no desire to loosen its grip on my finger.

"Hey, don't be scared..."

I tried calming the agitated fox with my best lines from popular anime characters, but it was no use. I just didn't have the ability to calm animals down. Out of options, I dragged the green fox from the cage by my finger, which it stayed dutifully latched on to.

"Mending Heal."

With the fox still biting down on my finger, I summoned my healing spell. A soft light enveloped the injury for a moment before dissipating. Possibly surprised by the sudden light, the green fox spread out its fluffy tail and jumped backward, staring up at me with its large eyes.

"Kyii?"

It cocked its head to the side inquisitively before attending to its hind leg, giving the injury several licks. Then it lapped at its front paw several times before brushing its face like a cat. Once properly groomed, the fox leaned back and sat on its hind legs, its large tail wagging as it looked up at me.

It seemed like it was done trying to run away.

I remembered the dried berries I'd bought that morning, which were still in my sack. The fox's nose perked up as it watched my hands closely pull out the berries. I smiled and poured some into my hand, offering them to the fox.

It was cautious at first, only sniffing at the berries in my hand. Then it made a decision and quickly bit down on one, running off into the corner to chew on it. After it had finished the berry, the fox walked back over to me, bit down on another one, and repeated the process. After going through this several times, the fox began eating the berries straight out of my hand.

The fear that I'd seen earlier seemed to have faded entirely. I chuckled to myself at the absurdity of it, wondering if it was really okay for a wild animal to become this friendly with people.

Once the fox had finished all the berries, I petted its head a few times, causing it to tense up. Its eyes narrowed slightly.

There didn't seem to be anything else of note in the cave, so I decided it was time for me to end my short break. The green fox jogged behind me on its short legs, hurrying to keep pace with me as I made my way toward the cave entrance.

I stopped and turned around, causing the fox to crouch on its hind legs in a sitting position. Its fluffy tail wagged gently as it looked up at me. It seemed like the creature had taken a liking to me.

I tilted my head to the side and looked down.

"Wanna come with me?"

I didn't exactly expect a response, but the green fox replied with a "Kyii!" and walked over to my feet, its tail wagging against my legs. It was almost like it could understand what I was saying.

I didn't know exactly what type of animal it was, but I didn't feel like "green fox" was cutting it. I wracked my brain as I tried thinking of a name.

Green...fox... Hmm...

"Which name do you like better? Oage or Tempura?"

I threw out the first two names that came to mind, but the fox's tail just drooped in response. Apparently, it wasn't a fan of either.

I glanced at the small creature's tail, covered with dandelion-like fluff.

"Hmm, how about Ponta, then?"

"Kyii!" The fox's tail popped up and wagged about excitedly.

I'd found a winner this time.

"All right, Ponta, are you ready to go?"

Ponta let out a squeak in response and jumped into the air, catching a gust of wind by spreading out its fleshy membranes. It almost looked as if it were floating atop some sort of invisible elevator.

"Whoa!" I gasped in astonishment, my eyes locking onto Ponta.

It seemed to be using some sort of wind magic. There was no way an updraft could occur inside a cave like this.

Ponta continued riding the breeze even higher, landing atop my helmet. Since we'd been facing each other, Ponta was now pointing toward my back, its large fluffy tail drooping down to obscure the slit in my helmet. I gently brushed the tail back and forth a few times, causing Ponta to readjust its position and clear up my view.

I knew I was in a fantasy world, but still, to meet such a mysterious creature, and one that could use magic at that, was beyond my expectations. I'd just figured it lived among the trees, gliding about like flying squirrels do.

I nodded once, amazed at Ponta's impressive feat, before collecting my bag and making my way toward the cave's entrance again.

Not wanting any further trouble, should anyone discover the bodies of the bandits, I used Fire to burn their

corpses. Ponta was surprised at first by the flames, but after it realized it wasn't in any danger, I could feel its tail swishing along the back of my helmet again.

Once the bandits had been reduced to ash, I left their base behind.

With the considerable loot I'd just acquired, my animal companion and I should be able to survive for a while without needing to work. It'd be nice to travel about wherever our whims took us, like birds on the wind. I felt like a newly minted retiree as I began considering the options.

I alternately walked and teleported as I thought about my options. When I finally made my way out of the trees, I was able to see the sky, which was turning a pale red.

Apparently, I'd spent quite a bit of time in the forest.

Off in the distance, I could see the walls of Diento. The vast fields around the town were devoid of any signs of life.

After walking upriver a ways, along the Lydel, I came upon the figure of a man, facing away from me. He was wrapped in a beige cloak, his green-tinged, blond hair blowing about in the wind. I assumed he was a man, but he looked different from all the other men I'd seen up to that point. From behind, I could see he had the elongated, angled ears that marked a certain species common in stories and games.

For some reason, I was incredibly excited to see one in person. I immediately teleported behind him using Dimensional Step and called out to him. "You're the first elf I've seen."

The elf jumped forward, spinning around in midair. As he landed, he drew a thin sword, pointing it, and a very stern look, my way when he landed.

He had green eyes to match his green-tinged, shoulder-length, blond hair. His slim body was covered in leather armor, his hand steady as he kept the sword tip trained on me. His demeanor was completely different from the bandits I'd encountered in the woods. I could immediately tell he was a soldier.

"Identify yourself, stranger."

Never once letting his guard down, the elf spoke in a low voice as he stepped back, putting more distance between us. His gaze seemed particularly focused above my head, or rather, on Ponta, who sat atop my helmet.

"I am Arc, a wanderer. Apologies for getting so excited."

The elf shot me a dubious look and lowered his blade ever so slightly. His eyes wandered over my armor, as if he were trying to see through it, to figure out who the man underneath really was.

"A human? I never knew a ventu-vulpis to take kindly to humans."

"Ventu-vul...?"

"Also known as the cottontail fox. That spirit creature sitting atop your head. What you humans call phantasms, I think? They usually travel in packs. Where did you find it?"

"You're a spirit, Ponta?"

Ponta responded with a curious cry, refusing to move down from its perch. The elf looked exasperated as he stared back at me.

"Not a spirit, a spirit creature. It's a type of animal a spirit resides within. If you don't already know that, then you're definitely no elf."

I could tell he was talking down to me, but I couldn't really blame him. He had no idea about my backstory.

"Apologies, this is the first time I've encountered a spirit creature. I found this fellow here injured in a cage inside a bandit camp, so I set it free. It seems to have grown attached to me after I healed its wounds and gave it some food, so I've decided to let it accompany me on my travels."

The elf facing me maintained a quizzical expression on his face as he listened to my story.

"Hmph. Spirit creatures are usually incredibly cautious. They rarely get close even to us elves. But I guess there are bound to be outliers."

Outliers... The elf seemed to lock his eyes on me as he said this word. Maybe it was just my imagination.

He lowered his sword, readjusted his cloak, and pulled his hood over his head, hiding his distinctive ears.

"What are you doing all the way out here?" I asked. "Are you heading into town? I haven't seen any elves there..."

Even though he had the hood pulled down low over his face, I could still see the dumbfounded expression the elf wore in response to my question.

"Are you really a human, stranger? Humans fear...no, *hate* all that is different or superior to them. We elves are granted long lives and possess strong magical affinity. Even here in the Rhoden Kingdom, where you've already entered a treaty with us, you continue hunting us if we don't stay out of sight. Apparently, you sell forest elves for large sums."

Deep within his cloak, his eyes burned with anger.

Officially at least, hunting elves was prohibited, but it sounded like no one actually enforced that treaty. Even without knowing the particulars, the look in this elf's eyes alone was enough to convey the atrocities committed by humans.

Maybe hunting wasn't quite the right word; it didn't sound like they were killing the elves. If elves were vicious, war-loving barbarians, humans wouldn't have entered a treaty with them in the first place. Nor would hunting and selling them for large sums be illegal. So, unless elf blood was some sort of all-encompassing cure, the only other possibility was slavery.

That meant this elf's reason for coming so close to a human town was...

"You're here to free the slaves, aren't you?"

The elf's face clouded over with suspicion, a dangerous look in his eyes.

"Hmph. You'd best not tell anyone about what we discussed here. Or even that you've seen an elf."

I sighed, letting my shoulders slump to show the elf he had nothing to fear. I spread my hands to indicate that I meant no threat.

"Not that I can trust the words of a human..."

Before he even got the full sentence out of his mouth, the elf was already lifting his sword again. Ponta screeched out from the top of my head, as if objecting to the man's actions.

"Kyii kyiii!"

The elf froze for a moment, but then the expression on his face eased up, and he lowered his sword.

"Well, you somehow managed to form a bond with a spirit creature, so I suppose an exception can be made. Don't forget what I said."

The elf quickly walked past me and disappeared into the forest. I hadn't even learned his name.

I'd thought this would be my chance to engage with a different species in this strange new world, but humanity's reputation was evidently too negative to overcome.

Well, perhaps we'd meet again. If elves were enslaved within the town, I could try to uncover some information. That way, if our paths did cross another time, I'd have some information to share.

With that objective firmly in my mind, I made my way back to town.

As the setting sun cast its glow over Diento's walls, nothing in particular seemed different or out of place. However, I looked on the town with new eyes, seeing only the darkness, a cloak that hid all of humanity's worldly desires.

Several days later, I woke up as usual atop my bed at the inn to the sound of the morning bells.

Ponta lay on the blanket, its face buried in the fluff of its green and white tail. From time to time, a low growl issued from the back of its throat and it would make chewing motions, as if dreaming of some delicious feast. Because of its foxlike appearance, I'd originally assumed Ponta was a carnivore, but it seemed to be an omnivore, with a preference for fruits and berries.

Ponta woke up, scratched behind its ears with a hind leg, then stretched its mouth wide open in a yawn. Hopping onto my shoulder, Ponta resumed its rightful perch atop my helmet. Apparently, cottontail foxes liked high places.

With Ponta on my head, I picked up the large, black cloak sitting nearby and draped it over my armor. The cloak was a recent purchase from a shop in town. Not only did it cover up my flashy armor, but it would also help me with covert activities.

But even when I covered up the gleam of my armor, my helmet still peeked out of the black cloak, which didn't help matters. I probably looked like some sort of black-cloaked, laser-sword-wielding villain right out of a certain sci-fi franchise.

Be that as it may, I was now able to disappear into a crowd of people far better than when I was showing off my armor in its full glory.

I went down to the first floor, offered up a greeting to the barkeep, who was busy in the kitchen again, and made my way outside. The bar only served dinner, so I'd gotten into the habit of buying breakfast from a street vendor in the mornings.

The road was lined on both sides with stalls, competing to draw the attention of prospective customers. As I walked between them, the world suddenly became dark as a certain cotton-like tail swung in front of my visor.

Whenever I walked past something Ponta liked, it would lock its gaze and turn its body to face whatever it had spotted, eventually obscuring my vision with its tail.

I reached up and turned Ponta around, then walked in the direction Ponta had been looking. It was a vendor selling a type of nut that Ponta had recently taken a liking to. The light brown shells housed a green inside, reminding me of pistachios.

"Kyiii!"

Buy it, pleeease! It wasn't hard to figure out what Ponta was saying.

I paid the woman at the stall five copper coins for a small bag then broke the shells of several nuts, feeding them to the creature atop my head. Ponta screeched in delight and gobbled them up. Though Ponta could take the shells off on its own, this resulted in pieces of shells falling in front of my visor as I walked.

I'd spent the past few days exploring the town, with Ponta perched atop my head.

I'd been looking around the nooks and crannies of Diento to see if I could uncover any information about the enslaved elves. However, since I couldn't just walk up to someone and ask them point blank if they knew where the slaves were kept, I was left wandering around without any specific destination in mind.

Buying and selling captured elves was likely a highly lucrative business, even if it was forbidden, which meant it was almost certainly happening under the direction of some powerful figure.

I had my suspicions that my search would be more fruitful not in the town itself, but the homes of the nobility closer to the center of Diento. However, my current appearance would draw immediate attention. There were many guards near the nobles' estates, but not nearly the same volume of foot traffic.

To be completely honest, I wasn't exactly conducting my search out of altruism. It wasn't that the concept of slavery didn't bother me, but, as awful as it was to admit, I was bored and simply had nothing better to do. There were probably better uses of my time, but I couldn't imagine just sitting around the inn without any clear goals ahead of me.

I didn't know what I'd do if I actually found the enslaved elves. For the time being, I was trying to keep a low profile. That way, if I did find myself in a situation where I could help them out, I could do so quietly.

It figured that when I'd finally met elves in this alternative world—something I'd dreamed of my whole life— it turned out they were being persecuted.

Come to think of it, I hadn't seen any other fantasy species since coming here. Did they even exist in this world? Judging by how the elf had spoken, I supposed that, even if they did, they were probably persecuted just like the elves. What a depressing thought.

I mulled these heavy thoughts over as I made my way to the mercenary guild office. I hadn't been there in several days, so it was nice to be back. Pounding the pavement wasn't getting me anywhere, so I figured I'd take on a job.

There were several mercenaries already crowded around the job board, picking through requests. I joined the group and began sorting through the tags, looking for something interesting.

One finally caught my eye. It was for a missing person.

The person had gone out into the woods up the Lydel River and hadn't returned. That was five days ago.

The forest upriver lined the base of the Furyu mountain range. It was commonly referred to as the Furyu Forest—same as the one near Rata. It stretched on and on, covering a vast area of land.

However, the forest on the other side of the Lydel River, despite being a part of the same mountain range, was known by a different name. People referred to it as the "Elf Forest" or the "Lost Woods."

Not only did powerful monsters run rampant there, but the elves living within the forest would give you no quarter if you came across them.

I wasn't interested in taking on this job right now. If I did, I wouldn't be able to complete the job until I either found the person or brought back something proving they were dead or alive. I'd heard an experienced mercenary telling a newbie earlier that for jobs like these, it was best to keep the information in the back of your mind, notifying the guild only *after* you found something.

I followed that advice and decided to look around in the woods upriver.

After leaving the guild office, I made my way toward the east exit, the gate closest to the Furyu Forest.

Unlike the north and south gates, which were often used by merchant caravans, the east gate was much smaller and only wide enough for a single carriage. This was also where the red-light district was located, the tiny alleys filled with questionable-looking shops. There weren't that many people out and about during the daytime hours, but come nightfall, the streets would be filled with women calling out to men as they walked past.

Since I was trying to stay out of trouble, I steered clear of this area at night. Besides, even if I wanted to go there,

there was nothing I could do with my body in its current state.

After passing through the east gate and the outer town wall, I crossed two wooden bridges spanning the moats and turned right to walk along the Lydel River. The Furyu Forest was twenty kilometers from the east gate, and the journey only took five minutes using Dimensional Step.

Once we entered the forest, I could feel Ponta wagging its tail excitedly against my armor.

I wondered if the light green fur was meant to be some form of camouflage for the forest-dwelling creature. A part of me was saddened by the thought that Ponta may return to them if we ran across any other cottontail foxes, but I ventured deeper into the woods all the same.

The forest was decently lit, allowing me a line of sight deep into the woods. The undergrowth, however, was thick, making it impossible to even see my own feet. Off to my right was a cliff. I could hear rushing water from the Lydel River echoing below. The forest was filled with bird calls and rustling leaves, giving it an altogether relaxing atmosphere. There were no fearsome monsters to be seen.

I continued my nature hike, basking in the sunlight streaming through the trees. But as I made my way farther into the woods, the air took on the distinct smell of rotting meat.

Up ahead, past some underbrush, the trees opened out into a small clearing. In its center, I found scattered bones, teeth marks gouged deep into them. I quickly realized what had caused such distinctive marks.

The mound of flesh in front of me, what had once been a human, was headless, making it impossible to identify. I couldn't find a head anywhere in the surrounding area either. I had no way of knowing whether this was the man from the job request or not.

Though it looked like the body had been gnawed on in several places by animals, its head had been severed cleanly. Assuming the man had been attacked and torn apart by wild animals, there was no way the neck would be cut like that. I wasn't even sure if monsters were *able* to do that.

The most likely scenario was that he'd been attacked and killed by bandits. There were no weapons or bags in the vicinity, and I had a hard time believing that someone would come into the dangerous woods unarmed.

I decided to look around in case there was another bandit hideout nearby.

Down in the grass, I discovered a trail of blood. Though it had already dried and turned black, it served as a guide through the forest.

The blood led me to the shore of the Lydel River, where it continued along the rocky beach. The river was wide here, but fairly shallow. It looked like whoever left the trail had crossed the water.

On the other side of the river was the so-called Elf Forest, which made me wonder if the man had been killed by elves. However, I had a hard time believing any elves lived at the edge of the forest, right along the river. It was too close to the humans. I thought it more likely that bandits had built a hideout here, in a place rarely frequented by humans and where elves would have a hard time finding it.

"Wanna play detective for a bit, Ponta?"

"Kyiii!"

Ponta had been drinking from the river when I called out, but it ran excitedly back to my side. I took a knee to allow the fox to jump up onto my shoulder and back to the top of my head. I cracked a few more pistachios and fed them to it, leading to more excited tail wagging as it gnawed on the nuts.

I crossed the river and entered the woods on the other side. Everything from here on out was the Elf Forest.

The forest itself didn't have a particularly foreboding feeling to it. If anything, compared to the woods on the other side, the massive trees here gave this forest a mystical, timeless quality. Light filtered between the leaves of the canopy above, illuminating the undergrowth at my feet.

There was no blood trail to be found anywhere, though I did uncover tracks that looked like a footpath. Maybe the man had been attacked as he was crossing the river, and he started bleeding on the other side. In that case, the bandits would be on high alert in this area, which meant it would do me no good to perform a meticulous search of the place or to continue following the tracks. I'd just have to walk around and see what I could find.

A short time later, Ponta and I ran across a bear. Or, rather, it had the body of a bear, the head of a wolf, and the long, drooping ears of a donkey.

The wolf-bear glowered at us and stood up on its hind legs, moving closer. I wasn't interested in hunting any wild animals today, so I gave the wolf-bear a quick punch, causing it to yelp and run back through the brush into the woods.

Ponta was still tense, fur standing on end, so I reached up and scratched under its chin. From the direction the wolf-bear had run off to, the cries of someone in distress echoed through the woods.

We were already deep into elf territory, so that meant the person was either an elf or some human up to no good.

Looking in the direction the cries had come from, I found a small path winding through the forest. The path—if you could even call it that—had been roughly hacked through the grass. It was barely wide enough for a single carriage.

I crept through the shrubs along the side of the path, using Ponta as a miniature ghillie suit for my head. As I moved along silently, a group of frenzied people came into view, weapons unsheathed and at the ready.

There were a dozen or so of them standing around a cart, their eyes alert and constantly scanning their surroundings. The wolf-bear I'd sent running just moments ago was dead at their feet, bleeding from multiple wounds. A thin, young man stood over the two-meter wolf-bear, spitting out epithets as he kicked its body.

"Dammit, don't scare me like that! All we've done today is knock around a bunch of stupid brats!"

He held an expensive-looking sword in his hand, though there was no sign of blood on the blade. It didn't look like he'd helped kill the beast.

An imposing man looked over, wide-eyed, at the young man and scolded him. "Keep yer voice down, Udolan. There could still be beasts lurking nearby."

Udolan's face contorted with rage. "Don't tell me what to do!"

The imposing man, possibly the leader of the group, averted his gaze from the young man as he screamed himself red, instead looking back at the men surrounding the cart.

"The cloth's slippin'. Ya better fix that."

There was a large, steel cage in the bed of the cart. Four young children with characteristic elf ears were packed inside. All of them had injuries, either on their hands or feet, and were crying quietly to themselves.

Several of the men standing around the cart picked up a large canvas, which had apparently fallen off during the encounter with the wolf-bear, and put it back over the cage, once again hiding the terrified elf children from sight.

Apparently, this group was involved in the capture, enslavement, and sale of elves. Seeing them, I recalled my conversation with the elf I'd met outside Diento several days earlier.

Even I'd known about the slavery, but seeing these children locked up in cages and treated like animals right in front of my eyes gave me a totally different perspective. I wondered if this altogether unpleasant feeling was related to the fact that I'd grown up in such a peaceful country. Even in my own world, there were probably those who couldn't distinguish between people from things, so long as they sold for a high price. But I was lucky to have never been around that.

I couldn't stand idly by and let these children be taken.

I was surprised to feel this focus, this calling, well up within me. I cocked my head to the side as I pondered over this, before returning my attention to the men in front of me.

They were evenly spaced around the cart, so even if I teleported in, there'd be no way to fend them all off at once. Plus, if any of the children were taken as hostages, it wouldn't matter how strong I was.

On the other hand, for all they knew, I was just some mysterious knight in a black cloak. If I came up behind them, I'd have the advantage until they figured out what I was there to do.

The next problem was the matter of timing.

As I watched the group from behind a bush, I detected movement in front of the traffickers.

"Who's there?!" a man at the front of the pack called out, quickly nocking an arrow and shooting it off into a bush near the cart. However, the only cry of pain that followed was his own.

Something flew out of the bush at blinding speed, ripping a massive hole in the chest of the man who'd shot the arrow. Before his body even had time to hit the ground, a gray shadow loomed out of the forest.

As blood erupted from the first man, the shadow broke into two tendrils that wrapped themselves around the necks and arms of two more men and pulled them to the ground. As they fell, I could see a lone attacker standing between them, readjusting the silver sword in her hand.

The woman was beautiful, wrapped in a dark gray cloak, thin saber at the ready. It was immediately apparent that she was no normal woman. Her flawless skin was light purple in hue, almost the color of amethyst. It was accented by her ruffled, snow-white hair, which was tied back in a ponytail and revealed elf ears, albeit shorter than those of the elf I'd met before. Her eyes glowed an eerie shade of gold in the rapidly darkening forest.

Underneath her cloak, the woman wore a decorative priest's robe, which was covered by corset-styled leather armor.

The soft lines of her figure still managed to show through her simple armor. She stood poised on long, slender legs that ended at well-formed hips, and her leather chest-piece strained to hold back her ample chest. And yet, she still reminded me of the knights of old.

"Release the children at once!"

She glared at the men with her golden eyes, her calm, measured voice filled with hatred as she spoke.

"An elf! Keep yer guard up, men!"

Despite having just seen three of their own slaughtered, the men responded in unison to their leader's orders, forming a semi-circle around the elf. The two men

on the ends rushed at her from both sides, trying to stay in her blind spot. However, she didn't seem to be in any real danger.

An instant later, the elf warrior bounded high up into the air, easily evading the two attacking blades. She quickly slashed her blade while still in midair before landing out of reach of the encroaching group. Her aerial strike cut one of her attackers' faces open, causing blood to pour out everywhere. The other man fell to the ground where he stood, three arrows jutting from his back. I caught the briefest of glimpses of an elf archer deep in the forest before turning my attention back to the woman.

Apparently, the slave traders had been ambushed by *two* elves.

"Don't let yer eyes fool ya! These are elf soldiers!"

The group of men was beginning to look more uneasy now that five of their own had been felled in a matter of minutes. However, they all hoisted their shields and withdrew slightly to readjust their formation.

The female elf gritted her teeth and scowled. Even though she'd gotten the drop on the group, there were still more than ten slave traders remaining, and they'd been able to pull their ranks in quicker than she'd anticipated. It made sense though; if you were operating in such dangerous woods, you'd have to be able to work as a team.

The two sides glared at each other, their hatred palpable. Udolan, the attractive young man from earlier, stood behind the protection of the men near the cart, waving his sword around frantically as he yelled.

"Surrender while you have a chance, hag! These men are about to chop you into ribbons! The same goes for your friend in the forest!"

Udolan's veins bulged, spittle flying from his mouth as he yelled. The young man seemed nothing like the rest—he definitely wasn't a regular member of their group.

The children, still locked away in their cage atop of the cart, suddenly found themselves at the other end of Udolan's blade.

"So, now you use children as a shield?! And you have the gall to call yourself a human, you cowardly beast?!"

The white-haired elven woman shot an intimidating glare at the young man before readjusting her stance and moving toward the group. However, Udolan's next move stopped her cold.

"Oh, shut up, will you? Take one step closer and I can't vouch for their safety!"

The moment the words left his mouth, the man thrust

forward with his sword, plunging its tip into the leg of one of the young girls in the cage.

Even with the gag in her mouth, the young girl's scream could still be heard far outside the cage. The other children cowered back into the corners, sobbing uncontrollably with fear.

The elf woman's face grew even fiercer, but she didn't dare move closer while the children were hostages.

"Kyiii."

Ponta, who was concealing my head with its light green fur, chewed lightly on a paw as it watched the events unfold.

Now that the light purple woman's advance had stopped, thanks to Udolan's threats, the slave traders seemed to relax a bit as they slowly encircled the woman. Her snow-white hair was in disarray, her eyes burning with hatred as she watched the oncoming men. They hesitated momentarily, but it would only be a matter of time until they made their move.

The male elf in the forest seemed at a loss for what to do, his bow hanging limply at his side. At this rate, it seemed clear they would both be captured.

Tired of watching the men make their painfully slow advance, an agitated Udolan pointed his sword at the woman and began screaming. "Don't even think of continuing to resist! Men, go in and get that dark elf. Looks like we've caught ourselves a pretty prize. I'll need to inspect this one myself."

A lustful grin pulled at the corners of Udolan's lips, the meaning behind his words readily apparent.

So, this woman was a dark elf, which was quite different from a run-of-the-mill elf. Back in the game, dark elves usually had dark brown skin, red eyes, and long, pointy ears. Apparently, things were a bit different in this world. From the way Udolan was talking, it sounded like they were a rare breed.

The dark elf's face contorted in a look halfway between fear and anger. Udolan's smile only grew with each passing moment.

If these were simply bandits roaming through the woods, I may have ignored the situation. But now that children were involved, I could no longer stand idly by.

I looked into the cage on the cart. The young girl who'd been stabbed held her leg, moaning as tears rolled down her cheeks.

No matter what the situation, it was absolutely unforgivable to threaten innocent children and use them as shields.

Since the men were focusing all their attention ahead of them, it'd be easier for me to get in a surprise attack now.

Figuring things were about to get dangerous, I took Ponta down from my head and put it around my neck, like a scarf. Then I used Dimensional Step to send myself behind the young man. Just as I'd hoped, neither Udolan nor the other men seemed to notice me, their attention fixed on the white-haired elf in front of them.

As I pulled back my fist to attack Udolan, I surveyed the surrounding area. My eyes locked with the dark elf's, her surprise evident in her wide pupils.

"You seem to be in a bit of trouble. Would you care for a hand?"

Upon hearing my voice, Udolan began turning toward me, but it was already too late for him.

"Gyaugh?!"

Unlike the last time, when I'd punched the other bandits with all my might, this time, I merely pushed my closed fist into the young man's back. I could feel his spine break, but rather than exploding like before, he flew into the group of men like a bowling ball into a row of pins.

Everything seemed to stand still for a moment.

Considering that the men had just seen a black-cloaked knight in brilliant silvery armor appear behind them, it was understandable they'd be speechless. The man I'd punched, as well as the two men he'd collided with, lay motionless on the ground.

Everyone in the vicinity was stunned, though the dark elf was the first to regain her composure.

She fell upon three of the men who were still staring blankly up at me, ending their lives with some skillful swordplay. From where I stood, a mere novice, her swordsmanship was poetry in motion.

The gruff leader of the group lunged forward to stab the elf in the chest. She spun deftly out of the way, no more than a paper's thickness of space between her body and the blade as she returned the blow. The rest of the men screamed aloud as they watched the events unfold.

The formation broke down and men took off into the woods. At that very same instant, the male elf began launching a volley of arrows at them.

One of the slave traders took off toward me, swinging his sword wildly, the deftness he'd displayed against the elf earlier now a long-forgotten memory.

I turned toward my attacker.

"Armor Lariat!"

With no time to draw my sword, I crossed my armor-clad arms, clasped my elbows, and ran into the man. I could hear a dull thud as I hit his sword, followed by the snap of his neck as I threw his body into a nearby tree.

In a matter of moments, the forest had returned to

its usual silence, the only sounds those of the insects and the wind.

With the threat now gone, my first priority was to set the children free and heal the girl's injuries. As I turned toward the cart, a harsh male voice rose up behind me.

"Stop right there!"

I turned around and saw that the male elf had left the forest. He had his bow trained on me, drawn and ready to fire, a fierce look in his eyes.

I raised my hands to show that I had no intention of putting up any resistance.

"I am but a simple traveler who happened upon..."

Even as the words came out of my mouth, I barely managed to suppress a chuckle at how absurd they must have sounded. I was no mere traveler. But still, I tried to explain myself.

"I said don't move! Ariane, look for a key to the cage!"

The male elf barked a command at the white-haired woman, who seemed hesitant. The look of uncertainty on her face only grew more intense.

"Wait a moment, Donaha. He helped us back there, didn't he?"

"I understand. But we're in elf country, and no one here wears massive armor like that. He must be a human, just like those abductors."

Ariane's eyes widened upon hearing this. She shot me a suspicious glance.

"Get the children from the cart and begin administering aid."

The female elf responded to Donaha's command and began searching for a key to the children's cage. Apparently, simply being human was enough to mark me as untrustworthy.

While Ariane searched the cart and the pockets of the dead slave traders, Donaha motioned for me to lower my hands, though he kept the bow trained on me, his eyes alert.

"Thank you for your assistance. However, we do not trust humans, especially those who keep their faces hidden."

I slowly lowered my hands, my palms still spread out, suppressing a laugh. It made perfect sense for him to be suspicious of an armor-clad man who'd suddenly appeared out of nowhere.

"Unfortunately, I cannot remove my helmet. The reasons are various, but personal."

Just then, Ponta's triangular ears perked up. After running a quick loop around my neck and checking the surroundings, Ponta hopped back on top of my head and cried out.

"Kyiii!"

Upon seeing this, Donaha's eyes went wide in disbelief. He lowered his bow ever so slightly.

"Is that...a ventu-vulpis?! Are you a human or aren't you?!"

Much like the elf I'd run into before, he was also taken by surprise upon seeing Ponta. It must have been pretty rare to encounter one of these cottontail foxes. Ariane looked up from her search for the key, shock registering on her face as well.

"The other elf I met was surprised, too. Yes, I am indeed human. I helped this creature out when it was injured and gave it food. It's grown attached to me. Lately, it's taken a liking to these."

I went back to the bush where I'd left my sack and retrieved the bag of pistachios. I poured a few out into the palm of my hand and raised it above my head. Ponta started chewing through the nuts' shells, stuffing their delicious innards into its cheeks.

Donaha seemed to be having a hard time believing what he was seeing. Though the look of caution never quite left his eyes, the drawn bow lowered farther as he continued his line of questioning.

"Who is this elf you said you met before?"

"I ran into him outside the town of Diento. He was working to set the elves in town free."

Though the man had asked me not to tell any humans of our interaction, I figured telling elves should be fine, especially elves with the same goal. Donaha's expression softened slightly, as if he may know the man I was referring to.

"You met Danka? Were you the one who..."

"No, this is the first time I've spoken of the encounter." I hurried to head off the man's suspicion, though I couldn't be sure he believed me.

Just then, Ariane called out to us. "I found the key, Donaha!"

She ran over to the cage and undid the latch, letting the door swing open with a heavy, metallic clang. The injured elven children inside looked relieved to see her, though they still wore black metal collars around their necks. Ariane lifted the girl who'd been stabbed out of the cart first.

Hoping to gain some points with them, and to smooth over my relations with the other elves of this world, I decided to offer Donaha the use of my magic.

"If anyone has been harmed, I may be able to heal them. Would it be all right for me to look at the child's injuries?"

"You say you're a human, so why would you help us? You must be aware of the relationship between humans and elves."

"Not all humans view elves as their enemies. There's nothing more to it than that. Like you, I cannot stand by while barbarous acts like kidnapping, hostage-taking, and violence against children are carried out in front of me."

Donaha turned his gaze from Ponta to Ariane and the girl in her arms. He put the arrow back in his quiver.

"I shall trust your word, for her sake. Can you heal this child?"

I took that as permission.

I left Ponta, who was busily munching pistachios, in my hand as I approached the girl. I thought the fox may keep the children calm. One hid behind Ariane, and the rest cowered slightly as I approached. I put Ponta on the ground and knelt to bring myself closer to their eye level.

The girl Ariane was holding tried burrowing herself deeper into the woman's arms, her face tensing up. She had blood-stained bandages around her leg from injuries she'd sustained prior to the recent stab wound. She probably had a hard time walking under her own power. I assumed the men had done that to keep her from escaping.

I spoke in the softest voice I could manage, to try and keep the girl calm.

"Stay still. I'm going to use a healing spell on you."

I reached out and summoned Mending Heal. A soft

light enveloped the girl's injured leg, and the wound started closing.

Everyone around me looked surprised, from the young girl herself to Ariane and all the other children. They crowded in around the girl for a closer look.

Donaha, who'd been hanging back as he watched on, spoke up.

"You must be quite powerful to use a healing spell without chanting. Judging by your armor, I'd figured you for a knight."

Evidently, one generally needed to chant in order to use magic. There was a cooling down period in the game before spells could be used again, but they were automatically cast the moment they were selected, without any need for chanting. I was thankful Donaha only thought of this as something uncommon, rather than something impossible.

Once the girl's leg was fully healed, she dropped down from Ariane's arms and tested her leg. After she was satisfied, she turned toward me, eyes facing downward.

"Th-thanks, mister..."

"Do you have any other injuries?"

The girl quickly shook her head.

Seemingly reassured, the other children came forward to have me heal their wounds as well.

Just then, an eerie wail broke the silence of the forest. Donaha narrowed his eyes, looking around the dusk-colored woods for the source of the noise.

"Sounds like a scavenger."

Seeing the children's concerned expressions, Ariane gently patted their heads to soothe them.

"We should do something before any other scavengers arrive," Donaha said. "Can I leave the bodies to you?"

Ariane nodded and immediately went about moving the slave traders' bodies all into one location. She was much stronger than she looked.

Keeping one eye on Ariane, Donaha turned toward me, looking as if he wanted to say something but couldn't find the words.

"Excuse me, but you are...?"

I realized then that I hadn't yet told him my name.

"They call me Arc. I'm a wandering mercenary."

"Pleased to meet you, Arc. I am Donaha, and this is Ariane. I hate to ask this of you, but would you mind healing the other children as well?"

I nodded in response to his request, which was surprisingly timid. I then went about casting Mending Heal on the remaining three children, each one thanking me quietly in turn.

After I finished, I looked over to Donaha, who'd been

watching us the entire time. He had a rather conflicted expression on his face.

"Are those mana-eater collars? They won't be able to use magic if we don't take them off. But I have no idea how to..." he muttered to himself as he looked at the black metal collars locked around the children's necks. There was a series of strange symbols carved into the surface of each one.

"What's a mana-eater collar?"

The term was completely foreign to me.

Donaha explained that the collar was cursed and would sap its wearer's magic ability, preventing them from casting spells. It also prevented elves from using their spiritual abilities.

"Ariane will be meeting with Danka after this. That leaves me to watch over these children and take them to the nearest village...with their ability to use magic blocked."

As Donaha examined the now-healed children and tried figuring out his next move, Ariane paused in her work with the bodies and approached us.

"Arc, was it? Can't we ask him to accompany you on the way to the village? I recall hearing that a mercenary is a type of human who will accept money to carry out a task."

Donaha furrowed his brow and turned his gaze toward me.

"That may be so, but..."

It was clear what he wanted to say. He probably didn't want to bring this strange human anywhere near where the elves lived. It was fine to make requests out here, but trusting humans was something else entirely.

"He helped us and the children, didn't he? We should be able to trust him on some level."

Ariane continued advocating for me, pushing through Donaha's hesitation. I wanted to tell her that she shouldn't be so trusting of people; there was something about her innocence that awakened a protective instinct within me.

It looked like Donaha was about to cave, so I decided to offer a suggestion of my own. I watched their expressions as I spoke.

"I have a spell that can remove curses. But I don't know if it'll work on the mana-eater collars."

There were several spells in the Monk class line that could lift curses, specifically Uncurse from the mid-tier Bishop class and Holy Purify from the top-tier Priest class. Uncurse would remove curses caused by items and status effects, while Holy Purify would remove all curses as well as cause major damage to the undead.

However, I'd never actually used them, so I couldn't be sure if they'd have the effect I was hoping for.

Donaha looked back at me, surprised. "You can remove curses?"

"Well, I can certainly try."

I turned to one of the children and waved my hand over his mana-eater collar while I called forth the Uncurse spell. The symbols running along the collar absorbed the light coming from my hand. A moment later, I heard a distinct crackle followed immediately by the thud of the collar breaking off and hitting the ground.

The child ran his hands along his neck, beaming up at me.

"Thank you, Mister Knight!"

I smiled inwardly at this, happy to be able to do something to help. The other children crowded around me, so I lined them up and removed their cursed collars one by one.

"Thank you so much... We can now bring these children back to their parents." Seeing how happy the children were, Ariane came over to thank me, using a hand to obscure her eyes slightly.

Donaha let out a sigh of relief. Now that the situation had been resolved, he scolded the children.

"Didn't your parents tell you all not to leave the village? I can't believe how careless you were!"

"I'm sorry... I saw a spirit moving about begging for help, so I went to see what I could do. I meant to come right back."

The child had tears in her eyes as she explained. Ariane followed up with another question.

"What was this spirit doing?"

A different child spoke up in response. "It kept saying 'help me, help me,' so I went after it. I found a tied-up cottontail fox covered in injuries. The humans caught me as I tried to help it..." His voice trailed off.

Ariane and Donaha turned their eyes to me, the appreciation that had been there only moments ago now a mere memory. A grave misunderstanding was playing out right in front of me.

"Before you jump to any conclusions, I just want to say that I found Ponta tied up in a bandit hideout. I had nothing to do with drawing out or capturing the elven children!"

"This is true... Cottontail foxes would never trust a person who'd caused them so much pain... I apologize for suspecting you."

Donaha gave me a weak smile and slumped his shoulders as he apologized. The suspicion faded from Ariane's gaze as well, and she began brushing off her armor. At least I'd been able to nip that problem in the bud.

I looked down to find Ponta surrounded by the elven children, on the receiving end of various pets and scratches. Everything I'd heard suggested that cottontail foxes rarely grew close to people, but I had a hard time believing that given the sight unfolding in front of me.

"Well, it's about time for me to take the children to the nearest village. If we don't get going now, we won't make it before sundown. Now that you can use magic again, I'm sure you can all watch out for yourselves, right?"

The children responded enthusiastically to Donaha and began making their way toward the bushes that led off into the forest. Apparently, with their magic, even these small children could protect themselves from the dangers that lurked in the forest.

Donaha collected his bags and began leading them. "We'd best be off."

"Take care, Donaha," Ariane called after him.

Donaha looked back over his shoulder and offered a quick response before he and the children disappeared among the trees.

Once they were out of sight, Ariane turned toward me, a carefree smile on her face.

"Thank you, Arc, for helping the children back there. I am Ariane Glenys Maple, an elf soldier."

I nodded my acknowledgement to her introduction. I had to admit, her name had a sugary-sweet ring to it.

"You may call me Arc. I am a simple wandering mercenary. This little guy is Ponta."

"Kyiii!"

Ponta had been brushing its tail against my legs when it heard its name called out, inciting a squeal. Ariane's expression melted, and she knelt to pet it. Ponta's eyes narrowed contentedly, and its ears twitched with each pat.

"I always heard humans were nothing more than barbarous beasts. I was so surprised to see a spirit creature this attached to a human."

"I'm not like most humans, so I may not be the best example to base your opinions off of."

It wasn't that I was special, just that I wasn't from this world. My values were quite a bit different from those here.

Ariane looked surprised at my response, though the edges of her lips began turning up ever so slightly.

"Well, I suppose if anyone is qualified to say you're different, it'd be you."

I coughed in embarrassment at her response and decided to change the subject.

"That reminds me... You were still in the middle of cleaning up the bodies. Shall I give you a hand?"

I glanced over at the haphazard pile next to the cart.

"If you could."

I rummaged through the belongings of the dead men as I added their bodies to the pile, taking weapons and other valuables I could find. Ariane made a face as she watched.

"You would take things from the dead?"

I could see where she was coming from; it wasn't exactly civil.

"You need money to live in the human world. Traveling about isn't cheap, either. Do elves have no use for money?"

Ariane looked back at me angrily. "We have our own money!"

According to Ariane, elf villages functioned mostly on a barter system, though elven money was used when performing trades between villages.

Elves used pure gold for currency, unlike the alloys used by humans, making it much more valuable. Ariane bragged that human merchants would even do business with the elves just to get their hands on the elven money.

At first glance, Ariane looked like a glamorous, refined woman, but when she went on excitedly about the greatness of the elves, she looked somewhat cute. I was pretty sure she'd fix me with an intimidating glare if I said as much, so I kept my mouth shut.

It sounded like there was at least some form of economic transaction between elves and humans. That pre-existing relationship was probably the reason Ariane and Donaha had trusted me, at least somewhat, despite my rather sinister appearance.

After gathering all the bodies into one spot, Ariane stepped forward and ushered me back.

I retreated a few paces with Ponta, who weaved in and out between my legs before sitting on its hindquarters. Its ears twitched as it watched Ariane's movements attentively.

"Great earth, I call upon you to swallow these up!"

Ariane put her hand to the ground. The earth surrounding the mound of bodies began rippling, then split wide open, swallowing the bodies like a giant beast. A moment later, there was no sign that the bodies had ever been there at all.

Ariane brushed her hands together, wiping the dirt away.

"That should keep the buzzards from coming."

Ponta tilted its head in confusion and began scratching at the ground, digging where the bodies had been.

Seemed like a pretty useful spell for disposing of bodies.

"So, is that spirit magic? I've never seen it before."

Though I'd heard about it several times already, I was impressed to see it performed in front of me.

"Strictly speaking, no. Spirit magic is the type of magic used by spirit creatures."

"Hmm. I see."

I watched Ponta scratch at the ground. That meant the wind magic the fox used from time to time was this so-called spirit magic. But I couldn't really distinguish between what Ponta did and normal magic; it all seemed the same to me. The only real difference was that when Ponta used magic, its fur would glow ever so slightly.

Now that the bodies were taken care of, Ariane removed the saddles from the horses attached to the cart and unhooked them, giving each a slap to send them on their way. The only remaining evidence of the battle was the cart and steel cage that sat in it. They both looked like they'd fetch quite a bit of money, but I'd definitely stand out if I tried selling them in town. I figured we'd just have to leave them behind.

"Where are you going next, Arc?"

Ponta gave a squeak before I had a chance to respond. As I followed the fox's gaze up into the sky, I could see a bird with beautiful turquoise wings swooping toward us.

Ariane also took notice. The bird deftly weaved through the trees and landed silently on her outstretched arm. It was just slightly smaller than a crow. The white feathers of its crest stuck up askew, as if it had just gotten out of bed.

Ariane explained. "This is a Whispering Fowl—it's also a spirit creature."

As she brushed the bird's turquoise feathers, it began speaking in a clear, masculine voice.

"I was sent with a report from Danka. He has found the hideout in Diento. Ariane, you must meet up with Danka and help him save the elves."

As soon as its report was finished, the Whispering Fowl closed its beak and cocked its head to the side. Ariane retrieved a small, red berry from a leather pouch attached to her waist, which the bird quickly snapped up. She brushed the bird's crest as she spoke back to it.

"We were able to save four children. Donaha is escorting them back to the village. I'll head to Diento now to meet up with Danka."

Once she finished speaking, she shook her left arm, causing the Whispering Fowl to take off into the air. It deftly swooped between the trees again, disappearing into the depths of the forest.

Apparently, the Whispering Fowl was used like a carrier pigeon, though it acted more like a voice recorder. I couldn't help but wonder if it would convey the message in Ariane's voice once it returned to whomever had sent it.

Ariane picked up on my surprise and laughed.

"You humans aren't used to dealing with spirit creatures, I guess. Is it hard for you to pretend something like this is a normal occurrence?"

Ponta was busy grooming itself at her feet, bringing a smile to Ariane's face before she turned her gaze back up to me.

"I'd like to ask you something, Arc. You said you were a mercenary, right? So, does that mean I could hire you?"

Ariane's golden eyes held mine as she pulled five gold coins out of a pouch at her hip.

"I'll pay you five elven coins up front and five when you're finished. Not a bad deal, eh?"

She was trying to recruit me for the mission to save the elves from Diento that the Whispering Fowl had mentioned.

I wondered if the elf I'd met a few days ago had figured out where the slaves were being held in town. All the time I'd spent walking the streets hadn't even turned up anything.

But why would an elf like Ariane want to hire me, a human? Judging by Donaha's reaction, humans were generally not to be trusted. It didn't make much sense for her to so readily trust an unknown entity like me, especially one covered in armor. Did she figure my actions here were reason enough to do so?

"Wouldn't Danka object if you were to hire me?"

Ariane crossed her arms, taking on a stern expression. Her golden eyes seemed to look straight through me.

"I have my reasons. Not only did you rescue us and the children, but this creature here has also grown close to you. It's not like I trust all humans."

She glanced down at Ponta, who was still sitting at her feet. The ability to form a bond with a spirit creature seemed to be held in high regard among elves.

"And, of course, there was the way you came to help us. Did you use teleportation magic?"

I gulped, remembering the moment our eyes met when I teleported in.

So, elves knew of teleportation magic. That meant it wasn't unheard of in this world. But the fact that Ariane would want to hire me because of that magic implied that she couldn't use it. Perhaps not many people—or elves—could.

I scratched the back of my head and shrugged my shoulders. "Yes, I can use teleportation magic."

Ariane's response was a mixture of surprise and amazement, though the serious expression remained fixed on her face. "I knew I wasn't mistaken! I never thought I'd see such legendary magic with my own eyes..."

Evidently, teleportation magic was something only written about in legends, or perhaps passed down in oral stories, not something normal people used.

"Will you help us, Arc?"

There was hardly any reason for me to turn her down. This would surely put me in good graces with Ariane and the elves. Plus, with my teleportation magic, it would be a standard infiltrate and escape mission. If I did everything successfully, I wouldn't even draw any attention to myself.

"I'll accept your offer."

"It's decided then!"

After shaking my hand, Ariane gave me the initial payment of five elven coins.

These were rather different from the currency used throughout the country. They were about the size of a one-hundred-yen coin and had intricate designs carved into both sides, lending them a far more professional look. Judging by the currency alone, the elves seemed to be far more advanced than humans. It was easy to see why humans may value elven coins more highly than their own, especially if they were made of pure gold.

"So, shall we use your teleportation magic to travel back to Diento?"

"Certainly. It's probably best to get back to town before the sun sets."

I nodded and summoned an image of Diento in my mind. Ariane readjusted her gray cloak, covering up her ears and skin, and nodded back.

"Let's head to Diento. Transport Gate!"

As soon as I summoned the spell, a three-meter-wide, pale blue column of light appeared at our feet.

It was already late in the day, and the forest was filling with the dark shadows cast by the trees and overgrowth. Sunlight bathed the trees in a supernatural glow as everything around us suddenly went black. A split second later, the trees were gone, and we were somewhere else entirely.

Ariane's golden eyes opened wide as she took everything in, the surprise apparent on her face.

Night was rapidly approaching, the sky taking on a light purple hue. All around, we could hear the sounds of the grass and leaves rustling in the wind. Ahead of us was the familiar stone bridge made of six successive arches that crossed the Lydel River. Beyond sat the town of Diento and the walls that surrounded it.

"I can't believe it. You can teleport without even chanting!"

"That should make the rescue easier, no?"

"Absolutely. You'll be a great help to my friends."

After considering our surroundings, Ariane turned back to me with a broad smile on her face. The rescue was looking much more promising, which seemed to have put her in great spirits.

"Unfortunately, this spell isn't without its flaws. I can

only teleport to places that I have a clear memory of visiting. And I'm unable to teleport to plains, forests, caves, or any other indistinct locations."

"That's fine. Elf villages are all connected by teleportation spots, but we can only go to specific locations, and it takes a ton of magic. You're the only person I know who can use teleportation magic at will."

I was surprised to hear this. "So, elves can use teleportation magic, too?"

Ariane made a face, as if cursing herself for saying something she shouldn't have. "Listen, umm, don't tell anyone I said that, all right…?" She waved her hands in a panic, bowing her head several times.

From the way she spoke, it sounded like only elves were able to use the teleportation spots to travel between towns. Come to think of it, I hadn't seen anything like what she was describing in any of the human settlements I'd been to. The humans would definitely be far more advanced if such teleportation spots existed. It'd make distribution channels more boring, but it'd go a long way toward modernizing the world.

If humans—who weren't exactly on the best terms with elves—learned of this teleportation magic, it could be enough to start a war between the species. I wondered if that was what she was worried about.

I supposed the same could also be said about me though, since I was able to use the magic as well.

I gave her my word that I'd keep it to myself. "Understood. I promise I will tell no one of the elves' transportation abilities."

With that out of the way, Ariane let out a deep sigh of relief.

"Well, we can't just stand here looking out at the town forever."

"You're right. We'll need to sneak into Diento." Ariane seemed to be back to her normal self. She pulled the hood low over her face and tied the gray cloak tightly around herself, practically disappearing within its folds. Together, we began walking toward the town.

Her soft, light purple skin certainly made her stand out from humans, and even other elves, so covering up was the only way for her to avoid being spotted immediately.

I was in the same boat, unable to let anyone see the skeleton body lurking inside my armor. At least in my case there was a sense of excitement at my new circumstances. For her, this was something she'd lived with her entire life.

I pulled my own cloak tighter around myself as well to hide the gleaming armor underneath and let Ariane lead the way.

Even as night fell over Diento, a large number of people and carriages still stood on the far side of the bridge, waiting to enter the town. They reminded me yet again that Diento was a transport hub. All the traffic seemed to be going one way, however, with no one heading out of town.

We crossed the bridge and joined the throngs of people, passing through the outer gate and making our way to the second. The crowds took notice of my black cloak as I approached, opening a path in front of me. I hardly minded the special treatment and moved on silently toward the inner gate.

I showed the guard my mercenary license then gestured to Ariane, who stood a few steps behind.

"This one's with me. How much is the entry tax?"

The guard glanced at Ariane, but he seemed more interested in the large number of people waiting behind her. He quoted the price for entry in a well-rehearsed manner.

I pulled a silver coin from the leather pouch at my waist, handed it to the guard, and made my way into town with Ariane following.

Irregularly placed lamps lit the darkened town as its inhabitants continued bustling about the streets. We passed through the south gate's square, doing our best to avoid the crowds.

"Well, we've made it to Diento. Where to next?"

"I was told to meet in the square right after the gate in front of the bridge, so, right about...here. Let's wait around a bit. I'm pretty sure Danka will be able to find us."

Ariane stepped out of the throng of people and made her way to a corner of the courtyard. We stood there with our backs against the wall, watching the crowds pass us in silence.

I recalled that Danka had also used a hood to cover up his elven features, so I started scanning the area for anyone dressed in a similar fashion.

A short time later, I spotted someone making their way toward us. The figure was wearing a brown cloak with a hood drawn low over their face. Even though I couldn't see their eyes, I could tell they were watching us.

As soon as Ariane spotted the figure, she stepped away from the wall and approached them.

"Who is this man, Ariane?"

The brown-hooded figure stopped in front of us, shooting me a glance while he spoke to Ariane in a low voice. I recognized the voice immediately as that of the elf I'd met outside of town.

"Listen, I've been through a lot. This man is a mercenary. I hired him to help us out."

"You can't be serious..." Danka's voice betrayed his incredulity.

It made sense. Hiring a human to help save elves that had been enslaved by humans did seem absurd.

Ariane responded politely. "We'll draw attention to ourselves if we stand around talking like this. Let's find somewhere to sit down."

With that, she began leaving the square. Danka must have realized it would do him no good to get into an argument here and started after Ariane, though his dissatisfaction was clear in his body language.

I followed, and Ponta made up the rear.

In the thoroughfare, rows of stalls lined the street, selling a variety of foods. There were tables and chairs set up in front of each of the stalls, giving it something of a festival feel. The tables were filled with noisy revelers who'd bought food and liquor from nearby vendors to enjoy with their friends.

"I'll go buy us something."

Ariane began making her way toward a vendor, but Danka stood in her way, keeping his eyes trained on me.

"I'll go. You get a table." He headed off to purchase food, leaving us behind.

Ariane bowed her head slightly in Danka's direction before making her way to an empty table nearby. She spoke to me as I sat down, though her eyes never stopped scanning the crowd.

"Are you going to eat something, Arc?"

"No, I'll be fine."

The sizzling meat from one of the stalls smelled delicious, but I couldn't take my helmet off with all these people around. Even though my body never really grew hungry, I still had trouble overcoming my desire to eat.

"I'll take the meat skewer, some of those beans over there, and..."

Danka made small talk with the vendor as he ordered before handing over some money. He seemed to be able to blend in easily with humans.

While I watched him, Ponta hopped down from my head to the table, assuming a sitting position. The smell of all that food was probably overwhelming, and the fox let out a sad cry.

"Kyiii..."

Moments later, Danka returned with two wooden cups filled with alcohol, some meat skewers, and a dish full of beans that looked like peanuts. After setting all the food on the table, he finally took a seat.

As soon as he sat down, Ariane gestured toward Danka and began making introductions.

"Arc, this is Danka Niel Maple. He is also an elf soldier, and he came here to collect information on the town.

Danka, this man in the armor is named Arc. He saved Donaha and me from a pretty sticky situation with some slave traders."

Danka furrowed his brow at this, his face contorting into a scowl.

Did she just say Maple? I knew that I'd heard that name somewhere else before—the woman in front of me, in fact. Ariane Glenys Maple.

"If I recall correctly, you also introduced yourself as a Maple. Are you two siblings?"

Danka's scowled deepened. Ariane made a face and laughed, shaking her head all the while.

"Elves have three names. Your first is your given name, then the name of your same-sex parent, followed by the name of the town you belong to. So, we're from the same town, but we're not related. We're from the Maple borough in the forest province of Canada."

That was a completely different naming pattern from the one I was used to in Japan.

And what was this about the Canada forest province? And Maple borough... Just hearing the name made me think of a town covered in syrup.

"Is this Canada forest province the same one the humans refer to as the Elf Forest or the Lost Woods?"

"I believe that's what the humans call it. Canada forest

province is the largest elf city, named by the first elf chief. He also gave Maple borough its name."

I had a hard time believing that the Canada and Maple connections were mere coincidences. Perhaps people like me were brought to this world from time to time. Though the way she explained it, this sounded like it happened a long time ago.

"When was Maple built?"

Ariane tilted her head to the side and glanced at Danka.

"Hmm... About eight hundred years ago or so?"

Danka nodded noncommittally then coughed. "That's not really important right now, is it? Shouldn't we be focusing on our plan?"

Danka turned the conversation back to strategizing for the rescue.

Ariane glanced around then waved for Danka to lean in closer. She whispered something in his ear. Even from under his hood, I could see the shocked expression on his face. Danka turned toward me and began questioning me in a low, harsh tone.

"You can use teleportation magic?!"

"With certain limitations, yes." I doubted anyone could hear us over the din of the surrounding crowds, but I kept my voice low, just to be safe.

Danka looked from me to Ariane, still in disbelief. Ariane was busy feeding Ponta a skewer, tugging playfully at the cottontail fox's ears as it ate the meat. She let go of Ponta's ears and went back to patting its head, then turned to face Danka, a serious expression on her face. "Anyway, you found their base, right? What's it like?"

Danka finally seemed to regain his composure and returned to business mode.

"Aah, right. Their base is located near the red-light district by the east gate. There's so much foot traffic in the area immediately after sunset, so I plan to sneak into their base in the middle of the night. They have a lookout posted at the entrance, and I believe there are quite a few people inside."

Apparently, the abductors' base wasn't near the nobility at the center of town like I'd thought. I hadn't spent much time in that area, since I was trying to avoid getting involved with any unsavory sorts.

"Do you know how many they've kidnapped?"

"My source said there were four elves, though they're planning on bringing more in soon."

"We put an end to that plan earlier today. But that means there are still four who need to be rescued. With Arc's magic, it should be relatively simple to get out of there."

I could feel her eyes on me.

Danka readjusted his hood, leaned back in his chair, and closed his eyes.

"Understood. So, for now, we just need to kill time until we make our move?"

I hadn't realized we had so much time left. "In that case, I have a few errands to take care of."

As soon as I stood up and grabbed my bag, Ponta stopped rolling around on the table and crawled out from Ariane's hand, jumping up to my shoulder with an energetic "Kyii!" Ariane looked on jealously.

Danka watched me out of the corner of one eye. "Don't be late."

I guessed that was his way of saying he agreed to have me along. I assured them I'd be back shortly.

Danka watched as Arc grew smaller and smaller in the distance. Then he turned to his sister-in-arms, sitting across the table from him.

"I'm surprised you'd bring someone along for this. And a human, at that."

Ariane looked away, her expression unreadable under the darkness of her hood.

"I was reckless, and the slave traders took one of the children as a hostage."

She continued staring at a fixed point on the table, her voice quiet and full of shame.

"If he hadn't come to our aid, Donaha and I very well could have been taken as well. I overestimated my abilities and tried taking on a small group all by myself. I should have waited for backup." Her voice was a mere whisper.

Danka's shoulders slumped as he sighed. "Eevin would've taken them head-on without ever putting the children in danger."

Ariane's head jerked up in response.

Eevin was the most powerful soldier in Maple and Ariane's sister. Ariane had chosen the path of a soldier in the hopes of one day becoming as strong as her. But it sometimes led to Ariane getting in over her head.

Danka gulped down his liquor and cast her a look.

"I get that you look up to her, but constantly comparing your achievements to hers will drive you crazy. You're incredibly strong for your age. Build up more experience, and eventually a day will come when you're as strong as she is."

This was no small compliment. Ariane was already stronger than Danka, and she was still only fifty years old. Danka let out a sigh. It was probably easy to underestimate your own abilities when you had someone like Eevin in your family.

"Still...I can't get over the idea that there's someone who can actually use teleportation magic. Are you sure he's human? What does he even look like?"

Danka changed the subject to try and improve the mood. Ariane seemed to pick up on this and slowly raised her gaze from the table.

"I haven't seen his face. He doesn't seem to want to take his helmet off."

Danka furrowed his brow at this.

"Trying to keep his identity a secret, maybe? You really picked a strange one to hire. Anyway, I sent a spirit to follow him around, just to be on the safe side."

If Arc was working with the enemy, he'd probably be making contact with them right about now.

"That cottontail fox seems pretty fond of him, too. I can't quite put my finger on it, but there's something about him that reminds me of my sister."

Danka shook his head. Try as he might, he couldn't find anything in common between Eevin and the armor-clad man. Maybe it was something only someone who had lived with Eevin for years, like Ariane, could see.

He recalled that Arc was keeping the timid spirit creature as a pet.

"Well, if he won't show his face, maybe that means he's one of the mountain people?"

Elves, the so-called "forest people," weren't the only species with an affinity for spirit creatures. The "mountain people," who were treated by humans as if they were monsters, also had a history of bonding with spirit creatures.

They, too, were often enslaved whenever they crossed paths with humans. Danka had heard rumors of a group of mountain people who were also trying to free their enslaved allies. That would explain Arc's need to hide his face. The mountain people had beast-like ears and tails, making them easily distinguishable from elves—and humans.

Ariane began poking holes in Danka's theory. "Mountain people and elves are hardly hostile to each other, so it doesn't seem like a good reason for him to hide his face from us. He also seems pretty powerful, magically speaking, which the mountain people usually aren't."

"That's true. But even among the mountain people, the wolfmen have stronger magical abilities than humans. Those who are particularly gifted are even employed as mages in Fabunach, so it's not entirely impossible."

Fabunach was the mountain people's capital, located on the southern continent on the far side of the south-central sea. It even included mages selected from those with the greatest magical potential.

"I suppose that's possible…"

Ariane furrowed her brow, not entirely convinced. She hadn't gotten that impression from her interactions with Arc.

"Well, in any case, he'll be back soon." Danka crossed his arms and leaned back in his chair once again, closing his eyes.

My greaves creaked rhythmically as I walked through the quiet streets of nighttime Diento. After parting ways with Ariane and Danka, I traveled down the thoroughfare to a district full of shops.

As usual, Ponta sat on its perch atop my head, dutifully swishing its tail back and forth against the back of my helmet.

All the shops were already closed, the lonely streets illuminated by the occasional street lamp and the stray glow of light coming from the shops' windows. I arrived at the shop I was looking for, but it was also closed, its sign marked with a sword and shield and the name of the armorer written underneath.

I could hear a young man mumbling to himself.

"Aww, it's already closed… I guess I'll just have to come back tomorrow."

Behind me, a cart had parked in front of the armorer's shop, a man in his early twenties sitting in the driver's seat. Judging by the various boxes stacked behind him, he was some type of merchant.

"Do you have any business with this armorer, merchant?"

"I, umm... Oh! G-good evening, Sir Knight."

The young man's eyes went wide with shock momentarily when he saw my face. Or, more accurately, when he saw the gleaming helmet that poked out of my black cloak. He hurriedly climbed off his cart and bowed his head.

"I am a mere mercenary, a wanderer. You need not bow for the likes of me. Do you have any business with this armorer?"

"Hmm? Oh! Uh, right. I was here to purchase some weapons, but I got into town much later than expected."

The young merchant gave me a chagrined smile. What an amazing turn of fortune! I was getting tired of dragging around the weapons I'd taken off the slave traders.

"How interesting. Actually, I was just here to sell some weapons to the armorer when I found out they were closed. Would you perhaps be interested in buying them?"

"Really? Well, could you show me what you have?"

"Certainly. These are prizes I picked off some fallen bandits."

The young merchant looked disappointed, though he

quickly put on a smile. Perhaps I shouldn't have mentioned I'd taken the weapons from bandits?

I hefted the sack off my shoulder and onto the ground, then opened it up, pulling the weapons out and handing them over. The merchant carefully drew each sword from its sheath and gave it a close inspection.

His business-like smile was soon replaced with a look of excitement. The man had no poker face, which would prove detrimental to a merchant. As a customer though, that was fine with me.

"Did you really take these from bandits? The blades are made of some high-grade steel! I won't even need to do any smithing. Maybe just some sharpening and I could sell them right away!"

They were technically elf slavers, not bandits, but I figured that wasn't worth mentioning. Judging by the way he spoke, bandits didn't usually carry high quality weapons. Maybe that was why he'd been disappointed when he'd heard these blades were from bandits.

After the young man finished inspecting all the items, he crossed his arms and surveyed the weapons laid out neatly in his cart.

"All fifteen of these swords are of superb quality. This one here is particularly amazing. However, I don't think my budget will allow me to buy it..."

The sword he held had belonged to the man they'd called Udolan. Despite his complete lack of skill, he'd wielded the best sword of the bunch. From the craftsmanship of the sheath to the gleam of the blade, it was truly superior to all the rest.

The merchant continued mumbling to himself, almost as if he was taken in by its beauty. He should have kept that information to himself to buy the weapons cheap and resell them at a higher price. I was somewhat worried about whether this young man would even be able to succeed as a merchant.

"There's no way I could buy them all with the money I have on me...but which do I pick? Hmm..."

I really didn't want to carry the weapons with me while I was sneaking around.

"How about 10 sok each, 150 sok for the whole lot?"

It hadn't cost me anything to acquire them, so even if I sold them cheap, I was still turning a profit. Besides, I wasn't hurting for money.

"Are you sure? These would normally go for thirty sok each!"

"You really shouldn't talk so much, merchant."

After I scolded him for being forthright about the market price, the young merchant quickly put his hands over his mouth. He seemed like a good man, so I was happy to help him profit. I assured him my price still stood, despite what he'd said.

"Thank you so much! With all the monster attacks along the border to the north, weapons and raw metals have been shooting up in price, which is what brought me down here."

"Huh. I'd heard there was a rather large monster that appeared up the road from here recently, in a town called Luvierte."

"Really? Thank you for telling me!"

The young man grinned from ear to ear, bowing low in appreciation. He packed up the weapons and climbed onto his cart, heading off in the direction of the inn. He turned back to bow his head multiple times as he made his way down the road. Even though I'd just met this man, I really hoped for his success.

Ponta wagged its tail from side to side, as if waving back. I was sure the young man would become fast friends with any spirit creatures he ran across.

With that out of the way, I put the 150 gold coins into my pouch and readjusted the much lighter bag on my shoulder. I knew I should probably start making my way back to Ariane and Danka.

When I arrived at the food stalls, the two of them were still at the table where I'd left them. I sat down in the empty chair.

"That was fast. Did you finish your errands?"

Ariane used one of her meat skewers to try and draw Ponta in closer as she spoke. Danka was in the same position as before, arms crossed and eyes closed.

"Yes, I was able to sell the weapons I took off the men from before."

"Oh, right..."

Ariane shot me a look, letting me know she was less than impressed. She finally coaxed Ponta down onto the table with the meat and immediately took hold of the fox, rubbing its stomach affectionately.

We spent the rest of the time making small talk while Ariane played with Ponta.

Once it was late enough, and most of the surrounding stalls had closed, Danka finally stood up from his chair. Ariane silently stood as well.

"Let's get going."

Ponta woke up and ran over to me. I put the fox on its perch on my head, grabbed my bag, and followed after Danka.

Hopefully, this plan will go off without a hitch, I whispered to myself as we made our way through the dark, empty streets.

CHAPTER 4

Operation: Elf Liberation

THE RED-LIGHT DISTRICT was located near Diento's east gate. Its narrow roads were lined with all manners of shady establishments. Drunk men stumbled down the alleys on uneasy legs, cheerfully humming as they went.

However, it seemed like it was already past closing time for most of the establishments. Light spilled from no more than a few windows. Lit only by the sporadic street lamp, the alleys were practically blanketed in darkness. Even the bright moonlight couldn't pierce the gloom of the densely packed buildings, making it difficult to distinguish between fellow pedestrians and shadows.

Danka, the elf soldier, led the way through the dimly lit alleys. His heavy footfalls echoed loudly on the cobblestone road in the silent night.

After walking a ways, Danka suddenly stopped. Ariane stopped right behind him.

Danka peered around a corner then turned back to Ariane, motioning ahead with his chin. Ariane looked in the direction he indicated—a building. Apparently, this was our destination.

Peeking out from our cover, I spied a three-story stone building. It stood on a relatively wide road—or at least, wide for the east district. The buildings here were built so close together that there was hardly any space separating them. The front entrance to the building sported a steel gate, watched over by two men armed with staffs. Beyond the gate was a yard, illuminated by four small lamps. These were held by even more men, sitting around and chatting, their indistinct conversation occasionally broken up by raucous laughter.

Even if we were able to dispose of the two guards out front, the gate would leave us completely exposed to those in the garden, making it difficult to launch any sort of surprise attack. The dense steel would easily put a stop to any frontal assault. It'd be nearly impossible to do this all in one go.

Danka's eyes searched Ariane's for a plan. She passed the same searching look on to me. I could see the corners of her lips curve ever so slightly upward underneath her hood.

Danka realized what she was thinking and shot me an angry glance.

"Do you really want to send this clanking hulk in after we've snuck here under the cover of darkness? The noise'll give us away!"

Even though my armor made far less noise than its cheaper, creaking counterparts, it wasn't exactly silent. It wasn't the best choice for a stealth mission, but I didn't have any other choice; I was just a skeleton underneath.

Before I had a chance to say anything, Ariane responded, "The whole point of us being here is to help our comrades. Whether they figure it out sooner or later, it's all the same in the end."

She was right. If we left any of the slave traders alive after saving the elves, someone was liable to get hurt. The best option would probably be to kill them all.

"Arc, do you think you can teleport up there?"

Ariane pointed toward a small window on the building's roof, completely dark inside. It had a small, triangular outcropping above it and looked like it could be a window into the attic.

"Easily."

"Great! We'll move a little farther back into the alley, then you can teleport. I don't want the glowing magic circle to alert the enemy."

"That only happens with Transport Gate. I'll be using Dimensional Step to teleport this time. It works better for short distances."

Ariane raised her eyebrows. "You have special teleportation magic for short distances? Just who are you really?"

"Let's go to the roof. Hang on to my shoulder."

Anything touching me would be taken along with me during Dimensional Step, while anything not in direct contact would be left behind. Since Ponta was always riding atop my head, I never had any problems bringing the fox.

After checking that Ariane and Danka had each grabbed a shoulder, I focused on the roof.

"Dimensional Step!"

The scenery around us changed instantaneously. We were now looking out over the moonlit roofs of the surrounding buildings. Gone were the cobblestone streets beneath our feet, replaced with tiles. We had to lean back to maintain our balance on the slanted roof.

Teleporting onto a rooftop was quite stressful. I was worried it would give way beneath us at any moment.

Danka took a knee next to me and surveyed his surroundings. "That was amazing..."

There were few other three-story buildings in the area, which gave us an unobstructed view of the surrounding town. Off to the southwest, I could see the inky outline of the marquis's castle sitting atop a hill, looking rather imposing against the backdrop of the starlit sky.

"I'll go first," Ariane whispered.

She leaned over the outcropping and peered into the small window. Only the slatted, wooden shutters kept out the elements. Glass was still a highly prized material in this world and apparently wasn't worth wasting on roof windows.

"It's clear. There's no one inside."

Ariane opened the window all the way and slipped inside, though she had to wiggle a bit to get her ample chest through the small opening.

The window looked much smaller up close than it had from the street. Ariane and Danka were slender, but even they could barely fit through. There was absolutely no way someone outfitted in bulky armor could ever make it inside.

After Ariane was through, Danka slipped in after her. Now that my turn was up, I looked through the window, called up Dimensional Step, and teleported inside.

Ariane scowled. "You coulda just done that first, you know!"

I wondered if she was embarrassed about all the

wiggling she'd had to do to get inside. Even in the dark, I could see her cheeks were flushed a light crimson. But I didn't see any reason for her to be embarrassed.

Danka ignored her objections, speaking in a low, easy-going voice as he surveyed the room. "It looks like this is just storage."

Boxes were scattered about the room, though the space seemed largely unused. There was a musty smell to the air, as if the room was rarely used.

Danka moved slowly, trying not to make any noise on the wooden floorboards. Once he reached the thin stairwell at the far side of the room, he looked down and quickly brought a finger to his lips.

Ariane locked eyes with Danka and nodded. Danka slowly made his way downstairs.

We could hear him moving about in the room below, before he popped his head up from the stairwell and gave us the "go" sign.

Ariane and I followed him down the steps.

The room below the attic was occupied by two sets of bunk beds. Men with blood gushing from their throats lay in each of the beds, filling the air with the smell of warm, rusty iron. Danka stood at the center of the carnage, busying himself with putting blankets back over the men to make it look like they were sleeping. Ariane made her way to the door at the center of the wall and peered outside before beckoning us over.

Once Danka's work was done, he and I made our way over to Ariane. She detailed her plan with hand gestures: Danka would go right, Ariane would go left, and I'd move through the center. Once we'd all nodded in agreement, she opened the door.

The door opened into a hallway with an open atrium at the end of it. Each side of the atrium was lined with three doors, with an additional door located at the far side of the room, presumably leading to the floor below.

The building was dimly lit by lamps lining the halls. This would let us see down to the floor below, but it also meant that we could be seen. Checking the rooms on either side would prove dangerous.

Ariane and Danka crouched down, trying not to make any noise as they each approached a door and put an ear to them. A moment later, they silently opened the doors and slipped inside, leaving me alone in the hallway.

There was no way I could cross this floor without making any noise, so I used Dimensional Step to teleport to the door at the other end of the room. I worried for a moment that my legs would become useless if I travelled everywhere using magic, but I put that aside for the time being.

Unlike the other doors in the room, the one in front of me one was of much heavier construction and was adorned with carvings and a gold-colored knob. I could sense a person on the other side of the door, moving around cautiously. But it didn't seem like they were about to sound the alarm.

Figuring I couldn't just wait around forever, I put my hand on the doorknob and slowly turned it. Locked. I leaned forward and peeked through the keyhole. The last time I'd looked through one of these was probably in elementary school, when I'd tried to break into the old storeroom.

Through the keyhole, I focused on a specific location and summoned my Dimensional Step.

I reappeared in a narrow, brightly lit room, still in the same crouching position. The walls were lined with ornate furnishings. A low-backed leather sofa sat in the center of the room, an amber-colored desk near the far wall. A well-dressed, heavyset man sat behind the desk, motionless. As I glanced around the room, the bloodstained bodies of three armed men stood out in the flickering lamplight. They all appeared to be dead.

A shadow suddenly lunged toward my face.

"Waugh?!"

My right fist connected with the shadow, making a

metallic clang as a weapon similar to a kunai glanced off my gauntlet. Out of the corner of my eye, I saw another shadow dash toward me, trying to stay in my blind spot.

This shadow was a young girl, dressed from head to toe in black with a red scarf trailing behind her, almost like a tail. She wore greaves on her legs, gauntlets on her arms, and a band around her head with a metal plate that had been burnt black. Her mouth was covered with a mask, and she wielded two short swords.

The black-clad girl came in low from the floor, lunging to stab at the gaps in my armor. I deflected her blades with my gauntlet, and she flipped backward through the air, putting space between us.

"How did you get in here? The door was locked." The girl's mask slightly muffled her voice.

Instead of answering her question, I blurted out the first thing that came to my mind.

"You're a ninja..."

The black-clad figure raised an eyebrow in response. Just then, I noticed a pair of cat-like ears sticking out of the top of her head, complimenting her beautiful—yet cold—azure eyes. One of the ears twitched. Upon closer inspection, I could see that the belt she wore around her waist was twitching occasionally as well. It wasn't a belt at all, but a tail.

The ears and tail appeared to be real, and not mere decorations. Some sort of animal ninja girl was standing right in front of me.

While I came to terms with the unexplainable feeling welling up inside of me, the ninja girl took notice of the green fox sitting atop my head, her eyes narrowing. The next moment, her hand disappeared inside her cloak and she threw something into the air. I was too lost in my own thoughts to respond in time; Ponta, however, reacted instantly.

The fox dove off my head and caught the red ball midair before doing a single flip and landing on the ground. It started chewing on the ball—apparently some form of fruit, slightly smaller than a plum. Ponta gnawed noisily as the girl leaned down to pet it, her eyes smiling.

I'd heard spirit creatures didn't warm up to people easily, and yet, three seconds after meeting her, Ponta was comfortable with this newcomer.

Wait a minute, hadn't this girl been throwing knives at me mere moments ago? I asked her about this.

"I apologize for that. You're not the one I'm looking for. What are you doing here?"

The ninja girl looked up at me, her head tilted inquisitively to the side. I was at a loss for words. Even if we were

no longer enemies, I still wasn't eager to tell a stranger why I'd snuck in.

Before I could come up with an answer as to what I was doing there, the ninja girl took a guess.

"You're here to save the elves, right? In that case, they're locked in a dungeon, in the basement."

She caught me completely off guard with her response. There was nothing about my armor-clad appearance to suggest whether I was a human or an elf. And Ariane and Danka were still searching the other rooms, so I had no idea how she'd been able to figure out why I was here.

I glanced at the bodies of the former guards lying at her feet.

Had she done this? If so, her delicate figure belied her fighting prowess. Had she found out about the elves from them?

Seeing my reaction seemed to bolster the girl's confidence in her guess.

Now that things had settled down slightly, I decided to ask her a question of my own. "Did you also sneak in here to set the elves free?"

She shook her head. "I was looking for something, but apparently it isn't here. I wasn't sure what to do about the elves, but it sounds like I can leave that to you."

The girl picked up a large, heavy-looking leather bag off the desk and strapped it to her back, tying it tight with a rope. She hesitated, as if remembering something, and moved behind the desk. A moment later, she handed me a scroll made from sheepskin.

"Here you are." She spoke in a flat voice, her face unreadable.

"What is this?" I looked back at the girl as I took the scroll.

"There are six more of these in the building. I expect you'll be needing them."

The girl walked over to the open window at the side of the room and put her foot up on the sill. She turned back to me to offer her parting words.

"The rest is up to you, but I feel our paths will cross again, when the time comes... Oh, one more thing. There are two elves being held in the marquis's castle."

As soon as she was done speaking, she grabbed the roof above her and effortlessly swung out of the room, not encumbered in the slightest by the heavy, rattling bag on her back. She disappeared into the dark night, easily fading away into the silhouettes of the buildings.

After she was gone, I peered around the desk she'd been hiding behind. In its shadow, I found a small stone door, wide open. A sturdy lock lay discarded on the floor beside the door. It had apparently failed in its task to keep the door shut.

I looked inside and found a small storage space, its shelves lined with all manner of rings and valuables...and six more of the sheepskin scrolls. It was some type of vault.

I'd wager the heavy bag the girl carried on her back was full of gold from the vault. Judging by her demeanor, however, I had a hard time believing she was just here for money. Not that I'd hold stealing money from such evil people against her. I had no idea what she'd been looking for, but at least it didn't seem to affect our plan at all.

Her parting words still echoed in my mind. She'd mentioned that the marquis held two elf slaves, suggesting he condoned the hunting of elves.

I had to tell Ariane.

After this rescue was accomplished, our next mission would be to infiltrate the marquis's castle. I should probably charge extra for that.

As I mulled this over, I reached into the vault and pulled out a scroll. It was a purchase contract, and for no small sum; the price was listed at over 10,000 sok. Since the only products within this house were elves, that meant they were being sold for over 10,000 gold coins apiece.

Including the scroll the ninja girl had given me, that

made seven contracts in total. I needed to figure out if these were contracts for the elves currently imprisoned here or for those who'd already been sold off. The contracts listed the names of the buyers, so, once I figured out who they were, I'd be able to rescue the elves.

From what I could tell, elven men sold for higher rates, which went against my expectations. I wondered if there was any special reason for women being in lower demand.

I shoved all seven contracts from the vault into my bag.

Ponta sidled up next to me and let out a "kyii," a wide grin on its face.

"Oh, Ponta... Do you just trust anyone who'll give you treats?"

Even I could hear the tinge of jealousy in my voice. Ponta looked back at me curiously, so I picked it up and put it on my head.

With nothing left to do in the room, I made my way back to the door, unlocked it, and stepped out into the hallway where Danka and Ariane were finishing their respective searches.

"There were just a few thugs in here. Ariane?"

"I didn't find anything."

It looked like they'd both struck out on the side rooms.

Danka turned his green eyes toward me, as if to ask what I had found.

"I gained some interesting information. Apparently, the captured elves are being held in a dungeon beneath the house. I also found these."

I pulled one of the scrolls I'd taken from the vault out of my bag and handed it to Ariane. She looked it over suspiciously before undoing the string and unrolling the parchment, letting her eyes run across the contents. Her brow furrowed, and deep wrinkles formed on her forehead.

"It's..."

"An elf purchase contract. I found seven of them. I think they can lead us to the buyers. I also found out something else of note. I learned there are two elves being held in the marquis's castle."

"Where did you learn that?"

Ariane glanced up at me before turning her attention to the room I'd just left. The room was rapidly growing cold, and the large, dead man still sat at the desk, as if he were a mere decoration.

She probably figured I'd gotten my information from him. Hopefully that'd be enough for her for now. We needed to focus our efforts on saving the elves.

Personally, I felt I could trust the young ninja girl, and it wasn't just because of her adorable little cat ears. I may not have had solid proof, but I felt like it was extremely unlikely I'd happen across a person like that in a slave trader's hideout who wanted to feed me misinformation.

"I guess we'll have to head to the marquis's castle after we finish up here. Arc, will you come along with me? I'll gladly pay you an additional fee. I normally wouldn't even think of sneaking into a castle, but with you there..." Ariane stared straight at me with her golden eyes.

There was something indescribably cheering about having a beautiful woman rely on you. I found myself smiling.

"I've already come this far. I may as well see it through."

"Thank you, Arc. I'm sorry to keep asking for favors, but there's something quite different about you, you know."

I nodded, and Ariane bowed her head in return, a smile forming on her lips.

"The very idea that the marquis himself would be involved..." Danka spat, an angry look burning in his eyes. "We'll have to tell the others as soon as we get back."

Judging by the high purchase prices, the people buying elves must have all been nobility, or well-off merchants. We also knew there were at least nine elves currently being held captive.

"We should head to the basement, where our friends are being held," Ariane piped up. "We can deal with the marquis's castle later."

Danka agreed, and the two left the room. I teleported after them to avoid making any noise. If there had been anyone watching us, it probably would have looked as if a large, ghostly suit of armor followed the pair.

We took the stairs from the third floor to the second, then crossed the atrium and descended to the first floor. After passing through a hallway, we found ourselves in front of a massive staircase on the first-floor hall. There were several tables in the room, with chairs scattered about, giving the impression of a bar. Several rough-looking men stood about, but they hadn't noticed us yet.

Danka gestured with his hand, indicating we should retreat, so we went back up to the third floor.

"There's no way we can make it down to the basement without being noticed. I'll take the second floor. Ariane, I'll leave the first floor to you."

Ariane replied eagerly to Danka's order. "Understood."

Danka turned his attention to me but said nothing. I guessed Ponta and I would just have to respond to whatever happened.

Ariane drew her sword and led the way down to the first floor, where she peeked around the corner to take stock of the situation. After taking a steadying breath, she dove into the room.

The gathered men stood awestruck for a moment as

they watched Ariane fly down the stairs at them, blade held ready.

"Fire, I implore you. Light this sword ablaze!"

Ariane murmured a spell, and moments later, fire danced across the blade. Blood spewed from the first man she slashed as his body burst into flames.

"Gyaaaaaaugh!!!"

The man's death cry echoed throughout the large hall, sending men running out from the rooms on the second floor to see what was unfolding below.

The burning corpse dropped to the floor, landing between the tables and chairs, sending sparks toward the furniture. Men rushed over to put out their comrade, but Ariane slew them all, creating more and more human torches as she went.

Danka stepped from a second-floor room and began cutting men down where they stood, before they even had a chance to join the fight on the first floor. His swordsmanship was nothing short of amazing. The men never stood a chance.

I'd heard elves were renowned for their magical abilities, but watching the way these two wielded their swords gave me a newfound appreciation for their martial prowess.

I saw several men leave a second-floor room to surround Danka. After forming my hand into a fist, I summoned up my Rock Shot and fired at them. The massive stones that leaped from my fist not only burst through the men, but also the wall behind them.

I realized it would only be a matter of time until the men outside heard the noise and joined the fray.

I used Dimensional Step to reach the entrance on the first floor and locked the massive door to keep anyone from getting in...or out.

"Get 'im!!!"

A man let out a scream from behind me and came running in to strike. I spun around and punched him with my fist, shattering his skull and sending his body flying through a table and chairs before embedding itself in the wall.

Since I was at level 255, fighting these men was nothing short of overkill.

One of the men Ariane had set ablaze stumbled into the kitchen. Moments later, large flames erupted from the doorway. There must have been some sort of oil or gas inside.

Even if the house itself was made of stone, there was still plenty inside that could catch fire. Flames roared as the blaze crawled up the wooden pillars and spread throughout the building.

"Kyiiiiii..."

Ponta crawled off my head and onto my shoulder, wrapping itself around my neck and burying its head near my ear. As flames erupted everywhere, I felt like I was wearing a fur scarf.

Danka came downstairs, apparently finished cleaning up the men on the second floor. Ariane extinguished her flaming sword and sheathed it so she could search the surrounding area.

I could hear the faint sounds of someone frantically banging on the massive door at the entrance, yelling something indistinct. The door was much thicker than I'd guessed. With the lock firmly in place, they wouldn't be getting in anytime soon.

"I found the stairs to the basement!"

I moved toward Danka's voice, flames already spreading throughout the first floor and all around me. Behind the massive staircase was a wooden door, behind which a staircase descended into the darkness.

The room had grown rather hot, so Ariane pulled off her hood. I caught a glimpse of the scowl on her face before she turned away to lead us down the stone steps. Danka followed, and I pulled up the rear.

"Just who do you—gyauuuggh!!!"

Below, I heard a man yell out, followed by a scream of agony and the clang of clashing swords.

"Damn, how'd they get down here?! Just what're those lazy sacks of—uruugh!!!"

Something fell to the ground with a thud. By the time I reached the bottom of the stairs, it was all over.

The basement was much more spacious than I'd imagined, the walls lined with cells, each with their own iron-barred door. The whole place smelled like dirt and rotting food. Three dead men lay at my feet, their blood pooling together. Ariane ripped a key ring off one of the bloody men's belts and made for the cells.

"My name is Ariane Glenys Maple. I've come to save you!"

I could hear several people moving around behind the cell doors.

"It can't be! A soldier from Maple has come to rescue us?!"

A young woman, who looked no older than seventeen, sprang up behind one of the doors, her expression a mixture of shock and excitement. A moment later, several younger girls appeared next to her. All of them wore the same black metal collars that I'd seen on the children in the forest.

Ariane flipped through the keys, trying each one in the lock until she found one that fit. The lock opened with a loud clink, which the girls took as their cue to leave the cell.

While they thanked Ariane and Danka, I noticed that

the fire had spread to the door at the top of the basement stairs. We didn't have much time. I'd have to deal with the mana-eater collars later.

"Miss Ariane, the fire has already consumed the first floor. We'd best get going."

The young girls turned at the sound of my voice, a few letting out squeaks of fear as they ducked behind Ariane.

Evidently, helmeted men covered in black cloaks weren't popular among young girls.

"It's fine, I hired him to help save you. Is this everyone?"

The girls all nodded, eliciting a relieved smile from Ariane.

"That's it for us here, Arc. Let's get going."

"All right then. We'll teleport outside the town limits."

I stepped close to Ariane and the four young girls, making sure Danka was also in the area of effect before summoning my spell.

"Transport Gate!"

A large magic pillar appeared at our feet, its blue glow filling the room and overpowering the dim illumination of the lamps. The circle of young girls tightened around Ariane, their faces tense as they watched the magic unfold. They shuddered as we were plunged into darkness. A split second later, we found ourselves in the middle of a grassy plain.

The oppressive atmosphere of the dark, cold basement was instantly replaced by a gentle evening breeze blowing across us, the burbling sounds of the river echoing in the distance. The stone bridge, illuminated by the moon, appeared as if it were floating above the dark river. On the far side of the Lydel, I could see the man-made structures of the town and the walls surrounding it.

For a moment, the young girls around Ariane didn't seem to realize what had happened, though their faces slowly took on expressions of surprise as they looked about. Danka, too, let out a gasp when he saw where we were.

The loud clang of the town's bell suddenly joined the sounds of rustling grass and burbling water, probably to notify the townsfolk of the blaze.

Off in the distance, within the town walls, I could see faint red flames licking into the sky, a pillar of smoke spreading above. All eyes were undoubtedly on that one spot.

A man stood in a room deep within his fortress at the center of the town of Diento.

Despite the fortress's stark outward appearance, the rooms within were all elaborately decorated and expensively furnished. The sleeping quarters were outfitted with intricately carved poster beds covered with soft, beautifully embroidered duvets.

In this particular room, a woman lay atop the large bed, her hands held fast by wooden bracelets, her body by metal chains. The single layer of silk the woman wore barely covered her, leaving her pale white body and faintly pink breasts exposed. Her crossed legs blocked her nether regions from view, but the wooden bracelets prevented her from covering her upper body.

The woman's green-tinged, blonde hair, punctuated by large, pointed ears, was splayed out on the duvet below her, looking almost like a palm tree frond. Her eyes blazed with contempt for the person standing over her.

"You elves always come up short with your bosoms. But your bodies... I just can't get enough of them."

The older, pudgy man standing at the foot of the bed grinned broadly. It was Marquis Tryton du Diento, the ruler of the town and surrounding area.

"If you're gonna do it, just get it over with already, you stupid prick!"

The man fixed her with an intimidating glare as she hurled insults at him. However, his smile only grew wider, as if he enjoyed her response.

"Oh, Sena, you always keep me on my toes with your spunky attitude. Hehehe!"

Two chambermaids stood expressionless off to the side of the room, ignoring the elven woman's pleading gaze.

Tears welled up in the corners of Sena's eyes. Tryton looked quite pleased with himself over the elven woman's response. He reached down to grab her snow-white ankles, preparing to lay his massive frame on top of her. Sena's face expressed both shame and disgust.

A lone man ran down the long corridor toward the marquis's chambers. The castle was eerily quiet, but the sound of the warning bells outside could be heard reverberating through the hall's windows.

The massive double doors leading to the chambers were made of wood so thick it was nearly impossible to hear what was going on beyond them. Intricate gold inlay gave the doors a further air of extravagance. A guard stood on either side of the door, their eyes lighting up as the disheveled man approached.

The man was Celsika Dourman, the envoy to Diento. He banged aggressively on the massive doors, almost as if he were out of his mind, though neither guard made any attempt to stop him.

"Master Tryton, it's me, Celsika. I have urgent news for you! Please, open the door at once!"

The pale, nervous-looking man wasn't usually one to

be easily shaken, but this evening his face was flushed in desperation, and he was sweating profusely.

"Celsika? What are you doing here at this hour...? Fine, fine, come in." It was clear from the marquis's expression that he was upset at having his evening activities interrupted. He ordered one of the chambermaids in the corner to open the door while he put his gown back on.

As soon as the doors opened, Celsika muttered a greeting and stumbled into the dimly lit room.

Tryton plopped his plump figure onto the bed and watched the frantic man enter.

"Master Tryton, I would like to see you alone..."

Tryton stroked his white beard and glanced over at the chambermaids. They quietly bowed their heads and made their way outside.

"What's so urgent?" The indignation was evident on Tryton's face.

Celsika glanced over at the naked, bound woman on the bed before returning his gaze to Tryton.

"There are currently four fires running rampant in the city..."

The longer Tryton listened, the more apparent his displeasure grew, his face contorting into a scowl.

Celsika sped up his explanation.

"All of the blazing buildings were slave markets, including our own!"

"What did you say?!"

Tryton was up in an instant. "We're almost at the deadline for handing over the product to Revlon! What happened to our goods?!"

"According to the surviving guards, some mysterious figure infiltrated the building before the fire broke out."

"How can that be? We have guards in place to prevent such a thing! What the hell were those idiots up to?!" The marquis was now completely enraged at what he was hearing.

"Apparently, someone locked the front door from the inside. They could hear screams coming from within. The building is surrounded on all sides, and there are no other points of entry, so the only possibility is that one of our men is a traitor."

Tryton strode to the window, glaring out at the city beneath him as he combed his fingers through his white hair. His anger had yet to subside.

"Dammit! Send the castle guards to the building and put out that fire at once! The basement is made of stone, so it should still be intact!"

"Don't you think it would look strange if we only dispatch guards to one location? We should send them to the other three as well..."

"Don't waste time telling me this! Just gather the guards and send them out!"

A vein bulged in Tryton's forehead as he rounded on Celsika. Sensing the oncoming onslaught, Celsika turned and stumbled out of the room with the same desperation as when he'd entered.

"If it's not one thing, it's the next! The men we sent out to collect the phantasms have been decimated, and now this!"

Tryton breathed heavily, his throat parched from all the yelling. He reached for a nearby pitcher and gulped down the water.

"I suppose I should be thankful that idiot son of mine is running late in delivering the goods. Worst-case scenario, I can put off other domestic orders and send what we have to Revlon..."

The Marquis du Diento rubbed his temples as he tried to figure out what to do next.

From my spot on the far shore of the Lydel River, I watched as smoke rose from several fires throughout Diento.

How strange... The slave trader building we'd set on

fire was in the red-light district near the east gate, but there were also flames cropping up in other parts around the city.

"Did you set those fires around town, Miss Ariane?"

I considered the possibility that Ariane's comrades had set the other fires to keep the town on edge. But she shook her head in response, a look of concern on her face.

"We had nothing to do with that. Danka and I were the only ones who went into town, so something else must have caused those. But this works out great for us! It may even draw out the castle soldiers if they're conscripted to put out the blaze."

Ariane didn't appear to be lying. Danka and the children also looked confused as they gazed at the growing flames.

She was right, this could turn out to be a great opportunity. If my own secret organization was under attack, I'd send reinforcements immediately. Hopefully Marquis du Diento would act the same way.

"You're right. Assuming Diento dispatched some of his soldiers to assist with the fire, the castle will be low on guards. This could be the perfect opportunity for us to infiltrate it."

Ariane twisted her lips into a beguiling smile before directing her gaze toward Danka and the children.

"Danka, can I leave the children with you? If you head up the Lydel and into the forest, you should only be about a day away from the nearest town."

"Good plan. We should be able to make it to the Rivulet River by dawn. You're a better fighter than me, so I'll leave the castle to you. We'll wait for you near the forest."

"Thank you. Oh, and Arc, can you do something about the mana-eater collars before we go?"

"Certainly."

Ariane nudged one of the elven girls forward. Doing my best not to frighten her, I reached out with my hand and held it over her collar.

"Uncurse."

Symbols glowed in front of my hand as I summoned the spell which were quickly sucked in by the collar. A second later, a loud "clink!" rang out as the collar shattered.

The other girls couldn't believe their eyes. One by one, I cast Uncurse on their collars, setting them free. Once all the collars had been removed, they all thanked me together.

"You can even remove curses? There's so much I don't know about you, mysterious stranger..." Danka spoke in a soft voice, clearly surprised.

Ariane tapped me on the shoulder and fixed her gaze

on the castle at the center of Diento. Apparently, that was her sign it was time to go.

I nodded in acknowledgement, then moved Ponta from where it rested around my neck back to the top of my head. Ponta gave a small cry to let me know it was ready.

I used my Dimensional Step first, to teleport to the other side of the river. The sound of the bell grew louder.

Thanks to the proximity between the south gate and the river, there were no houses outside the wall, and no one in sight. Due to the late hour, there were also few sentries manning the top of the outer wall.

After using Dimensional Step to teleport to the top of the wall, I quickly teleported again to the inner wall.

Unlike its external-facing counterpart, there were no sentries atop the inner wall. I imagined it was built purely for strategic reasons, in case the fortress came under attack. There wasn't much use for sentries here in times of peace.

However, just to be on the safe side, I kept my body low as I peered out between the parapets.

I spied smoke rising from various places across the town. It looked like there were four fires in total. The odds of four separate fires breaking out at the same time seemed rather suspect, but I didn't have time to think about that.

Ariane's gold eyes gazed out at me from under her gray cloak, urging me to hurry up. Her light purple skin seemed to disappear in the darkness of her cloak, making it look as if only her eyes existed within, bringing to mind the conductor from a certain anime about an express train in space. Unlike the anime character though, a dynamite body lurked beneath her cloak.

I could see the marquis's castle at the center of the town, towering above everything in the area. Under the dim moonlight, it looked pretty far away. The buildings near the base of the castle were swallowed in its massive shadow.

Ariane poked me to get my attention. It wasn't like I was just gawking. I was trying to figure out a way to teleport close to the castle, but I couldn't find any favorable destinations. Teleportation magic wasn't much use in the dark. I decided to focus on the moonlit roof of the castle and was able to easily teleport there with Dimensional Step.

Since the castle had been built atop a hill, the town below suddenly seemed all the smaller. I had a great view of the whole area. It'd be an amazing sight to see in the middle of the day.

Ariane, surprised to find herself up so high, lost her balance for a moment and grabbed my arm, letting out a small shriek.

"Eek! H-hey! Don't just go teleporting onto roofs like that, okay? I need a moment to get my bearings!"

We were standing atop the slanted roof of a tower. The angle was steep, and if you lost your balance, you'd fall straight to the ground below. It was no wonder she was upset.

She stood close enough that I could detect a delightfully feminine fragrance wafting off her. Despite her chest pressing so tightly against my arm, I couldn't really feel anything on account of her leather and my steel armor.

"My apologies."

She narrowed her eyes and shot me a look. Her demeanor quickly changed, however, when she caught sight of Ponta atop my head, tilting its head adorably to the side. I decided I owed Ponta some raisins after all this was over, for resolving the tense situation.

It seemed unlikely that the marquis would have planned on intruders coming through the roof, which allowed us to look around freely without having to worry about anyone noticing.

The castle lacked the dignified air you would commonly associate with nobility, looking more like a foreboding fortress. In addition to the double walls, it also sported twin moats, making a straight-forward invasion all but impossible.

Between the inner wall and the castle itself, there was a large, open expanse leading up to the front gate. The space contained barracks and barren patches of land likely used for training.

The castle itself had six towers along its perimeter, while the center portion contained a building that appeared to be the residence of the marquis himself, which was connected to another, smaller building by a hallway.

Our vantage atop the tower nearest the marquis's residence gave us a view of the entire complex.

The castle was vast, so looking around blindly in the hopes of finding the elves would only end in us being discovered.

The tower we stood atop served as a lookout for the fortress. Underneath, it would likely house a storeroom full of grains for use during a siege. Far below, there were likely dungeons, where they'd lock up prisoners and other criminals, but I had a hard time believing the marquis would spend all that money on an elf just to lock them up.

"Miss Ariane, I hesitate to even ask this, but what are elf slaves used for after they're caught?"

Her golden eyes glared at me from within her hood, her face clouding over in annoyance. "Does it matter?"

"Not particularly. I just thought we would have an easier time finding them if we know what they're used for."

After a moment of silence, Ariane spoke in a low, solemn tone. "Women are usually used for pleasure, like playthings. I've heard the men are used to impregnate noble women."

"According to the purchase contracts, men typically fetch much higher prices. Is that the reason? Why would a human woman want to bear the child of an elven man?"

"When a mixed-species child is conceived, it takes on the species of its mother. Didn't you know that?"

I nodded along with her, even though this was all new to me.

"However, the child is also born with the magic of an elf. I hear that's the reason many noble families among the humans possess strong magical abilities. They've been intermingling with elves for generations. Though, they're still not able to use spirit magic."

So, that was one of the ways humans had been able to survive on this monster-infested continent. They'd been forcefully taking the elves' power for themselves to build up their magic. If many of the nobles possessed magical abilities, that suggested money and strength were closely equated with power in this world. So why had the country sworn off relations with the elves, if they could use them to increase their strength?

I had a hard time believing that people in a feudalistic

world like this would do it out of respect for human rights. It had to be some sort of plot by those in power. But I didn't have time to untangle all of that just then. We were there to rescue the enslaved elves.

I doubted the marquis would keep them in a dungeon if they were being forced to have sexual relations with humans. The marquis's residence seemed like the most likely location. Fortunately, there were few guards currently patrolling the building. I wasn't sure if this was because they'd been dispatched to deal with the fire, but I was thankful either way.

"Let's head to the marquis's residence."

Ariane already had a hand on my shoulder. I teleported down from the roof of the watch tower to the hedges near the residence.

Through one of the glass windows that lined the building, I could see a wide, empty hallway, so I teleported us inside. We were now fully exposed.

The hallway ran along the perimeter of the residence, its walls decorated with an eclectic selection of furnishings.

Ariane walked lightly to keep her footsteps from being heard. She approached one of the doors lining the hallway and quietly opened it, peering inside.

She waved her hand, indicating for me to follow her into the room. Inside was a wooden table and chairs, all polished to a shine, sitting atop a decorative wooden floor. The walls were also covered with massive paintings. At first I thought it might be a reception room, but a closer look suggested it would be better suited for meetings. The room was dimly lit, making it difficult to see anything.

There was another door directly across from the one we'd just entered. Ariane crossed the room and opened it a crack.

The residence had looked deceptively small from the top of the tower, but now that we were inside, it felt rather spacious. I wondered if this building also had its own dungeon in the basement.

Ariane stepped through the door and out of the meeting room. I followed a few steps behind her.

The next room appeared to be another hallway, about half as wide as the one running along the perimeter. Both sides of the hall were lined with doors, the spaces in between adorned with small paintings. The hall turned to the left at the end, so I couldn't see what lay beyond.

I teleported to the end of the hall and slowly stuck my head around the corner to get a better look. The hall ended in a wooden door with a latticed window. In front of the door, a guard dozed in a chair. Compared to the other doors in the room, this one seemed strange.

I teleported next to the guard, wrapped my arm around his neck, and began choking him. His eyes opened instantly and his limbs started flailing, but that lasted only a moment before he lost consciousness. Once his body went limp, I put him back into his chair so it'd look like he was still sleeping.

I found a key attached to the guard's waist with a leather strap, so I ripped it from his body and tried it in the nearby door. The lock released with a satisfying click. I slowly turned the knob and stepped into a small, square room. The only thing inside was a stairwell leading down. Since we were already on the first floor, that meant these stairs led to a basement. Taken together with the guard posted at the door, that suggested my initial hunch was correct.

I called out to Ariane, who'd followed me to this section of the hallway and was busily searching the other rooms.

"Miss Ariane."

Even though I'd spoken in a low voice, she quickly turned her head in my direction. Apparently, elf ears really were that sensitive.

I gestured with my chin and she nodded, following me into the square room. After checking the stairwell in the center of the room, Ariane led the way down.

Despite the wooden steps, Ariane was somehow able to reach the bottom without making a single sound, almost like a ninja. There was absolutely no way I'd be able to do that in my armor, so I teleported after her. I thought briefly about imitating a certain fire-breathing Indian character from a popular fighting game, if it came to using any of my flame attacks down here, but my thoughts were interrupted by the sounds of battle up ahead.

I could hear a man groaning, followed by the thump of something slumping to the floor. Apparently, there'd been another guard standing watch.

I found myself in a hallway illuminated by several lamps. On my right was a stone wall with three steel-reinforced wooden doors. There were no windows in the doors, and I had no idea what could be on the other side.

"My name is Ariane Glenys Maple. Are any of my comrades being held here?"

Ariane knocked on the first door and identified herself. A reply came back almost instantly.

"A soldier from Maple? I can't believe my luck! Please, get me out of here!"

Evidently, Maple soldiers were known for their fighting prowess. The woman on the other side of the door sounded slightly nervous, but her relief and excitement were clear.

Ariane rolled the dead guard over to search his body

for a key so she could let the woman free, but she came up empty.

She shouted in annoyance, "I can't find any keys!"

An answer came from the other side of the door. "The owner of this place has them. They put a mana-eater collar on me, so I'm not able to use any spirit magic to break down the door."

So, only the marquis held the keys? It made a certain amount of sense. If the guards held keys to the room, they could take advantage of the captives whenever they pleased. But if the door could be broken with spirit magic, then we didn't need to worry about the keys at all.

"Please, step back from the door."

I took a deep breath and gave the steel-reinforced door a solid kick.

An awful clang resonated throughout the basement as the locking mechanism shattered. The door, covered in only a thin plate of steel, screeched as I shoved it aside, bending under the pressure. With this much power, I could probably escape any jail on my own, if it came down to it.

A thin, pale woman stood on the other side of the twisted door, a look of shock on her face. She had the long ears and green-tinged, blonde hair typical to elves. Her beautiful body was covered in nothing but a thin robe, under which I could faintly see the outline of pink nipples. I quickly redirected my eyes to her hands, which were bound by wooden shackles held together with nails. Elves weren't known for their brute strength, so it was probably enough to keep her restrained.

For me, however, the wooden shackles broke easily. The enslaved woman rubbed her newly freed wrists before bowing her head low.

"Thank you for your help. Are you also a soldier from Maple?" she spoke, in a slow, gentle voice. Her bob-cut hair shifted gently as she tilted her head to the side, fixing me with a curious look.

"No, I hired him to help me save you." Ariane popped her head out from behind me, a chagrined look on her face as she explained the situation. "He may look intimidating, but he's a good guy. You have nothing to worry about."

She asked me to remove the mana-eater collar. I nodded and summoned the Uncurse spell. A moment later, the metal collar dropped to the ground with a clang.

The woman rubbed her neck gently. "I can't believe it! I didn't know there was anyone out there who could lift curses without chanting!"

"Please, take this, if you'd like." I removed my black cloak and handed it to the scantily dressed woman.

"Thank you so much! W-Wow, this is pretty big..."

After draping the cloak over herself, she looked around the room. Maybe it was my imagination, but she seemed to be in remarkably good spirits despite having been locked away. I couldn't tell if she was just used to living on the cusp of death, or if all elves were like this. Either way, she came across as quite strong.

"By the way, I heard there were two elves being held here. Do you know anything about that?"

The woman slammed her fist into her hand as if she'd just remembered something.

"That's right! They took Sena off to the marquis's room tonight!"

So, Diento had decided to have the other elf brought to him. That meant we'd need to get close to the marquis himself to rescue this Sena. The situation had just gotten much, much worse. If I rescued an elf from the marquis himself, I'd undoubtedly be putting myself on the bad side of the influential people. Considering Diento was violating the laws of the kingdom, he probably wouldn't want to spread the story about me, but he could still make it difficult for me to move about freely.

"What if we come back for her later? We don't even know where the marquis is located."

It wasn't an easy suggestion for me to make, but Ariane quickly shot me down.

"We can't do that! If we let this opportunity go, they'll increase security, and it'll be even harder to get in next time."

Of course, she was right. We needed to take advantage of the situation tonight. We'd already come this far. I just needed to steel myself for the next part of the mission. Besides, I couldn't really leave the other elf in this place.

"The marquis? He's up in his bedroom on the top floor. I can show you!" The once-enslaved elf made a fist with her right hand.

"I see. Are you familiar with the layout of his residence?"

"Of course I am. I've been here two years after all..." She frowned, her eyes drooping slightly.

"Two years... That's quite a long time."

"We elves have long lives, so it's different for us. But I can't say it's been short either."

Ariane stepped up to hurry us along. "We've gotta hurry. You said you could lead us to the marquis, umm, Miss...?"

"Oh, I'm Uhna. Pleased to meet you, Ariane. Now, follow me!"

The woman introduced herself quickly, then took the lead and jogged up the stairs. Ariane took off after her, and I followed before they could leave me behind. Given how big this place was, I'd never be able to find them again if I lost them.

I followed the two elven women up the stairs to the first floor, out of the room with the stairwell, into the hallway, and out through another door that led to the first floor's main hall.

Directly in front of the building's entrance sat a massive staircase that led up to an open hall on the second floor. At the top of this staircase hung a massive portrait of a pudgy, white-haired man. A giant chandelier hung above the central hall, and expensive decorations covered nearly every surface, speaking volumes about the power of the man who lived here.

The expansive room looked like something from a movie. While I was busy taking it all in, Uhna spoke up in a quiet voice.

"Isn't it strange, though? There aren't any guards..."

A flame flickered in the palm of Uhna's right hand. Apparently, she'd summoned her spirit magic to take care of any guards.

"I assume they sent people out to deal with the fires in town." I followed Uhna into the hall as I explained what had happened.

"That's pretty lucky then! We should be able to go straight to the marquis's chambers and get our revenge!"

"Sounds good. Let's take care of this and get you two back home."

Uhna shot me a wide grin before taking off. An unnaturally strong breeze blew through the room. The cloak covering her body fluttered about as she ran up the stairs to the second floor. Ponta cried out excitedly as soon as it caught sight of her. The two of them shared an affinity for wind magic. Ariane and I followed after her, all the way up to the third floor.

There was something unsettling about the conversation the two elves had earlier that stuck with me. I could understand the desire to take revenge on the man who'd kidnapped these women, but we were talking about nobility here. Understandable or not, this wouldn't end well. Still, there was so much I didn't know about the relationship between this country and the elves that I wasn't in a position to say what was right or wrong.

At the very least, I'd do whatever I could to make sure the marquis didn't learn who I was.

Something caught my eye as we made our way up. I took it in my hand and looked it over, but Ponta began crying out to get me to hurry up.

"Kyiii kyiiiiiiiii!"

I used Dimensional Step to move to the base of the stairwell leading up to the third floor.

When I reached the top of the stairs, I heard a man and a woman screaming, followed by a hideous crashing sound. A thud reverberated down the hall, and several chambermaids appeared, running toward me. I put my back against the wall and stood still next to another suit of armor, pretending to be a decoration. These chambermaids would be witnesses to the events of this evening. I hoped to avoid them telling their friends about the imposing, armored man they'd seen with the attackers. Since this world lacked any form of radio, the information would stay local, and with all the other people wandering around town in armor, the impact would likely be minimal, but I figured it was better to be cautious.

Ponta seemed to catch on to what I was doing and stood stock still as the women ran past us. From a distance, Ponta's fur probably looked like the crest on a Roman soldier's helmet.

I turned to head in the direction that the women had come from.

The massive double doors, which looked as if they'd once been quite beautiful, had been blown wide open. Body parts that I could only assume belonged to the guard were scattered about. It was a pretty disturbing sight. I wondered which of the elven women had done this.

I stepped over the carnage and went into the bedroom. Everything in the room, at least to me, looked incredibly expensive. At the center stood a massive poster bed, decorated with intricate carvings.

The room was illuminated by an object that looked like a candelabra, though, instead of candles, there were glowing crystals inside it.

At the far wall of the bedroom stood a man whose face I'd just seen at the central stairwell. The plump, white-haired man looked rather pathetic with his bottom half exposed. A knife had been stabbed straight through his right hand, pinning him to the wall.

A long-haired elven woman struck the man between his legs with a powerful kick.

"Gyaaaaaaaaaugh!!!"

The man—the marquis, I assumed—let out a scream like I'd never heard before. Even though I was made up of nothing but bones, the power behind that scream made the space between my own legs ache.

Unable to drop down since his hand was pinned to the wall, the marquis shuddered as he tried to keep standing, sweat pouring off his body, drool dribbling down his chin. He struggled to control his breathing as he glared at the intruders.

"Y-you think you c-c-can get away with this, do you?! I am a marquis in this country, and if you think you can just..."

The marquis's thighs trembled with the effort of standing. His gaze grew harsher, as if the women he was looking at were so much trash.

Ariane removed her hood, exposing her purple-tinged skin and untidy white hair, which took on a slight blue glow under the light of the crystals. Just the sight of her made the room feel cooler.

The way she spoke even made my blood run cold.

"Even if we were to kill you where you stand, this country holds no power over the elves of Canada. After all, it's the people of Rhoden who broke their word first, is it not?"

She ripped off a corner of the bed sheets and shoved them into the marquis's mouth. After looking him over once more, she turned her back to him.

A magical aura emanated from the two elven women standing behind Ariane—Uhna, who had led us here, and the long-haired woman who'd just kicked the marquis. I assumed this was Sena, the other enslaved elf. She was practically nude, her long hair plastered to her back with sweat, eyes ablaze with hatred for the marquis.

Ariane looked at me suspiciously. "Why are you wearing a curtain over your head, Arc?"

I'd figured it would help conceal my identity, like a veil, though it really just made me look like a person

313

pretending to be a ghost at a student-operated haunted house.

"We can talk about that later. Don't you think it's unwise to kill Rhoden nobility?"

I tried dodging the subject. However, Ariane just looked at me as if I were some bizarre creature.

"They were the ones who broke their promise first. What's wrong with me collecting a penalty?"

It seemed like this world didn't have any sort of international conventions. Not only were rules different from group to group, but what was natural and expected even differed among species. I was just a mercenary here. Now that I'd raised my objection, all I could do was watch the situation unfold.

I shrugged my shoulders and shook my head. "Nothing."

Ariane looked over her shoulder and locked eyes with the other two women. All three of them nodded in agreement.

As if on cue, Uhna and Sena began brutally beating the marquis, his screams echoing through the room as his blood showered the walls. It looked like a gang initiation that I'd seen on some TV program. Even with my incredible strength, I wouldn't want to anger these women...

No longer needing to conceal my identity, I took the curtain off my head and walked away.

I looked around, trying not to think about the murder being carried out behind me. On the other side of the room, I spied a sturdy-looking door with a heavy lock on it. The lock was covered in intricate carvings, and it piqued my curiosity.

I drew my sword and cut through the door in a single diagonal slash. The two pieces of it fell away, as if I'd dragged a sharp knife through paper. The lock was now a useless decoration. I ripped what remained of the door off its hinges and stepped into the room, a small space filled with expensive pieces of artwork and other knick-knacks whose purposes I couldn't even begin to guess.

In the back of the room were several wooden chests stuffed with gold coins.

Part of me couldn't help but wonder why humans were so drawn to gold. The other part of me, the human part, felt like I'd just uncovered a treasure trove, causing my face to ease into a smile... Or, it would have, if I still had facial muscles.

There was no way I could take all the gold with me, but I could at least shove a fair amount of it into my sack. Ariane said the marquis had acquired his wealth through illegal means, so it wasn't like I could be criticized for this.

I hurriedly stuffed my sack with gold coins. I let out

a self-deprecating laugh as I realized that my actions weren't that far off from what the women were doing in the other room. Still, I needed to be careful. Given the weight of gold, I risked having the bag tear open if I got too greedy.

Then I noticed a sword mounted to the wall. The gleaming silver blade was covered in symbols. A lion's head was carved into the hilt, its eyes a pair of red jewels.

I'd seen this sword before...

Back in the game, it was known as the Sword of the King of Lions, an incredibly rare blade that boosted the user's speed and attack power. I had no idea if that would be true in this world though.

I decided to take it with me. It'd be a shame to leave it here collecting dust.

I took the sword off the wall and slid it into the sheath hanging below before putting both of them into my bag of treasure. Just then, I heard loud noises coming from the bedroom.

"There are bandits in the marquis's chambers!"

"Let no one escape!"

I heard soldiers pouring into the room, one after another, their swords scraping together as they crammed through the blown-apart doors. Moments later, I began hearing explosions, followed by men's screams.

A particularly loud explosion shook the entire building. It was followed by the sounds of something crumbling, then the roar of flames.

The building was on fire.

Ariane entered the room and called out to me in an exasperated voice.

"Just what are you doing, Arc?"

The dark elf stared at me with her arms crossed, a look of annoyance on her face. With her cloak now discarded, her crossed arms rested atop her leather corset, propping up her full chest from below, further accenting the twin peaks barely contained by her armor.

From her point of view, it probably looked like I'd snuck off to steal a bunch of gold. If only I had green cheeks, the look would be complete.

If there had been a chimney nearby, I might look like Santa Claus instead. But there wasn't one in sight.

"It'll cost quite a bit of money to get the organization back together."

"Huh?"

She looked at me suspiciously, not understanding what I was saying. Finished with their work, the other two elven women appeared behind her.

"Assuming someone wants to create another slave trading organization, they won't be able to do it without this

money as starting capital. If we bring the money with us, it will slow down their activities."

I thought this was a nice-sounding excuse for why I was taking all the money. To be fair, there was an element of truth to it.

Ariane exchanged looks with the women flanking her. After nodding in approval, they also stepped into the room and begin shoving gold into leather bags. Sena was now wearing Ariane's gray cloak, who also joined them.

"I'm impressed you can hold such a heavy bag without even breaking a sweat. It's gotta be at least three times the weight of mine."

"I agree with what he said, but just how are we supposed to get out of here with all of this weighing us down?"

"Yeah, it's heeeeeeavy."

The three women looked at me, surprised at the size of the bag I was carrying.

"Don't worry about that. He can use teleportation magic. It looks like we're done here, so let's get going!"

"Wh-what?! Teleportation magic? By himself? I thought those were just fairy tales!"

"Hmph, I need more practice..."

While the three talked among themselves, I could hear more sounds coming from downstairs. If we didn't leave soon, things were about to get much more complicated.

The three of them had finished collecting the rest of the gold in the room, so there wasn't much else for us to do here.

"Time to leave town! Transport Gate!"

As soon as I summoned the spell, a magic pillar began glowing around us. The next moment, we were standing on the opposite shore of the river in a grassy plain, looking out over Diento.

"Looks like we escaped! I can't believe how convenient that teleportation magic is. I wonder if there's some way I could use it..."

"No... No way! Was that really magic?!"

"*Yaaaawn.* I'm tired... Where are we anyway?"

The three elven women looked around in surprise. I was also surprised, but for a different reason. Everything in the magic pillar had teleported with us. All the pieces of artwork and various knick-knacks that had adorned the room were now lying about in the open field.

Fires continued raging across the river in Diento, smoke rising into the sky. In fact, it looked even worse than before. I remembered hearing the sound of fire crackling in the marquis's residence.

"So, I suppose my job is complete?"

Ariane looked away from the scene unfolding across the river and shot me a wide grin. She pulled ten elven coins out of her waist pouch, put them in a bag, and tossed them my way.

"You were an incredible help. Here's your fee, plus the extra amount I promised. I assume that's enough, though it's probably nothing compared to the money you stole."

I caught the bag in one hand and tossed it into the sack on my back.

"Much appreciated."

Ariane dropped the bag of gold from her shoulder and fixed me with a serious look.

"Listen, Arc... We're heading over to Lalatoya. It's the closest village. Why don't you come with us and meet the village elder?"

I was taken aback by her suggestion, but I really did want to see an elf village. On the other hand, I also wanted to avoid running into anyone important, and that included village elders.

"I would love to come with you. But...is it necessary for me to meet with the elder?"

"Of course it is. We need to get permission from the elder just to invite an outsider into the village. And, to be completely frank, I was hoping we could work with you again in the future. To prove how much I trust you, I want to introduce you to the village elder, one of the people I trust most in this world."

The two women standing beside Ariane looked surprised by her words, but they didn't voice any objections.

"If you've come to trust me that much, then I won't lie to you. I'm afraid I can't meet the elder. Not if it means taking off my armor."

"I mean, you would have to at least show your face. You won't change your mind?"

I simply nodded.

"May I ask why?"

It was hard to respond to that. I didn't want to lie to her, but I couldn't tell her the truth either.

"If I were to take off my helmet, I may end up on the receiving end of your blade."

"What if I promised I wouldn't do that? Would you show me your face then?"

Her golden eyes were locked on me.

Would she turn against me? Or might she understand my plight? If I could see the reaction of a person who'd grown to trust me this much, it may actually help me decide how to continue living my life in this world. After all, there'd probably be many trials waiting for me in the future.

I put my hands on the sides of my helmet. Ponta hopped off and landed easily on my shoulder.

I slowly pulled the helmet from my head and faced the women.

The expressions on their faces betrayed their surprise.

Standing in front of them was an armor-clad skeleton, light blue flames flickering from deep within its eye sockets, like a pair of disembodied souls.

The two elves on either side of Ariane took fighting stances and began summoning their magic.

"Stop it!" Ariane threw out her arms, holding back her comrades.

"Arc, is that really... What happened...?"

Ariane did her best not to let her voice betray her surprise, but I still caught a hint of it.

Obviously, I couldn't tell them that I'd woken up in a different world from my own and was now living as my video game character. There was no way they'd understand.

"I don't quite know myself. But one day, I found myself in this body, all alone in the country of Rhoden."

"He's not undead, is he?"

"A super strong undead in armor? That'd be awful!"

Sena and Uhna maintained their fighting stances and continued glaring at me. Ariane remained calm, maintaining eye contact with me.

"He doesn't have the corruption of death on him. Besides, a spirit animal like the cottontail fox wouldn't get so close to an undead monster. He was also able to perform healing spells."

Ariane's words had the desired effect of at least getting the other two to stop and think.

"Huh? Now that you mention it, *is* that a cottontail fox on his shoulder? A spirit animal? What's going on here?"

"That's right. Corrupted undead can cast curses, but they wouldn't be able to use the power of light to remove curses. This doesn't make any sense!"

Ariane laughed gently at their confusion. It seemed like the tension had eased slightly.

"Arc, you've done so much to help me and my companions. Your secret is safe with us. If you've been cursed, then the elder may have some information that could help you."

"That would be greatly appreciated. Nothing would make me happier than to remove this curse from my body." It *would* be nice to go back to having a flesh-and-blood body that could actually respond to the sight of the beautiful women standing before me.

I put my helmet back on, thinking over my past actions and wondering why it was that I'd ended up turning into my skeleton avatar in the first place.

"Let's start from the beginning. I am Ariane Glenys Maple, a soldier from the Maple borough in the forest province of Canada. I would like to ask you again, Arc. Will you come to our village?"

Ariane extended her right hand toward me. I reached out and took it.

"My name is Arc. I am on a journey to cleanse my cursed body. I will gladly take you up on your offer."

Now that I'd finally put it into words, I decided that returning to my own world would become my new goal.

I'd never actually considered that removing my curse could become the purpose of my journey. I didn't even know if I *was* cursed. But so long as I continued to live like this, I would face many hardships. If the elf elder had any wisdom to share with me, then it'd be worth the journey.

"Well then, let's head up the river and join our friends!"

Ariane smiled at me and hefted the gold-filled bag over her shoulder. I lifted my own bag from the ground and looked toward the forest, where the two rivers met.

It was still dark, and our path was lit only by the moon. But our course was clear.

"Let's get started, shall we?"

SKELETON
KNIGHT IN
ANOTHER WORLD

Epilogue

OLAV, THE CAPITAL of the Rhoden Kingdom, was built in the middle of a vast, fertile plain to the north of the Calcut mountain range, and was bordered to the east by the massive Lydel River that flowed down from the Furyu mountain range.

The castle and town were surrounded by four walls, successively added with each growth spurt the town experienced. Olav currently boasted a population of over 50,000, making it more than three times larger than the transportation hub of Diento.

The capital city was surrounded by farmland, broken up only by massive roads stretching off in the four cardinal directions. Goods traveled into the city from all over the country.

Rhoden was the third-most powerful country on the

northern continent, though it paled in comparison to the power of the Revlon Empire to the north. Rhoden was made up of several different land-owning nobles, the biggest being the royal family of Olav. This gave Olav the power to set the course for the kingdom's policies, though it wasn't strong enough to unilaterally dictate terms to the other nobles. Though the royal family certainly wielded enough power to control any individual noble, they would never stand a chance against all of them combined.

That said, Olav did have the ability to bring the nobles, and their military forces, together to combat any threat to the kingdom, whether it be an invasion, civil unrest, or any other situation the royal family deemed necessary.

Deep within the chambers of the Olav palace, a group of nobles had gathered to discuss the numerous theories and rumors surrounding the assassination of Marquis du Diento.

A figure sat at the head of a large, rectangular table in the middle of a beautifully decorated, narrow room deep within the royal palace. Along one side of the table sat three individuals, a seat left empty between each of them.

The man at the head of the table had deep wrinkles

etched into his forehead, giving him a rather gaunt appearance. However, his blond hair—marked with the occasional streak of white—thick beard, and piercing blue eyes made apparent the strength still lurking within him. This ornately dressed man was Karlon Delfriet Rhoden Olav—the country's ruler.

At fifty-five years old, he was already considered elderly in this world, where people rarely lived past the age of fifty. Being the ruler of a nation probably made him look even older than his true age.

Behind the king stood Duke Bionissa du Jackell, one of the seven dukes and the current in a long line of Jackells to serve as the country's prime minister. Despite not owning any land of their own, the dukes of Rhoden were the most powerful supporters of the royal family and lived on stipends provided by the king from levies on the country's citizens. They wielded great power over the kingdom.

Prime Minister Bionissa wore the relatively simple uniform of a court official, though his shaved head and intense, monocled gaze gave him the look of a bird of prey.

"What are we doing about the whole Marquis du Diento situation?" King Karlon spoke with a certain heaviness to his voice, looking straight ahead and turning only his eyes to address Prime Minister Bionissa.

The prime minister fidgeted with his monocle as he responded to the king's inquiry in a bored, monotone voice.

"We've sent Orhevo, Marquis du Diento's heir apparent, back to Diento from the Rhoden palace to see what he can learn. As for the culprit's motives, some are saying it's the work of freed slaves, given that multiple slave trading houses were attacked and the beastpeople are missing. However, we have yet to come up with any concrete proof."

A cold voice spoke up the moment the prime minister finished. "I have been hearing rumors that this was the work of elves."

Sekt Rondahl Karlon Rhoden Sahdiay—the first prince to the Rhoden Kingdom—was one of the three sitting at the table. He brushed his fingers through his light brown hair as he spoke in the practiced voice of one who had grown up among nobility, a smile gracing his handsome face. He exchanged glances with the young man sitting next to him, giving the man an odd smile.

The man on the receiving end of Sekt's gaze had a small but muscular build and short, cropped hair. He wore a military uniform decorated with gold trim. His name was Dakares Ciciay Vetran—the second prince. In contrast with Sekt, he was a spirited military man through and through, and completely lacked the former's royal grace.

King Karlon let out a heavy sigh, as if he were used to the hostile interactions between the first and second princes, before making an inquiry of his own. "Why would you give voice to such gossip, Sekt?"

Sekt's smile grew wider as he turned to face the king.

"Well, actually, I've heard that Marquis du Diento was capturing elves and selling them off to the eastern empire."

The tension in the room was palpable.

Dakares made no effort to conceal his contempt as he glared at Sekt. "That's nothing but hearsay, no? Unless you have any proof, dear brother."

Sekt responded with the same eerie grin. "And why are you so interested in standing up for the marquis, Dakares?"

"You're spreading rumors about Rhoden's nobility!"

The king cleared his throat, drawing attention back to himself and putting an end to the young men's quarreling. The wrinkles in his forehead grew even deeper.

"That's enough. It's unbecoming to speak ill of the marquis without any proof. However, it is true that we cannot turn a blind eye to these rumors. We should dispatch a group to Diento immediately to perform a formal inquiry. Yuriarna, what do you think of this?"

The king turned his gaze to the only woman in the room. Though the dress she wore was rather reserved in its design, the fabric and needlework made it apparent what a true masterpiece it was. The woman fit to wear such a beautiful dress was Yuriarna Merol Melissa Rhoden Olav—the second princess of the kingdom.

Yuriarna, who had been sitting silently throughout the preceding arguments, ignored both the young men and turned her gaze to King Karlon. After a brief pause, she opened her mouth to speak.

"I, too, have heard rumors. If true, they would mean not only that the elven treaty the Frivtran family worked so hard on has been broken, but also that friction with the other countries could be imminent. We should get to the bottom of this situation at once and enter into discussions with the elves."

Despite her youth, Yuriarna spoke calmly and steadily, without the slightest hesitation in the face of the king's scrutiny.

Beside the king, Prime Minister Bionissa spoke up in approval. "It is as Miss Yuriarna says. If the elves were to restrict trade with Limbult as revenge for this act, we would be at the mercy of the other countries."

The king turned to the prime minister, making no effort to hide his displeasure. "This is true. Magic tools

would, of course, be an issue. Moreover, if they were to re-strict our access to the crop fertility runestones, we could be looking at a food crisis, or even flat-out revolt from the other Rhoden nobility."

"Understood, Your Highness. I will put together a for-mal group of inquisitors and make for Diento."

The king nodded. "That is all for today then."

The moment the king finished speaking, Bionissa clapped his hands. The servants waiting outside entered the room and lined up along the walls.

Sekt and Dakares didn't even look at each other as they stood and quietly walked out. A moment later, Yuriarna slowly began standing. Karlon called out to her.

"Yuriarna."

"Yes, Father?"

"I hope to open communications with the elves as soon as possible. I would like you to go to Limbult. Could you speak with Seriarna about this matter and ask her to make the arrangements?"

The king's expression had completely changed. He no longer spoke as a monarch, but as a father asking a favor from his daughter.

Yuriarna smiled back at him.

"Of course, Father."

Two men joined Dakares in his private chambers, one of whom sat on a leather sofa directly across from him. All the servants had been sent away, leaving the three men alone.

Dakares, who just moments ago had been bickering with the first prince Sekt, sat stiffly in his chair, his blue eyes burning with rage.

"Dammit! We're right in the middle of concentrating our power and now we lose our biggest financial backer?!" The second prince's well-chiseled face twisted in anger as he spat out the words.

The large man sitting on the sofa across from him nodded deeply. The man's muscular physique gave the impression of youth, though his white-speckled, brown hair and impressive mustache betrayed his true age. His name was Duke Maldoira du Olsterio, and he was one of the seven dukes, serving as the general in command of the third royal army.

General Maldoira made a face as he discussed the situation.

"Yes, as a result of this incident, Marquis du Diento's eldest son, Orhevo, has been sent back to his city. We should plan on him being absent from the capital for a while, until he's able to take control of the situation."

Dakares pounded his fist on his thigh. "We've got bigger problems! If that fool doesn't conduct himself properly, the inquisitors will figure out everything that's happened! We need to make sure he keeps his mouth shut, one way or another."

"You don't need to worry. I've dispatched several good men along the route to Diento. He will never make it home."

"My, my! You truly are fast!" Dakares readjusted himself in his chair, looking more relaxed now.

The general smiled. "I will graciously accept your compliment."

"The servants who saw the events unfold are saying it was the work of elves, but could that really be it?"

"It's hard to tell. There are reports of people seeing elves around town, but we also know a band of liberators attacked three other slave trading houses on the same night, resulting in over forty-four of the beastmen escaping. Many say the assassination was also the work of these so-called liberators."

"I don't care if the beastmen were the ones to perform the assassination, but I can't see any reason why they would risk killing the marquis if their goal was to save their enslaved brethren. Do you think they were working with the elves?"

"I cannot say. It's possible they wanted it to look that way. Sekt could have done this intentionally to weaken Diento's position by exposing their crimes. Meanwhile, Yuriarna is trying to reconcile with the elves. If she discovers what we we're doing, she may reveal your violation of the king's wishes, further restricting your power. I've ordered the servants to keep their mouths shuts about what they saw, but we've already lost track of one of them. It's possible one of your siblings offered them asylum."

"Isn't that a problem? If the servant reveals what they knew, then..."

"It's still the word of a single, insignificant servant. The real problem, however, is what became of the funds that Marquis du Diento was supposed to send. Elves generally aren't interested in money, and, even if these ones were, the amount taken could have never been carried away by such a small number of them. This could be some sort of conspiracy to weaken our faction."

Prince Dakares frowned. This situation went far beyond a simple loss of funds to support his bid for the throne. If it all went public, this would bolster Prince Sekt and Princess Yuriarna's own bids to be named Karlon's successor.

Sekt's faction had already won the support of three of the seven dukes. Plus, he had the support of the Revlon

Empire to the west. The deck was already heavily stacked in his favor.

Just as General Maldoira had said, the only possibility was that this was a plot to further impede Dakares's ambitions. Yuriarna was straightforward and honest, and Dakares was convinced she'd never do something as dirty and underhanded as stealing Diento's money while making it look like an elven raid. His half-brother Sekt, however, would readily commit such an atrocity, all the while maintaining a façade of innocence.

"We must act before Sekt has a chance to. Cetrion, it's time for you and Houvan to begin your preparations."

A man in his thirties, dressed in military attire, stepped out from behind General Maldoira and bowed deeply in response to Prince Dakares's command.

"As you wish."

The man's name was Lieutenant General Cetrion du Olsterio, one of the three royal generals and heir to the Olsterio dukedom. He looked just like a younger version of his father, General Maldoira.

Prince Dakares smiled, imagining his sneering brother wreathed in flames.

At that very same moment, Sekt—the first prince to the Rhoden Kingdom—was also joined by two others in his private chambers.

The prince slumped back in his luxurious chair. It was made of amber-colored wood and covered with a cushion adorned with floral designs.

His blue eyes, set deep in his well-chiseled face, were inherited from the king, and he dressed in nothing but the most princely of clothes.

A beautiful, refined woman stood next to him, sipping daintily from a cup, her light brown hair neatly arranged. She shared facial features with Prince Sekt, though it was hard to identify them under her heavy makeup. She wore a gorgeous dress that blossomed out into a wide skirt.

The woman's name was Lefitia Rhoden Sahdiay—the second-class queen and Sekt's mother. She set her teacup down on the table as she spoke.

"Dakares's camp is scheming as we speak. Are you just going to rest on your laurels, Rondahl?" As his mother, Lefitia still referred to Sekt by his given name.

Calling a member of the royal family by their given name was an honor reserved only for close family members and others with an intimate relationship. It would be considered nothing short of a grave insult coming from anyone else.

"Dakares and his gang are just trying to clean up after themselves, Mother. They did a respectable job concealing the truth, but it was painfully apparent where all the marquis's money was going. I doubt we need to do anything, considering how much this whole debacle will set him back."

The other man in the room nodded in agreement before speaking up. "In my humble opinion, Princess Yuriarna is the only one currently being proactive. If she uses this opportunity to take greater strides toward her own goals, it could very well endanger your bid for the throne."

Despite this small-framed man's polite smile and priestly attire, he had a rather vile air about him. He was a Hilk priest, named Boran, and he was only in the capital to proselytize and spread the Hilk faith.

"That's true. She's also popular among the subjects. If she uses this situation to gain the upper hand, those standing on the sidelines, and even the dukes who have aligned with us, may back her. We need to find out how the people are leaning and make our move. Boran, I assume you can call upon your magic-using followers, if necessary?"

The priest responded with fervor. "Why of course! We, and our Father up in heaven, will bring a thousand blessings upon you, Your Highness. My devout followers and I eagerly await the opportunity to be of service to you."

Sekt struggled to maintain his composure in the face of Boran's exaggerated proclamations. "Boran, we are equals, are we not? There is no need to speak so formally with me. And please, call me Rondahl."

Boran looked perplexed for a moment before bowing low. "I am deeply touched by this great honor you have bestowed upon me, Master Rondahl. However, I'm afraid I must be going now, for there is much to do to ease Your Highness's worries."

The man was so excited he practically danced out of the room, though he still managed another polite bow before making his exit. Once he left, Lefitia let out a sigh.

"Did you really need to say that, Rondahl? Won't this come back to bite you once Princess Yuriarna is disposed of?"

"Not in the least. Boran has been playing both sides for a while now, though his real goal is to get rid of Yuriarna. After all, she's the one pushing Father to put a stop to Hilk proselytizing. Once I've used Boran to destroy Yuriarna, I'll get rid of his private army. Religious inclinations are relatively weak here in Rhoden, so letting the Hilk infiltrate any further would only lead to more problems."

Lefitia took a sip from her teacup. "I suppose so. On

the other hand, it's also worth considering the massive population increase an influx of Hilk followers and their temples would bring. Though, I've heard a rumor that the emperor of Revlon has turned away the Hilk's high priest, so that may not be possible while the Revlon Empire supports you."

"Right. It would be a pretty poor move to form an alliance with a rejected religion while we're trying to stop their spread to the south, even if it would grant us access to the Holy Revlon Empire's glacier-free port. First, I'll have Boran figure out what Yuriarna is up to, then we'll dispose of Dakares. After we reveal what really happened with the marquis, I'll put an end to the Diento family and give the domain to the Hilk."

Sekt let out a sinister laugh before picking his cup up from the table and downing the tepid tea in one gulp.

Elsewhere in the palace, while Sekt was busy plotting her downfall, Princess Yuriarna sat beside a window overlooking a beautiful garden.

The man across the table from her had long, wavy blond hair. His beautiful brown eyes seemed entirely unsuited for the angry look they held.

A chambermaid poured tea into their cups with a well-practiced hand before bowing lightly to the Princess and stepping back out of sight.

"Thank you, Ferna," Yuriarna said. Ferna had been at her side ever since childhood.

After taking a sip of her tea, Yuriarna let out a deep breath and turned her attention to the man across from her.

"We almost had Dakares exactly where we wanted him. What are the odds that the ruler of Diento, where our spies were currently operating, would be killed? Do you think this was an attempt by Dakares to conceal the evidence of his treachery?"

The middle-aged man facing Yuriarna sat perfectly straight in his chair, wearing the crisp military uniform reserved for lieutenant generals.

Carlton du Frivtran—one of the kingdom's three generals—paused for only a brief moment. "No, m'lady. The marquis was a major source of funding for Dakares's camp, and a powerful supporter, so it's hard to believe Dakares would kill him. As for the servants who provided statements about what they saw, we attempted to secure them as soon as possible, but we could only get our hands on one. I've already issued orders to hand the servant over to the Grand Duchy of Limbult."

Yuriarna knitted her eyebrows and frowned. "According to the witnesses' statements, the castle was attacked by elves. Was this just revenge for the marquis's kidnappings? There are also reports that beastpeople were set free from various slave trading houses around town, so I wonder if they were working together. I'd heard that Diento is a rather sturdy fortress, so it's hard to believe that elven soldiers could succeed in an attack all on their own."

Yuriarna wasn't looking for an answer exactly. Rather, she was letting her mind work through the problem. Her eyes narrowed as she stared into the steam rising from her cup.

Carlton wore a thoughtful expression. "The elves and beastpeople have relatively stable relations, so it's entirely possible. However, without some sort of inside help, it would have been difficult to sneak in. The biggest mystery for me is how the beastmen were able to steal all that money and burn down half the castle's main residence, all without any witnesses seeing anyone other than the elves. Perhaps it was one of Sekt's people, trying to weaken Dakares's position."

"In any case, Rhoden citizens living near the elves must be trembling with fear. After all, even a massive fortress wasn't enough to stop them from getting revenge. I fear our trade routes will become even more constrained. I can't believe my idiot brother would do something so foolish! He's trying to abandon a 400-year-old treaty!" Yuriarna let out a heavy sigh.

"However, this incident will greatly weaken the power of Dakares's camp, sending even more nobles our way. Going forward, we'll need to keep an eye on Sekt's movements."

"That's true, I suppose. Sekt is also likely to use this situation to try and win over Dakares's supporters. We should have proper talks with the elves to discuss the situation as well. Let's start in the Grand Duchy of Limbult, since they're the only ones who have any regular trade established with the elves."

Yuriarna slumped her shoulders and picked up her cup, taking a sip of her herbal tea. The scent of it brought back good memories, putting a smile on her face.

"I wonder how Seriarna is doing..." Her older sister, Seriarna, had married into the Ticient family—the Grand Duchy of Limbult.

A sigh escaped Yuriarna's lips as she turned to gaze out the window.

High above the castle, dark gray clouds had rolled in, blanketing the sky. The sound of heavy rainfall drew closer.

SKELETON
KNIGHT IN
ANOTHER WORLD

Lahki's Merchant Diary, Part 1

ALONE HORSE PULLED a cart down a darkened road in Diento. The sun had set, and night cloaked the land.

A young man in his twenties with curly brown hair hummed to himself as he sat in the driver's seat, holding the reins. Though dressed nicely, he didn't give off an air of wealth. A quick look at the crates stacked in the back his cart suggested this young man was a merchant. In addition to his leather armor, he carried a simple sword at his waist and small shield on his back. He was on his way to stay the night at his usual inn in Diento.

As the inn came into view, a muscular man with short blond hair standing out front waved toward the cart, as if he'd been waiting for its arrival.

He shot the driver a warm smile. "You're late, Lahki.

Did you bring any goods to sell?"

The young merchant known as Lahki responded quickly, suggesting that the two were friends. "Evening, Behl. Actually, I got a bunch more than I expected!"

The other man, Behl, had the massive body of a fighter. His face registered surprise at Lahki's words. "No way! Rea and I were jus' talkin' about how all the stores would already be closed."

Lahki looked around. "Where is Rea, anyway?"

"Heh, already back in the room, kicking her feet up."

Lahki parked the cart in front of the inn's entrance and unleashed his horse. After leaving his steed with the inn's stable hand, he pulled his bags out from the back. The inn locked carts inside a garage overnight to reduce the risk of theft, but it was still a wise idea to bring valuables into your room with you.

Lahki struggled with a particularly heavy bag. Behl reached out and picked it up for him.

"This is pretty heavy. You sure you bought weapons?"

"The weapon's shop was closed, just like you said. But I happened to run across a wandering mercenary selling weapons of his own. So I bought them off him."

The two walked past the counter downstairs and made their way to the second floor. Lahki almost always stayed in the same room.

Lahki knocked on the door and waited for the woman inside to respond. "Rea, can we come in?"

After getting permission to enter, Lahki and Behl entered.

The room was in the corner of the building and barely had enough space to contain the three beds crammed into it. A woman sat on the bed farthest from the door.

She'd taken off her armor, and her chestnut-colored hair hung loose past her shoulders instead of being tied up in its usual ponytail. Despite her boyish attire, she gave an impression of femininity.

Rea's face perked up as soon as she saw Behl and the heavy bag he was carrying.

"Whoa! You got the weapons?"

"Well, actually..." Lahki repeated the story he'd told Behl earlier.

"A mercenary, huh? So, what type of weapons didja buy?"

"I was wondering about that, too." Behl dropped the bag on the ground and began pulling out its contents. After he'd drawn every single one of the swords out of its sheath, he gasped in surprise.

"They're all pretty impressive. Each sword must've cost

you twenty-five gold coins, yeah? I'm surprised you could afford to buy 'em all."

"Look at this one! Isn't it great? It's totally different from all the rest."

Behl and Rea both gasped when they saw the sword Lahki was holding.

"They'll each sell for around thirty gold coins. The one Rea's got'll give us another sixty, maybe even a hundred."

Behl spoke in hushed tones. "How'd you buy all these...?"

Lahki scratched his head in embarrassment and leaned in closer, keeping his voice low as he recounted his story.

"Wha?! No way!"

The two could hardly keep quiet. Lahki quickly put his hands over their mouths.

"Are you serious? You bought all of this for 150 gold coins?"

"That's amazing, Lahki! We should make at least double that in profit if we can sell 'em all. Did the mercenary have any idea how much they were worth?"

Lahki shook his head. "He claimed he was a traveling mercenary, but it seemed like he was some sort of noble knight. I don't think he was hurting for money. More than anything, I think he just wanted to lighten his load."

Behl looked at the sword hanging from his own waist

and let out a sigh, as if he could feel the difference in social standing.

"Must be nice for swords as expensive as these to be nothing more than a bother to you…"

Lahki, noticing his friend's reaction, got caught up in the excitement of the moment.

"Listen, Behl, pick out whichever one you want. I'll give you one for free!"

"Wait, are you sure about that? I mean, that'd be amazing, but…" Even as Behl said this, he was already excitedly looking over the swords before him.

"Of course! You're always such a great bodyguard. Plus, if you have a better weapon, I'll be even safer in my travels."

Behl reached for one of the blades, similar in appearance to the sword he currently wore.

"Are you sure that's the one you want?"

"Yup! It's best to stick with what you're used to."

Behl clipped the new sword to his waist, smiling brightly as he checked the feel of it.

Lahki and Rea exchanged glances and laughed.

"Well, I think it's time we get some shut-eye. Sorry, Rea, for always making you stay here with us guys."

Lahki looked truly apologetic as he said this, but Rea didn't seem to care in the least. She simply waved her hand and dropped back onto her bed.

"No reason to make a fuss about it now. It's always been like this. I'm just happy to have three beds."

"Even if we only had two, we'd let you have your own! Lahki and I would just double up!" Behl looked up from adjusting his new sword to tease his two friends.

"Hey, I'm a refined young lady! I thought that was obvious!"

"Hmm...where is this refined lady you speak of?" Behl looked around the room with exaggerated confusion, glancing straight past Rea. This kind of banter was common between the two of them.

"All right, all right! Listen, it's getting late. Let's clean this stuff up and get to bed!"

Lahki spoke in a well-practiced tone. He was used to breaking the two of them up. After putting the weapons away, he extinguished the lamp and climbed into bed.

"Tomorrow, we head to Luvierte."

"Roger that, boss."

"G'night, Lahki!"

Lahki smiled at his companions' replies and closed his eyes. Soon, the room was filled with the sound of steady breathing, as all of them joined the rest of the town in its slumber.

The next morning, the trio took the road out of

Diento and headed northwest toward Luvierte. Lahki led the way in his horse-drawn cart with the other two following on foot.

Whenever they ran across a beast or monster along the route, Behl would take off to slay it, all too happy to try out his new blade.

Rea was supposed to be providing support magic, but she spent her time complaining about Behl's enthusiasm instead. Lahki didn't seem to mind—after all, this was par for the course.

Several other merchants and travelers maintained a steady distance from Lahki and his party. Not only were Behl and Rea both four-star mercenaries, but they were also magic users, so the others were all too happy to let them deal with any threats. This was a pretty common occurrence on their travels.

Four days after leaving Diento, the group finally caught sight of Luvierte in the distance.

From its moat, with water drawn from the Xpitol River, to the five-meter stone wall surrounding the town, Luvierte looked like Diento, but on a smaller scale. It'd been quite a while since Lahki had visited the town.

Behl looked around at the vast fields as he walked, speaking to no one in particular.

"Made it without any problems, and just in time for

lunch, too."

At the east gate, Lahki showed the guard his merchant guild license, identifying him as a seller of metal goods. The group was allowed to pass through.

The back of the cart was only filled with scrap iron, the weapons Lahki had picked up in Diento, and a few other commodities, making for a quick inspection.

Lahki took his cart straight to the blacksmith to have the swords sharpened. Since he'd blown all his money back in Diento, he figured it would be best to look for buyers here in Luvierte while the blades were being sharpened nearby.

Smoke billowed out of the blacksmith's chimney, and the sound of metal clanging against metal could be heard from within the shop. Lahki left Rea with the cart and went inside, Behl following close behind with the bag of weapons.

Deep inside the blacksmith's, two men were in the middle of a conversation, yelling to be heard over the noise of pounding hammers. The muscular, white-haired man appeared to be the owner of the shop, while the younger man was dressed in a military uniform commonly worn by knights. His physique put even Behl to shame.

"Ya can't just come in here and add a weapon to yer order! We're runnin' short on materials. And besides, I can't make tools for the townsfolk if I'm always makin' yer weapons!"

"Are you mad? How do you think the townsfolk will be able to go on if we don't have weapons to fight the monsters?! You can't have forgotten that we slew two giant basilisks mere days ago!"

The argument between the men continued heating up, as if they were competing with the temperature of the forge itself. Unfortunately, the more they debated, the further they seemed from a solution.

Behl's and Lahki's eyes went wide at the mention of a giant basilisk. A monster like that could easily wipe an entire town right off the map. The self-proclaimed mercenary Lahki met the other day had mentioned there were monsters in the area, but Lahki never imagined he'd been talking about giant basilisks.

The older man finally took notice of Lahki and Behl and called out to them.

"Whaddya here for? You a customer?"

Lahki had to yell to be heard over the hammering.

"Uh, yes! I'd like you to sharpen these weapons so I can put them up for sale!"

Before the blacksmith had a chance to respond, the knight got a word in first.

"What?! You're weapon merchants?"

The man crossed the shop with quick strides, striking quite the imposing figure. It was all Lahki could do to nod his head.

"Can you show those weapons to me?"

Lahki didn't have any good reason to object, so he glanced over toward Behl, who dutifully laid the fourteen swords on the blacksmith's workbench.

Lahki had given one of the original fifteen to Behl. Behl's old sword was back in the cart with the other scrap iron. He'd nearly had tears in his eyes, contemplating his beloved sword's end. But the blade itself wasn't in a condition befitting a four-star mercenary, so it was the most practical choice. It was actually quite impressive that Behl had made it up to four stars with such a poor blade.

The knight and the blacksmith looked over the swords, drawing each one to check its condition.

"The steel used on these is pretty impressive! About twenty-five sok, I'd guess?"

The blacksmith didn't immediately acknowledge the knight's question, instead inspecting the blade in his hand, the sharp look in his eyes making him appear much younger than his years.

"Where did you get this sword? This... Is this a mithril blade? It's gotta be worth at least five hundred sok..."

The surprise in the blacksmith's voice was nothing

compared to the surprise on Lahki and Behl's faces. They'd known it was a high-quality sword, but the possibility of it being a mithril blade hadn't even crossed their minds.

This was hardly the type of weapon an average merchant like Lahki would normally deal in, especially considering he'd bought all fifteen swords for a mere ten sok apiece. He'd never imagined they'd be talking these kinds of prices.

Mithril was said to reduce the power of magic. Putting a thin plate of it on a shield would reflect magical attacks, while forging it into a sword would allow you to cut through even the toughest of monsters with ease. It was incredibly valuable.

However, mithril ore was both relatively rare and incredibly hard to work with. This made it rather difficult to properly price mithril weaponry.

Historically, only elves and dwarves had possessed the skills necessary to work with mithril. By kidnapping these species, however, humans had managed to learn their craft. The human's actions ultimately led to the dwarves being hunted to extinction on this continent, and the elves fleeing to the forests. Despite having gone to such lengths to acquire these skills, the items humans produced still didn't hold a candle to the dwarves' work.

As a merchant, Lahki was pretty good at telling the

quality of an item, but this was far beyond his experience.

"I, uh, I just bought it off a traveler. He, umm, sold it to me—for pretty cheap, too."

Lahki broke out in a cold sweat. The self-proclaimed mercenary had said these swords were looted from some bandits. But it was inconceivable that a bandit would be carrying a mithril weapon. If they'd stolen it, news of the theft would have gotten around, and an order would have been issued to hunt the bandits down. Still, Lahki prided himself on being a good judge of character, and he hadn't sensed anything disingenuous about the mercenary. He almost didn't want to know where the swords had truly come from.

The knight's voice interrupted Lahki's thoughts.

"Merchant! Would you be willing to sell these swords to my master, Viscount Luvierte? We can offer you five hundred sok for the mithril blade and twenty-five sok each for the rest."

After some quick calculations in his head, Lahki realized this would fetch him more than five times what he'd paid for the weapons.

"You can have the mithril sword for four hundred sok. I accept your offer for the rest."

"What? You'll undercut my offer by a hundred sok for the mithril blade? You must want something in return."

The knight's eyes went wide as he inspected Lahki's face, trying to gauge the other man's motives.

Lahki decided it would be poor form to tell the knight that he'd picked up the sword for a mere ten sok. Instead, he came up with a different explanation for his behavior.

"I was hoping this could be an opportunity to put myself in the viscount's good graces."

The knight looked taken aback for a moment, then he reached out to slap Lahki hard on the shoulder, letting out a hearty laugh.

"Wahahaha! You merchants don't let a single opportunity pass you by, do you? My name is Horcos. I'm in charge of the knights of the Luvierte estate."

"You're the h-head of the knights? Apologies for my insolence, Commander Horcos, sir. I am Lahki, the merchant."

"Ahaha! Don't worry about it. I almost forgot, though. I need to run this conversation past Master Buckle. Wait here. I'll be back with your money shortly!"

With that, Commander Horcos left the shop, mounted his horse, and took off at a gallop toward the castle.

After watching this all unfold, the blacksmith finally addressed Lahki.

"Commander Horcos is always like that. You can wait

over there until he returns."

Lahki thanked the man, then asked if he'd be interested in purchasing some scrap iron, ultimately securing a sale. Iron ore usually reached Luvierte from the south, but lately it had been getting held up in Diento.

Considering this, Lahki had hoped he'd be able to sell the scrap above normal market value, but the blacksmith managed to talk him down in exchange for sharpening Behl's sword for free. Overall, Lahki was satisfied with the deal.

A short time later, Horcos returned with several of his men to collect the swords. After receiving his 725 gold coins, Lahki shook hands with the commander and made his exit.

In stark contrast to Lahki's expectations of a long, drawn-out sales push, he now found himself with more money than he'd ever held at one time. His hands trembled slightly as he accepted the money.

Just to be safe, he opened a compartment in the bed of his cart, revealing a chest. After putting the money inside, he covered it with dirt to keep it from rattling about.

"I still can't believe that was a mithril sword..." Behl spoke animatedly, his excitement obvious. Rea was quite surprised when she heard the story, but also delighted at their luck.

"This is great! You're so much closer to owning that shop you've always dreamed of!"

"I know. I was completely taken by surprise!" The excitement seeped into Lahki's voice as well as he steered the cart toward the town's merchant guild office.

Whether you wanted to know about the current year's crop yield, or about the recent monster sightings, or even about the various tax categories, the local merchant guild was a great source of information. Goods and tax rates in particular varied for every domain and ultimately affected the selling price of everything. Success depended entirely upon a merchant's ability to look at the taxes each town levied and find something profitable to sell.

Selling the swords had given Lahki a great deal of money to work with. He hoped the merchant guild would be able to help him find something else to sell before leaving Luvierte.

Unfortunately, despite having all this money at his disposal, Lahki had a limited carrying capacity in his current cart, and, with just one horse, the more he piled on, the longer it would take him to travel between towns.

Lahki's mind cycled through his options as he made his way to the merchant guild office. He wasn't sure where he wanted to go from here—down south to the capital or follow the Xpitol River to the port of Bulgoh off to the west.

He pulled his cart into the parking area and left Behl and Rea behind to watch it while he went inside alone.

Strictly speaking, the purchase counter at the merchant guild office was more of a wholesale shop than anything else. Sellers who didn't already have a specific buyer lined up could check the market value of their goods and sell them at the counter—at a slight discount of course. This service was of great use to mercenaries, since they could sell whatever they brought in, from monsters they'd slain to rare medicinal herbs.

Lahki mumbled to himself as he put together a plan in his head. "First, I'll check what sort of goods they have in their storehouse, and figure out where to travel next. Then I'll figure out the tax categories for towns along the route."

There were several people, buyers and sellers, at the counter haggling with each other over prices. Their voices jumbled together, creating quite a racket. As he walked past, Lahki overheard one man—possibly a guild member—arguing with a girl about a purchase price.

"That can't be right! Daddy sold less than this before and got ten more gold coins for it. Why are you only offering me ten, and for a larger amount?!"

"It's like I said, kid. Price is determined by demand.

First it goes up, then it drops back down. This is my best offer."

The girl stood just 150 centimeters tall, her soft, chestnut-colored hair tied back in braids that hung down past her shoulders. She had large, blue eyes and a healthy tan, and she wore simple clothes, like you might find in one of Luvierte's outlying villages.

"Gah, I can't believe you! I'm going to sell these somewhere else!"

The girl grabbed the handle of her pushcart, a large bag still inside it, and made her way toward the exit in a huff. Lahki picked up a sweet, familiar scent as she walked past.

"Yer not gonna find a buyer all on your own, li'l lady! Come back here and sell it at the offered price!" The man yelled after the girl as she left, but she ignored him, not even glancing back on her way out.

Lahki, who had watched the entire exchange, chased after the girl. It didn't take him long to find her. She looked utterly dejected.

"Hey, girl. Do you have a moment?"

She turned a suspicious eye toward Lahki, hiding the large bag behind her back. "Who? Me?"

"Ah, excuse my manners. I'm Lahki, a merchant. And you are...?"

"My name's Marca. Do you need something?"

Lahki spoke to the girl in a soft voice, despite her rather curt response. "That item you've got there... Is that kobumi by chance?"

Marca's eyes went wide. "You know about kobumi?"

"Well, it has a pretty unique scent. Would you mind letting me look in the bag? I'd be interested in buying it if the quality's right."

After letting Lahki's words soak in, Marca opened the bag and showed it to him. Lahki thanked her, picked up the bag, and looked inside. As soon as the bag's flap opened, his nose was filled with the familiar scent. Inside, the flowers were half dried. He plucked one out to check its quality; it seemed good. Satisfied, Lahki nodded and hefted the bag again to check its weight.

"Considering the quality and weight...how does thirty gold coins sound?"

"Th-thirty gold coins? Whoooa!" the girl yelled out, before she even knew what she was saying. Lahki quickly put his hand over her mouth.

Her surprise was only natural. As a girl living out in one of the villages, her household expenses probably didn't exceed even three gold coins a month.

Lahki took his hand off her mouth and put a finger to his lips.

Marca nodded, speaking just above a whisper. "Is that

really okay? That's so much money."

Lahki replied nonchalantly. "Of course. If I take this down to the capital, I'll turn quite a profit."

"If you're a merchant, do you know what type of illness the kobumi heals? No one back in the village will tell me, though they say they don't need it there."

"It's not exactly used for an illness. More like a...preventative measure? But yeah, I imagine you don't really need it in a village." Lahki wasn't quite sure how to answer. That was the best he could do.

Marca stuck out her lower lip and pouted. "You adults are all the same! Fine, I'll sell it to you for thirty. Now hurry up before I change my mind!"

Lahki smiled as he counted out thirty gold coins, put them in a small bag, and handed them to the girl. After checking to make sure they were all there and sliding the bag into her clothes, she looked much more cheerful.

"Thanks, mister! Good luck selling it all!"

Marca waved excitedly before dashing off. Lahki threw the bag of kobumi over his shoulder and headed back to the cart.

Behl and Rea were lying in the bed of the cart, bored out of their minds. Rea caught sight of Lahki first and called out to him.

"Welcome back! That was faster than I... Hey, what's

that sweet smell?"

"Oh, that's kobumi. It's used for medicines."

He showed them the bag he'd bought from Marca, recounting the exchange.

"That merchant guild guy was a real jerk. But still, I can't believe you spent that much... Just what type of medicine does it make?" Behl took the bag and looked inside, tilting his head in confusion.

"The kobumi blossom is used to make contraceptives. It can also be used to induce abortions."

"Contraceptives... Really? Wow, I never knew that. But I guess it makes sense that villages would have no need for them."

"Haha, yup! Having a bunch of kids is pretty much part and parcel of village life."

The three of them had all come from the same small village, making this type of medicine all the more interesting to them.

"Contraceptives... Now those have gotta fetch a ton of money."

"Yup. Brothels use them, and I hear even some nobles do, too. We'd make an absolute killing if we could sell them in the empire."

Rea looked confused by this. "Do kobumi blossoms

not grow in the empire?"

Lahki shook his head. "They don't grow at all up north, but that's not why you can sell them for so much. Have you ever heard of the Hilk?"

Behl puffed out his chest. "Nope!"

Rea looked at him through half-lidded eyes, wracking her mind for all of the information she could remember about the Hilk.

"They're the ones proselytizing across the entire northern continent, right? I've never been there before, but I know they've got shrines—churches?—dedicated to fire gods, water gods, and more all across Rhoden."

"That's right. The Hilk religion teaches that there is an all-knowing, all-powerful god that created all people. Beyond the port of Bulgoh, it's been spreading out to the west of the Hilk Kingdom."

"Must be lonely to be a god without any friends." Behl looked sympathetic. Of course, if a Hilk practitioner had heard him, there'd be no end to the lecture he'd receive.

"The Hilk teachings forbid abortions, and since Hilk is the state religion of the entire empire... Well, you know. It's forbidden even to have kobumi out in public. But there's a huge demand for it, so you can sell it at exorbitant prices."

Lahki's friends listened intently to his story, though

Behl didn't really catch most of what he was saying. Behl nodded along all the same. "So, we're going to the empire to sell the kobumi?"

"Gah, are you stupid or something? Lahki was just talking about how it's forbidden. If they caught him, they'd take off his head for sure!"

Lahki laughed at the all-too-familiar interaction. "I figure we'll head to the capital, where we can still sell it for a ton of money. I need more information about the route, so I want you two to stay with the cart."

He left the sack of kobumi with Rea and made his way back to the merchant guild office, his mind already focused on how they were going to get to the capital.

Afterword

THANK YOU so much for picking up *Skeleton Knight in Another World*. My name's Ennki Hakari, and this is my first novel. It's such a strange feeling to think of how your work has been released into the world.

It was all a rush in the beginning, full of exhausting trials and exciting experiences along the way, but I was finally able to get this book out thanks to the wonderful efforts of my manager, the amazing illustrator KeG, my editor (who pointed out my constant typos), and many, many others.

I'd like to take this opportunity to properly thank you all.

I wrote this story in the hopes of creating something that I would find interesting as a reader. I hope you will find it interesting, too. And if you want to read the next volume, well, that'd make my day.

If there are people out there like me who enjoy this story, then we may have a lot in common—or so I hope anyway.

Well, I'm looking forward to seeing you all again in the next volume. That's it for now!

MAY 2015—ENNKI HAKARI